THE MAYFAIR MYSTERY

'THE DETECTIVE STORY CLUB is a clearing house for the best detective and mystery stories chosen for you by a select committee of experts. Only the most ingenious crime stories will be published under the THE DETECTIVE STORY CLUB imprint. A special distinguishing stamp appears on the wrapper and title page of every THE DETECTIVE STORY CLUB book—the Man with the Gun. Always look for the Man with the Gun when buying a Crime book.'

Wm. Collins Sons & Co. Ltd., 1929

Now the Man with the Gun is back in this series of COLLINS CRIME CLUB reprints, and with him the chance to experience the classic books that influenced the Golden Age of crime fiction.

THE
DETECTIVE STORY
CLUB

THE MAYFAIR MYSTERY

A STORY OF CRIME BY
FRANK RICHARDSON

WITH AN INTRODUCTION BY
DAVID BRAWN

COLLINS
CRIME
CLUB

COLLINS CRIME CLUB
An imprint of HarperCollins*Publishers*
1 London Bridge Street
London SE1 9GF
www.harpercollins.co.uk

This edition 2015

1

First published in Great Britain as 2835 *Mayfair* by Mitchell Kennerley 1907
Published as *The Mayfair Mystery* by The Detective Story Club Ltd
for Wm Collins Sons & Co. Ltd 1929

Introduction © David Brawn 2015

A catalogue record for this book is
available from the British Library

ISBN 978-0-00-813708-3

Printed and bound in Great Britain by
Clays Ltd, St Ives plc

INTRODUCTION

Wm. Collins Sons & Co. Ltd. was celebrating exactly 100 years of book publishing when in the spring of 1919 Sir Godfrey Collins and his staff announced its first detective novel—*The Skeleton Key* by Bernard Capes. Capes, a prolific and versatile writer best known for his ghost stories, had delivered his manuscript to Collins shortly before falling prey to the worldwide flu pandemic in the autumn of 1918, and died before his most lucrative book in a 20-year writing career was published.

Sir Godfrey, who had served in the Victorian navy and later entered politics to become a Liberal M.P. and later Secretary of State for Scotland, had become head of publications at the Glasgow-based printing company in 1906 when his uncle, the ambitious and colourful William Collins III, plunged to an untimely death down an empty lift shaft in a freak accident at his Westminster flat. It is not known now whether Sir Godfrey had intended *The Skeleton Key* to be a one-off book or the start of a new initiative, but its immediate success coincided with a growing post-war interest in modern exciting fiction based on crime and mystery. Within ten years of *The Skeleton Key*, Collins had built up a rich stable of reliable and popular crime writers, among them Lynn Brock, J. S. Fletcher, Anthony Fielding, Herbert Adams, John Stephen Strange, Hulbert Footner, G. D. H. & M. Cole, J. Jefferson Farjeon, Vernon Loder, John Rhode, Francis D. Grierson, Miles Burton, Philip MacDonald, Freeman Wills Crofts and, in 1926, Agatha Christie.

Nearly all new novels in the early 1920s were hardback, usually costing 7/6 each, and the most popular titles were frequently rejacketed and reprinted in a 'cheap edition', still in hardcover but often smaller in size and always on cheaper paper. In fact, the idea of making cheap hardbacks out of popular copyright fiction by living authors (as opposed to nineteenth-century classics, as had been the convention) was one of Godfrey Collins' earliest initiatives. His revolutionary 'Books for the Million' first went on sale in May 1907, but to Collins' dismay rival publisher Thomas Nelson beat them into the shops with the same idea just three days earlier.

By 1928 Collins had pretty much cornered the market in this area with a rapidly growing number of different series, including *Collins Classics*, *The Literary Press*, *The Novel Library*, *The London Book Co.* and *Westerns* (later renamed *The Wild West Club*), with more than 2,500 cheap fiction titles now appearing in the Collins catalogue. It was probably therefore inevitable that Godfrey Collins would add another imprint to the growing range of sixpenny hardbacks: *The Detective Story Club*.

Launched in July 1929, the series included the whole panoply of crime writing: classic mystery novels from the previous century; tales of true crime; modern detective stories; and a growing publishing phenomenon, 'the Book of the Film', inspired by cinema's new 'talkies'. Twelve Detective Story Club books had been published by Christmas 1929, and another 60 or so would follow over the next five years. All had brand new colourful jacket designs with matching spines, finished off with the distinctive stamp of the masked 'man with the gun', an evolution of a sinister Zorro-like mask motif which had adorned 1920s Collins crime covers to distinguish them as detective novels.

Perhaps the boldest move was to change many of the book titles to make them sound more obvious: thus Bernard Capes' *The Skeleton Key* became *The Mystery of the Skeleton Key*; Israel Zangwill's *The Big Bow Mystery*—the first full-length 'locked room' novel—became *The Perfect Crime*; Maurice Drake's obscure thriller *WO2* was retitled *The Mystery of the Mud Flats*; and J. S. Le Fanu's classic *The Room in the Dragon Volant* became *The Flying Dragon*. Perhaps the oddest alteration was to J. S. Fletcher's accomplished short story collection

The Ravenwood Mystery, renamed *The Canterbury Mystery* despite there being no such story in the book.

The *Daily Mirror* reviewed the new series: 'Attractively bound in black and gold, with vivid coloured jackets, these books are bound to be immensely popular', and an advertisement for the Detective Story Club in June 1930 claimed that it was 'The Club with a Million Members!' with already 19 books 'sold by booksellers & newsagents everywhere'. The advert went on to state:

> The extraordinary popularity of detective stories shows no signs of diminishing. The late Prime Minister [Stanley Baldwin] has confessed that he enjoys them; eminent men and women of every branch of life find them a mental stimulus. There is room for the Detective Story Club, Limited, founded to issue stories from the best detective writers—from Gaboriau to Edgar Wallace at a uniform price of 6d. Membership of the 'club' is completely informal. Any member of the public can buy these books through the ordinary trade channels, and in no other way.

The Detective Story Club was a big success. It spawned its own monthly short story magazine, which also sold for sixpence, and within a year gave Collins the confidence to launch a dedicated imprint for its full-price 7/6 hardbacks. In May 1930 the Crime Club was born, publishing three new mystery books every month, again selected by a body of 'experts'. For its logo, the masked gunman evolved into a hooded gunman, and fans were invited to register by post for a free quarterly newsletter. The Crime Club ran until 1994 and published more than 2,000 titles, adding many new famous names to Collins' existing roster, including Anthony Gilbert, Rex Stout, Ngaio Marsh, Elizabeth Ferrars, Joan Fleming, Robert Barnard, Julian Symons, H. R. F. Keating and Reginald Hill.

The Detective Story Club continued alongside the Crime Club until 1934, eventually abandoning the classics, the true crime and the film tie-ins and becoming principally a vehicle for cheap reprints of Collins' earliest crime novels, such as 1920s titles by Agatha Christie, Freeman Wills Crofts and Philip MacDonald.

Then in 1935 the launch by publisher Allen Lane of his popular Penguin paperbacks sounded the death knell of the cheap hardback. Within a year, Collins launched its own paperback list, 'White Circle Crime Club', with stylish green and black covers showing a ghostlike gunman (and a knife-wielding accomplice), whose hood had now become a full-length shroud, and the original Man with the Gun was retired.

The resurrection of the Detective Story Club today is a chance to revisit some the best and most entertaining detective novels of the last century. The editors who picked titles for the Club chose well, although ideas about what constituted a detective story were obviously quite broad. Some books didn't even feature detectives, and many of the rules and disciplines that characterised the era that has become known as the 'Golden Age' had yet to be formalised. These authors were the pioneers of an emerging genre—some broke new ground by inventing new types of story like the locked room mystery, the police procedural or the serial killer, while still drawing on more old-fashioned styles of classical romance, whimsical satire or the supernatural. But these were books with thrills and spills that got under the skin of their readers, and as such offer a candid glimpse today of how people thought and behaved at the time they were written.

The Mayfair Mystery, originally published in 1907 as *2835 Mayfair*, is one such example. Author Frank Richardson had become very well known both in the UK and the USA as a satirist, his recurring theme a crusade against the Edwardian fashion for facial hair. He wrote more than a dozen books in just ten years, latterly collections of his widely published stories and parodies, including *Bunkum* (1907), its imaginatively titled sequel *More Bunkum* (1909), and perhaps his most famous, *Whiskers and Soda* (1910). These clearly endeared him to readers and reviewers on both sides of the Atlantic: 'Whimsical, audacious, unconnected, and discursive, irresistibly amusing' (*Daily Express*); 'A master of extravaganza: No one can take up his books without being infected by the light, careless spirit which pervades them' (*Daily Telegraph*); 'No living writer knows better how to amuse than Mr Frank Richardson' (*New York Herald*); 'One of the wittiest men in London' (*New York Evening News*); and so they went on.

Frank Collins Richardson was born in Paddington, Middlesex (as it was then) on 21 August 1870. He went to Marlborough College, where impending unpopularity amongst his peers from a 'versatile incompetence' at both games and work was seemingly averted by his ability to invent and tell vivid stories after lights out in the dormitory. After being 'superannuated' at Marlborough, he failed to get into Trinity, Oxford, where one Professor declaimed: 'Richardson, you will always be a fool, but your sense of humour may prevent you from being a damned fool.' However, he did get into Christ Church, but got out without a degree, and thanks to his father, the (inevitably bewhiskered) Chairman of the North Metropolitan Tramways Company, trained as a barrister and got work in all Courts, Parliamentary Bar, Chancery Bar, the Queen's Bench and the Old Bailey.

A consistent failure, however, or so he maintained, Richardson took up playwriting, with moderate success, and a breakthrough with the publication of a couple of short stories led to him being invited to write novels. Choosing subjects he knew, but with a comedic twist, his first, *The King's Counsel*, was published by Chatto and Windus in 1902, and three more followed in 1903, all with a strong vein of satire and gratuitous references to whiskers. Richardson is credited as coining the term 'face-fungus', and *Punch* called him 'Mr Frank Whiskerson'. His ability to write caricatures also developed into drawing them, and his later books and articles often featured his own sketches.

Like so many clowns, however, Richardson's life ended tragically. Widowed before he turned 40, his appetite for writing had all but dried up by the time he published a book of poetry, *Shavings*, in 1911. Although he may have exhausted his peculiar topic of humour, he had remained a popular figure, opening fêtes, signing books, drawing cartoons and judging seaside beauty contests. But on Thursday 2 August 1917, *The Times* announced his death, aged 46: 'Mr Frank Collins Richardson, barrister, and novelist, was found dead in his chambers in Albemarle-Street, Piccadilly, yesterday. An inquest will be held.' The next day, Westminster Coroner, Ingleby Oddie, heard evidence from Richardson's sister and ex-valet which showed he had been suffering from depression and was given to 'alcoholic excess', despite his successful business interests as director of two flourishing companies: a cataract had robbed him of sight in one eye, and he feared it would spread and he would go blind. He had died on 31 July from a cut to his throat, and the jury returned a verdict of suicide whilst of unsound mind.

Published in the second batch of Detective Story Club titles in November 1929, *The Mayfair Mystery* was the only one of Frank Richardson's books acquired by Collins for a reissue. Though none of his others were deemed suitable for the list, its predecessor, *The Secret Kingdom* (1906), set in the imaginary country of Numania, featured Sherlock Holmes and Dr Watson in one of their earliest parodies, and might have been an interesting contender.

DAVID BRAWN
April 2015

CONTENTS

CHAPTER I

THE DEAD MAN

THE body of a man in evening-dress lay on the dull, crimson carpet.

The black eyes were staring fixedly at the electric light hanging from copper shades. The jaw had dropped. The dead man's face was remarkably handsome. The forehead was broad, and indicative of considerable intellectual power. Strongly-marked black eyebrows jutted perhaps a little too far over the aggressive, aquiline nose. The chin was strong and determined. The close-cut, shiny black hair was silvered at the sides. But for a slight, almost dandified moustache, one would have thought that the features were those of a barrister, of an ideal barrister.

The small room in which the corpse lay had evidently been newly decorated. A smell of varnish was in the air. It was furnished simply and in good taste. The walls were panelled in dark oak, and the few ornaments proved their owner to be a man of excellent judgment in matters of art. A few books, the latest novels, illustrated and scientific papers, lay on a Sheraton table. In the grate burnt a fire of ship's logs, emitting a fragrant scent that battled with the smell of paint.

In *Who's Who?* the dead man's biography was as follows:

OAKLEIGH, Sir Clifford, First Baronet; created 1903. G.C.B., D.C.L., LL.D., F.R.S. Physician-in-Ordinary to the Princess of Salmon von Gluckstein. Born 21st August 1870. Son of John Oakleigh of Aberdeen and Imogen B. Stapp of Chicago. Education: Eton, Christ Church,

Oxford. First-class First Public Examination 1891; First Class Greats 1892; Edinburgh University, Gillespie Prizeman. Recreations: shooting, yachting and hypnotism. Address: 218 Harley Street. Clubs: Athenaeum, United Universities, Garrick, Beefsteak, Gridiron and Arthur's.

CHAPTER II

CONCERNING THE CORPSE

'Thank God, I've found you!'

As the servant closed the door, Reggie Pardell, in evening-dress, his flabby face pallid, almost ashen, sank into a chair.

George Harding rose hastily.

The K.C. looked down at the frightened figure in the chair, went into the dining-room, and returned with a brandy-and-soda.

'Drink that,' he said.

While Reggie drank with long gulps, his eyes stared at the gaunt barrister.

As he scanned the clear-cut, intellectual face, with its piercing grey eyes, its long, sinister, thin nose and tight-shut vigorous mouth, he felt a sensation of returning confidence. At the same time, also, there floated through his mind a feeling of irrelevant despair. Each was thirty-eight years of age. They had been at Christ Church together. George was a brilliant advocate and Reggie was—well, Reggie was an ex-black sheep. A passion for backing losers had been his undoing.

Harding took away the glass.

'Feel better?' he asked.

The other nodded.

'What's the trouble now?'

It was eleven o'clock, and from the library one could hear the sound of carriages and cabs passing along South Audley Street. In the home there was complete silence.

Reggie shook his head.

'It's not a trouble of mine this time, not directly. But it's the most awful thing that's ever happened. That's why I've come to see you.'

Harding smiled. His friends always came to him in time of trouble. There was something in the man's vigorous personality that invited sympathy; his vast reputation for acumen and knowledge of human life rendered him an invaluable adviser in moments of difficulty or danger.

He went back to his chair and lit a cigarette, waiting for his friend to speak.

The first words that came from Reggie's lips were:

'Clifford Oakleigh is dead.'

'Dead!' cried Harding, aghast at the news that his best friend at Eton and Oxford, and indeed in the world, had died. Horrified, he pressed for particulars.

'When did he die? How do you know?'

'I have just come from his house.'

'From Harley Street?'

'He doesn't use that as a house.'

'I know. He lives at Claridge's.' The K.C. corrected himself. Reggie shook his head.

'He has lately taken, or rather built, a little house in King Street, Mayfair; just near here. Didn't he tell you?'

'Never a word.'

'Well, he only moved in a week ago.'

'But what were you doing there? I thought that you and he were not quite . . .'

'No,' said Reggie, grimly. 'But he has been very good to me one way and another. He has lent me a lot of money; I wouldn't have gone to him again, but . . . the fact is I'm his valet.'

The barrister gazed at him in surprise.

'I was his valet,' repeated Reggie. 'He engaged me as a valet.'

'You were his valet?'

Harding stared at the prematurely fat young man with three pendulous chins and an unbecomingly large waist. It seemed incredible to him that Sir Clifford Oakleigh, one of the most famous physicians of his day, one of the most brilliant men of all time, had selected that mountain of adiposity as his valet. Further, it struck him as extraordinary that a man like Reggie Pardell, a scion of one of the oldest families in England, should be willing to perform these duties.

Reggie explained.

'You see it was like this, George . . . Harding. I was absolutely stony. Of course, I'd got clothes, and the run of my teeth, and so on. But I was broke to the world. Poor Clifford met me one day at Arthur's and he guessed how things were. He made me a sporting offer. He said: "Look here, old chap, you have failed at most things. The only thing you do understand is clothes. Come and be my valet. I will give you £500 a year." At first, I thought he was joking. But he wasn't, and he installed me in this little box of his in King Street. Only part of the house is furnished; his sitting-room and bedroom and my bedroom. He never has his meals there. The charwoman comes in every day and sees to the place; all I had to do was to look after his clothes. It really was the most extraordinary arrangement that I've ever come across. It was philanthropy on poor old Clifford's part, because my time was entirely my own.'

The other reflected.

'It's strange he never told me about this.'

'Dear old Clifford wouldn't,' rejoined Reggie.

'You see, he knew that I shouldn't like it to be known that I was doing a bit of valeting. Well, after all, what's the disgrace? My elder brother, Horace, is chaperoning the "Venus" at the Nasallheimers' Gallery in Bond Street. It is his duty to show financiers and peers and people of that sort the beauties of Titian. Of course, if he ever succeeds in selling it, he will lose his job as vestal virgin to the "Venus". And my cousin, Dartmouth, keeps body and soul and motor together by selling Stereoscopic Co. et Fils Cuvée Anonyme to unwilling aristocrats. Still, Clifford knew that I shouldn't like people to hear that I was his valet.'

The lawyer's knowledge of Reggie's character told him that interruption would be useless. He must tell his story in his own way. He merely showed his impatience by taking out his watch and clicking it.

'I know,' said Reggie, accepting the hint.

'Well, tonight I dined with three pals at White's. We were going on to the Covent Garden Ball. But, somehow, an extra man turned up and someone suggested Bridge. You know I've not got a very good reputation for solvency, and I could see they'd be just as well pleased if I didn't cut in, so at ten o'clock I left them. I thought at first of going on to the ball alone. But that struck me as being a dull scheme, and so I walked back to King Street.'

'Yes, yes?'

'I let myself in with the latchkey and went into the sitting-room, which is at the back of the house on the ground floor, the second room from the front. The front room is not furnished. And there I saw Clifford lying on the floor—dead.'

The barrister was silent at the horror.

'Dead,' he whispered at last. 'My oldest friend, my best friend! What could have happened?'

'That's the mystery,' answered Reggie. 'That's the extraordinary thing. What does a man, a man in robust health and strength die of . . . like that?'

'Heart disease?'

Reggie shook his head.

'No, not in this case. I know, in fact, that only three days ago Clifford went to his Life Insurance Office and increased his insurance enormously. Besides,' and he shrugged his shoulders, 'you know perfectly well that he was sound in wind and limb. You have shot with him. You know how deuced strong he was. Not an ounce of superfluous flesh on his body. No, no, it wasn't heart disease.'

'Then you suspect . . .'

Reggie leant over:

'I suspect nothing. I'm afraid they may suspect me . . . the police may suspect . . . me.'

Harding threw himself back in his chair and drew a long breath.

'Have you told the police?'

'No, I came straight here. I thought it would be better to come straight here. But the police must be called in. You see how much worse it makes it for me if I don't call them in at once.'

Harding rose from his chair and stood by the mantelpiece.

'I can't believe it!' he said, 'I can't believe it! Isn't it possible that you're mistaken?' he said, snatching at a hopeless gleam of hope.

Reggie shook his huge, flabby head.

'No, no chance of that. I know death when I see it. I was in the Boer War, you remember. Besides, his chin had dropped; his eyes were staring. Poor chap, he was very good to me.'

Quickly Harding spoke:

'I will go with you to the house. We must go at once. This is a terrible affair. No, we won't take a cab. We must walk.'

The two passed out into South Audley Street.

They walked rapidly in the direction of King Street.

There was a quick fire of questions and answers.

'Where did he dine?'

'I don't know.'

'What time did he leave the house?'

'At seven-thirty.'

'Was he dressed?'

'Yes.'

'What time did you leave?'

'At seven-fifty.'

'Did he know that you were going to the Covent Garden Ball?'

'Yes.'

'He seems to have given you a pretty free hand?'

'Certainly. I was practically my own master.'

'And no one else was in the house when you went out?'

'No one.'

'That seems extraordinary! What about burglars?'

'Well, you see, I don't think that anybody would know the house is occupied. The dining-room is shut up. There is nothing to burgle. There are only a few valuable vases and bronzes that wouldn't appeal to burglars.'

'So he would let himself in with his key, would he?'

'Yes.'

'How many keys are there?'

'Only his and mine.'

By this time they had reached the door of a small house in King Street. The house had been newly built. The bricks were red, the paint was white, and the door was green with dull red copper fittings.

Reggie opened the door, and they passed into a narrow hall and thence to the sitting-room.

Scarcely had Reggie turned the handle when he started back.

'My God!' he whispered, 'someone has been here. The light has been turned out!'

CHAPTER III

THE DISAPPEARANCE OF THE CORPSE

WITH hesitating fingers he turned on the electric light, and then fell back nearly into the arms of Harding.

'My God!' he said. 'It's gone! There's nothing on the floor!' With wild, staring eyes he looked at Harding.

Harding returned his glance curiously. The conviction gradually growing in his mind was that Reggie had gone mad.

'But I saw it, I saw it,' said the other, detecting the suspicion. 'I saw it, and I touched it. It was almost cold. It was lying there by the sofa—between the sofa and the fire. The head was on the ground. It seemed as though he might have fallen off the sofa. No, George, no. This is no hallucination. The body was there, as I told you, and it is not there now. Someone has taken it away!'

'Thank Heaven,' gasped Harding, 'he may not be dead!'

'Oh, yes,' replied Reggie, firmly, 'he is dead. Only the body has been taken away. That makes the mystery worse, more terrible.'

'Come with me,' said the lawyer, 'this may be a matter of life and death for you. We must leave no stone unturned. I must search the house in your presence.'

And they searched it thoroughly. The kitchen door proved to be securely fastened: the windows had all been carefully closed. There was not a nook or cranny in which anyone could hide. No means of egress could be discovered.

At length, they returned to the sitting-room. Harding, who had had considerable experience of criminal work at the bar before taking 'silk,' felt himself completely nonplussed . . .

provided Reggie was of sound mind. If the body on the floor was an hallucination, then the mystery ceased to exist. If his story—and he had told it lucidly and with no more excitement than the circumstances warranted—was accurate, that he had actually touched the dead man, then the mystery was so appalling as to be almost incredible. Either Clifford would return that night and, as a consequence, Reggie's mental condition would be inquired into by people competent for such an undertaking or . . . or there were more things in heaven and earth . . .

Vainly he cast his mind this way and that, seeking a clue. Automatically he stroked the bronzes on the mantelpiece. Suddenly he took up a pair of spectacles which were lying there, open.

'That's curious,' he commented. 'I didn't know Clifford had anything the matter with his eyes. He is one of the best shots I've ever seen.'

He was standing with his back to Reggie, who inquired:

'What do you mean by that? He has the most wonderful eyesight. What makes you think he hasn't?'

'Why,' exclaimed Harding, turning round, 'these spectacles. A man does not wear spectacles if he has perfect sight.'

'But Clifford never wore spectacles. These are not his spectacles.'

'Are they yours or the charwoman's?'

'Certainly not.'

'Who can have left them here?'

'My dear Harding,' Reggie answered, 'since I have been here, not a soul has entered the house. I tell you he never receives anybody here. I don't know what he keeps the place for except for the excuse for giving me my £500.'

'Nonsense,' replied Harding, 'you could have taken £500 a year all right without his putting himself out to run such an expensive hobby as a house in King Street, even a little house like this.'

'I tell you what it is, Harding, the whole thing beats me. I have never been able to understand why a man should have his consulting-rooms in Harley Street and sleep here. Of course, no man could live in Harley Street. It is like living in a dissecting-room. But with his reputation he could have brought his patients to . . . Bayswater or Tulse Hill.'

Carefully the barrister examined the spectacles. He placed them on his nose. Then he whistled.

'These are a woman's spectacles,' he said. 'I am almost sure of that. They are too small for a man's face. And the extraordinary thing about them is that they are plain glass, practically plain window-glass. Now what has he got these here for? How did a pair of woman's spectacles of plain glass come into the possession of an eminent medical man?'

'I don't know, Harding. I've never seen them before. I suppose he brought them here.'

'But why, in Heaven's name?' queried Harding.

'A woman does not give away a common pair of steel spectacles as a *gage d'amour*. You noticed they were open when I found them, as though they had just been taken off the owner's nose.'

'Well, what do you make of it?'

The lawyer shrugged his shoulders.

'Make of it? I don't make anything of it, at all.'

He affected an air of joviality.

'But I tell you what it is, Reggie. When Clifford comes home we will have you put away in an asylum for the term of your natural life. A man who comes to one's house late at night with cock-and-bull stories of corpses on carpets is not needed; there is no market for him. Now I'm going home.'

Reggie, as he let him out, asked: 'Do you really think that he's not dead?'

'The only conclusion to which I have come is that either he is dead or you are mad . . . if that is a conclusion.'

'Am I to tell the police?'

'No. Certainly not. Good-night.' He turned abruptly up the street.

Reggie remained at the door, looking after the tall figure that strode briskly along the pavement.

CHAPTER IV

THE ALLEGED ADA

'Oh, we're not proud at all, are we? Not puffed up with pride, not likely.'

Attracted by the unattractive voice, Reggie looked to his right.

A female servant at No. 35, a much larger house, was seeking to engage him in conversation. This was not the first, the second, nor the third time that she had sought to gain the friendship and—who knows—perhaps, the hand of the 'gentleman 'valet in the mysterious house.

'No, we're not puffed up with pride,' answered Reggie, 'but we don't converse with menials.'

'Not when we've got our white waistcoat on, eh?' the girl replied. 'My word, you *are* a toff! You're a deal toffier than your gov'nor. You're too good for your guv, that's what you are.'

'Look here, Ada, we don't need to go into that.'

The maid was not even pretty. She had a face of the colour and texture of pink blotting-paper. It was of the tint often to be seen on a hard-working hand, unbecoming on the hand, unpleasant on the face. He had no use for her.

'Not so much of your Ada! My name ain't Ada,' she said, tilting up her nose.

'I thought all scullery-maids were called Ada,' answered Reggie.

'That shows what little you know about scullery-maids, mister, and you don't know anything at all about me. I'm not a scullery-maid. I'm an under-housemaid. £16 a year and beer money. That's what I am. Scullery-maid, indeed!'

'I beg your pardon,' replied Reggie, who had no desire to prolong the conversation. He was on the point of shutting the door, but the girl was agog for a chat. 'Next door' was the great topic of conversation in the servants' hall. 'Next door' was a mystery, and the valet of 'Next door' was the most glorious valet there had ever been. Apparently he had a position which for lack of labour was the ideal that all gentlemen's valets strove to find. If his remuneration were in proportion to the comfort of his place, he would make a most desirable husband. That was the universal opinion in the servants' hall of No. 35.

'Don't go in, mister,' she pleaded.

'Why not, miss?' he answered.

'Don't call me miss: it's so stiff like. Call me Nellie.'

'I decline to call anyone Nellie. It's a most repulsive name. I regret that your name is Nellie, but,' he added judicially, 'I am afraid you deserve it.'

'Oh, don't start chipping me, and don't you go in, neither. Your guv. will be pleased to meet you when he comes back. It will be a great help for him to find you standing there.'

'What do you mean?' he inquired in surprise.

'Well, if he don't sober-up before he gets home, it will be a difficult job to get him indoors. He was that drunk! And I know something about drunkenness myself, Mr Man. I once had to give notice to one of my guvs for intemperitude. And he never was what you might call rolling drunk: he merely got cursing and fault-finding drunk. But I gave him some of my lip, I can tell you. A nice example to set the other servants!'

'Who are you talking about?' persisted Reggie.

'Who should I be talking about but your guv.'

'Well, then . . . Nellie, you're not talking sense. Sir Clifford is a teetotaller.'

The words had slipped from him in his surprise.

'Oh, he is a Sir Clifford, is he? Well, that's something to know. Sir Clifford what, pray?'

But he would go no further.

'Well, it's something to know he is Sir Clifford. I don't suppose there's so many Sir Cliffords kicking about that I shan't be able to find out what his full name is. Lor', he was that drunk I thought he would never get into the cab. I thought I should have died of laughing. Oh, he's a bad hat, your Sir Clifford is . . . to go about with a creature like that: a drab I call her.'

'Look here,' interjected Reggie, sternly, 'what are you talking about?'

'Oh, you want to know, do you? I've interested you at last, have I?'

She placed a value on her information.

'Give me a kiss, mister, and I'll tell you.'

She coquettishly put up her rough red face and he paid the price. He did not like paying it, and she did not regard his payment as liberal.

'Why, our Buttons kisses better than that,' she said. 'Being kissed by you is like catching a cold. It's a pity, isn't it, that gentlemen's servants aren't allowed to grow moustaches? That's where postmen have a pull. When I was living in Westbourne Terrace, I once walked out with a postman . . . he *was* proper, I can tell you . . .'

But Reggie stemmed the tide of amorous recollection. He insisted on knowing what she had seen.

Very deliberately, and in a manner entirely convincing, she said:

'Just about a quarter past eleven I happened to be standing here; never you mind what for, old inquisitive, but my folks were at the theatre and I do what I like and no questions asked. I should like to see anybody ask 'em. They wouldn't get any answer, not much . . . only a month's warning. Suddenly your door opened and a sort of untidy middle-class woman comes out with your guv. He was so drunk he couldn't stand. I thought she would have dropped 'im. She must have been a strong woman! But she got him into a four-wheeler as was waiting. Then she comes back and shuts the door, says something to the driver, jumps in, and off they goes. Such goings-on! And not the sort of woman a gentleman should keep company with, to my way o' thinking; but when the drink takes 'em, you never know. I had a uncle—a Uncle Robert—who was just the same; he was an oil and colourman, too, in a fair way of business. Oh, dash, there's our rubbish coming back. Must be going. So long!'

And she disappeared down the area as a motor-brougham, with the servants in conspicuous semi-military grey uniforms, dashed up.

Reggie, completely mystified, entered the house. A great weight was taken off his mind.

'It is much better,' he reflected, 'to be drunk than dead . . . not so dignified, perhaps, but on the whole better . . . infinitely better. . . . Besides, I shan't lose my job.'

CHAPTER V

AT THE GRIDIRON

ENGROSSED in thought, Harding scarcely noticed where he was going. His mind was full of the extraordinary circumstances that had occurred.

Automatically he stopped in front of his house. But he hesitated to go in. The December night was clear and crisp. It seemed to him improbable that were he to go to bed, he would sleep.

Therefore he walked on to Piccadilly, and eastwards past the Circus.

Suddenly he felt a hand clapped upon his shoulder, and a hearty voice inquired:

'Are you on your way to the Gridiron?'

He turned round to find himself in the presence of Lampson Lake, a jovial, middle-aged man whose chief characteristic was his extraordinary versatility in failure. He had failed at everything, and on that account, perhaps, was universally popular with successful men.

At the mention of the club's name Harding realised that he was hungry and the two turned into the Gridiron.

The single long room which constituted the famous club was desolate except for two men, Sir Algernon Spiers, the famous architect, and Frederick Robinson, a somewhat obscure novelist, who were seated together at the table.

The newcomers took two seats next them.

Robinson, a wisp of a man with a figure like a note of interrogation and hair brushed straight back without any parting, was, after his usual practice, dealing in personalities.

'I can't help thinking, Sir Algernon, that it is a very sound scheme of yours to wear your name on your face.'

'What the dickens do you mean?' asked Sir Algernon. 'How do I wear my name on my face?'

'I will explain. Your name is Algernon, is it not?'

'Of course, my name is Algernon,' replied the other, huffily.

'Well, don't you know the meaning of Algernon?'

'No, I don't.'

'It has a very curious origin. Waiter, another whisky-and-soda. A very curious origin. It would be idle for me to assume that you are not aware that you suffer from whisker trouble. In fact, you are at the present moment toying with your near-side whisker. You are massaging it for purposes of your own. Whether it will do any good I can't say. But both you and I and any intelligent observer must be aware that you cultivate a superb pair of white face-fins. Now, whiskers were originally introduced into England by the founder of the Percy family. He came over with William the Conqueror. He was known among his friends as William Als Gernons, or "William with the Whiskers"; whence, says Burke, his posterity have constantly borne the name of Algernon. Curious, isn't it?'

'It's damned impertinence, sir,' roared Sir Algernon, purple with indignation.

'On the contrary,' replied Robinson. 'It is merely useful information; very, very useful information. There is no need to thank me for the information.'

Then he turned his attention to Harding.

'Ah,' he said cheerily, 'here we have the woman-hater.'

Harding gave him the lie.

'I'm not a woman-hater,' he said. 'Life is only long enough to allow even an energetic man to hate *one* woman—adequately. If a man says he hates two women he is a liar or he has scamped his work, or he has never known a single woman worthy of his hatred. The ordinary "woman-hater" hates one woman and has no claim to the title. Would you call a man a football player because he has played football . . . *once*?'

He had no desire to talk. His desire was to eat a devilled bone and return home. But he had always considered it preferable to bore a man than to be bored by him. Also, he was in no mood for the absurdities of Robinson.

'Still, you have never married,' pursued the novelist.

'I told you I was not a misogynist,' replied Harding, with a perfunctory smile. 'No girl that I ever knew was so radically bad as to deserve me.'

'Nonsense,' broke in Lampson Lake, 'my dear old chap, I don't believe there is a man in England who is so anxious to marry as you are. You have got everything in the world except a wife. You are a huge success. You have got a beautiful house . . .'

'Thanks to the advice of Sir Algernon here,' Harding answered.

'Heaps of friends,' continued the other. 'A face that would not exactly frighten the horses. Why, my dear fellow, your whole life is directed with a view to a happy marriage. You are only looking out for . . . the impossible.'

'What do you mean by the impossible?' queried Robinson.

'Oh, not you,' replied Lampson Lake, glancing at the novelist, 'I don't go in for personalities. You needn't worry. The impossible is the perfect woman. And that is what Harding is looking for.'

And herein Lampson Lake was right.

Indeed, Harding, tall, sparsely built, handsome—in a non-theatrical manner, despite his clean-shaven face—with bright brown eyes and athletic figure, seemed rather a happily-married man than a man whose one grief was the fact that he had never yet met a woman with whom he had desired to live for the term of his natural life. He knew that life should be duet. The confirmed soloist is regarded with mistrust. If a man declines to take a partner into his life's business, surely that life must indeed be a dull and drab affair. And Harding was exceedingly popular with both men and women. Yet he had never come across a woman who could rouse in his heart any feeling warmer than the great affection he had for Clifford Oakleigh.

'But you're not married either,' said Sir Algernon to Lampson Lake. 'Are you looking for the perfect woman, too?'

'It is no good *my* looking,' he replied. 'No woman will marry a failure—a specialist in failures, that is.'

'On the contrary,' interposed Robinson, 'some of the most shocking failures I know are married.'

'Yes, but they married *first*,' explained Lampson Lake, 'they became failures *afterwards*. It is a great consolation for a man, who has made a muddle of his life, to throw the blame on his wife, especially if he can get his wife to believe it.'

'A perfectly trained wife will believe in anything,' was the architect's comment.

'Except in her husband,' corrected Robinson, who, not being married, knew all things about wedlock.

'A woman wants to marry a man who will succeed or who has succeeded, and I think most women prefer the first. It is surely the greatest privilege of her life to accompany the man she loves from poverty to riches, from obscurity to fame.'

'No doubt,' answered Lampson Lake. 'But I am not in a position, and I never have been in a position, to give a woman the chance. I am one of Nature's failures. And, mind you, I'm not complaining. The world has need of failures. It is a great pleasure to any K.C. who was called to the Bar at the same time as myself to realise that no sane solicitor would ever give me a brief. Besides, people are kind to me because they are not jealous. They give me their best in the way of food and wine because they know I am not too busy to notice such things. They trust me with their wives because they know I am not ambitious, with their daughters because I am too poor to marry. Oh, I have an excellent time, thank you.'

'Then, Lampson,' asked the K.C., 'you really enjoy not being a . . . success?'

'Well, I shouldn't like to be a failure . . . as a failure. I am, at any rate, the leading failure of this club. But that's not saying much, because we're all famous here; except, of course, Robinson. He is merely notorious.'

'Thank you,' replied Robinson, smiling. 'I know you meant to be rude, but you failed even at that. Fame is what we call the reputation of people who are dead, of great men who are dead. Notoriety is the reputation of great men who are alive.'

'What,' asked Lampson, 'would you call Clifford Oakleigh? Is he famous or is he notorious?'

'As he is alive,' replied Robinson, 'he is notorious. When he is dead he will be famous.'

Harding shot a keen glance at him. He was on the point of speaking. But his lips shut tight.

'He is a most extraordinary man,' said Sir Algernon. 'You know I built that house for him in Pembroke Street, No. 69. He gave me an absolutely free hand to do anything I liked, and I must say I was pleased with what I did. Everything went well until the house was almost finished, and then suddenly Clifford, who is one of the best chaps in the world as we all know, began taking a very great personal interest in the details. So keen was his interest that it became very awkward for me, as a professional man. And, mind you, I discovered that he knows a great deal about architecture. In fact, I have never come across anything that he doesn't understand. Well, we had a sort of amicable quarrel. We agreed to differ. And the result of the whole thing was that the completion of the building was taken out of the contractor's hands and he gave the job to some tenth-rate builder that he had discovered in Hammersmith.'

Harding had listened in astonishment to the statement made by Sir Algernon. He had never heard that his friend was building a house in Pembroke Street. Yet another house!

He turned to the architect.

'You surprise me, Sir Algernon. Clifford and I, as you know, are old friends, and he never mentioned to me the fact

that he was building a house. The ordinary man can't buy a
motor without boring his friends to death with the subject.
It is very strange that Clifford should not have mentioned to
me a little thing like that. How long has it been built?'

'Oh, about six months!'

'Six months!' exclaimed the other. 'But he doesn't live
there?'

'No,' replied Sir Algernon, 'I don't think he intends to.
I think the idea was to let it furnished. It is one of his
hobbies, I think.'

'A very expensive hobby,' interposed Lampson Lake.

'Fortunately, he can afford expensive hobbies,' said the
architect. 'I understand that it is superbly furnished. And
now I come to think of it I remember he said that if he let
it he would expect to get £2000 a year. No. 69 is one of the
smallest houses in Pembroke Street. The idea of £2000 a year
is absolutely preposterous.'

To the barrister's thinking, the whole scheme was preposterous. No matter what Clifford Oakleigh's fortune might be,
it would not stand a habit of building and furnishing houses
on which a prohibitive rent was placed.

'I should like to have a look at the place,' continued Sir
Algernon. 'But he made me understand,' he added laughing,
'that he would never receive me in the house . . . so as to
avoid painful memories as to my professional pride. However,
he gave me an excellent dinner at the Savoy the other night.
He is a very curious man; certainly, he is a very curious man.'

'Not for a genius,' interposed Harding.

It seemed to him uncanny that these four men should be
sitting up at night talking of a dead man as though he were
alive. Two or three times it had been on the tip of his tongue
to tell them of the tragedy that had just occurred. Had it not
been for the fact that Reggie might be hopelessly involved
therein, he would have spoken. Another reason that kept him
silent was the incongruity of his position. His best friend was

dead, and he was taking supper at the Gridiron. Why was he taking supper at the Gridiron? He himself hardly knew. His nerves had been shattered by the events of the night.

'You think he is a genius?' asked Robinson.

'Certainly he is,' Harding replied. 'Ever since I have known him he has been a genius. He was a genius at Eton, he was a genius at Oxford, and he has been a genius in London. He has one of the largest practices of any physician in London, and what is more he hardly ever has a failure. Then look at "Baldo". That was really one of the greatest inventions of the age.'

He was alluding to a preparation invented by Clifford that consisted of a white cream which one applied to one's face in the morning and it instantly removed the night's growth of hair. By this useful device, a complete substitute for the razor, Clifford Oakleigh had already made nearly half a million.

'A slight application of "Baldo" to your whiskers, Sir Algernon, would, I am sure, be efficacious,' said Robinson.

'Oh, damn my whiskers,' replied the architect.

Robinson politely responded: 'My sentiments entirely.'

'Directly Robinson begins to talk about whiskers, I go home,' said Lampson Lake, rising.

'I, too.'

Harding paid his bill and, incidentally, Lampson Lake's, and left the club.

CHAPTER VI

THE TROUBLE WITH MINGEY

THE next morning, when Harding reached his chambers in King's Bench Walk, he noticed that his clerk, Mingey, was looking more dismal and lugubrious than usual.

Were it not that the man was so excellent at his business, Harding could not have tolerated the presence of so lamentable a figure. Mingey was six feet tall, intensely lean, with a dank, black, uncharacteristic, drooping moustache, and a pallid face that looked as if it required starching. He always wore shiny black clothes, and presented the appearance of an undertaker with an artistic taste in his calling. Today there were red rims round his colourless eyes.

'Cheer up, Mingey,' said Harding, heartily,

'this is not your funeral, is it?'

'Excuse me, sir, but something terrible has happened . . . my daughter, sir.'

'Ill, is she?' inquired Harding. 'I'm very sorry . . .'

He went to the table and cast his eyes over his briefs.

'Worse than that, sir,' replied the clerk, 'she has disappeared.'

'Disappeared!' echoed the K.C. 'Perhaps she has eloped,' he suggested.

'No, sir, she is not that sort of girl. She never had, to my knowledge, any love affairs. She once did show a sort of feeling for one of our ministers, but he turned out to be engaged to a lady in Scotland, so nothing came of that.'

'Tell me all about it,' said Harding, seating himself at his table and preparing to listen.

Succinctly the clerk made his statement. His experience of the Law courts enabled him to do a very unusual thing.

He told a simple story in a simple way. It appeared that Miss Mingey was devoted to the creed which her father had discovered was, of all creeds, the most suited to his spiritual wants. [Mr Mingey was, by persuasion, a devout Particular Strict Baptist: an intensely select creed with only two places of worship, one in Peckham and the other in Monmouth Road, Bayswater.] An entirely good girl. She took no interest in clothes or young men. She was, as her father put it, 'an intellectual girl much given to book-learning.' As to her appearance, even paternal pride would not enable him to say that she was good-looking.

'Here is her photo, sir,' he added to prove his statement.

But the photograph did not quite bear out his contention.

Harding gazed at it intently.

It represented a girl of about twenty—nineteen Mingey maintained was her actual age. Her features, so far as one could judge from a full-face photograph, by a cheap and inadequate practitioner, were regular; she wore spectacles; her hair was done in an unbecoming way; her dress was abominable. It was rather clothing than clothes. With no evidence as to her complexion and her figure one could not say whether the girl was good-looking or plain; but the fact that she took no trouble with her hair, that her dress stood in no relation to the fashion—even, so far as he knew, to Bayswater fashion—that she was photographed in spectacles, proved that she regarded herself as unattractive. A girl who takes this view is almost certain to be right.

He handed the photograph back.

According to the father's story, after a meat-tea with her mother she had gone out to post a letter. She did not return.

'She was happy at home, Mingey, was she?'

'Perfectly, sir. She always attended service twice on Sundays. No, I have never known a girl who was happier, or who had more reason to be happy.'

'Quite so,' said the K.C. 'And no affair of the heart, you say?'

'Certainly not, sir.'

'But as to the minister who married the Scotch lady?'

'Sarah had too much self-respect, sir, to get mixed up with a married man. Directly Mr Septimus Aynesworth married, she—so to speak—cut him out of her life.'

'Did you go to the police-station?'

'First thing this morning, sir.'

'Well, my dear Mingey, I shouldn't be alarmed if I were you,' he said, trying to administer consolation. 'It may be some curious freak . . . some girlish whim. You will probably find her at home when you get back.'

Mingey shook his head.

'I'm afraid not, sir. You've noticed there have been two mysterious disappearances lately of young girls. They both met their death. There are always three of these things! Sarah will be the third.'

Shaking with grief, he shambled to the door.

'Wait, wait, wait!' cried the banister.

'Surely, surely it was to her that I gave a letter of introduction to Sir Clifford Oakleigh the other day. What did you say the matter was? Her nerves, wasn't it?'

'Yes, sir, nerves. It was wonderful the way he put her right then and there. And no charge, sir, to a friend of yours, sir. He's a wonderful man, sir. She only paid one visit and he cured her completely.' Woefully he added, 'And to think it was all no good.'

Then he went out of the room.

CHAPTER VII

MAINLY ABOUT LOVE

THAT night Harding fell in love.

It came about quite suddenly.

At first he did not know what was the matter with him, but gradually the conviction forced itself upon him that he, George Berkeley Harding, had fallen in love at first sight, just as a boy at Eton falls in love with a Dowager-Duchess.

It was during dinner at the Savoy that he became aware of his condition.

As the Courts did not sit on Saturday afternoons, he had walked up to King Street and inquired of Reggie for any news of Clifford Oakleigh.

Reggie had answered in the negative. He had suppressed the servant girl's story, because he had not been convinced in his mind that she was a witness of truth. She might only have been making fun of him—a course of conduct which he would have resented. If, in very truth, Clifford had left the house drunk with a 'creature' he would certainly return, and he would not like the disagreeable fact recounted even to his best friend.

Harding had been in two minds. It was obviously his duty or Reggie's to inform the police of the mysterious occurrence. But, at the same time, as the story was so completely incredible and rested solely on the evidence of Reggie, he thought it might be wise to wait another day. In the meantime, Clifford might return, or Reggie might develop some conspicuous symptom of insanity.

Throughout the afternoon he had vainly puzzled his brain for a solution.

With a clouded brow he had driven up to the Savoy to dine with old Mudge, the eminent family solicitor—solicitor incidentally to Clifford and himself.

From Mudge's company or from the guests likely to be invited by Mudge he did not expect much amusement.

He found his host and hostess in the hall waiting for him.

Mrs Mudge was obviously Mrs Mudge. She had no figure, no individuality, and no features. Neither had she any colouring. She was, indeed, so colourless as to be almost invisible. When she was with Mr Mudge one could recognise her as his wife. Apart from Mr Mudge one would never have seen her at all.

Harding's heart fell. He had expected, at worst, a party of men. However large the actual party was to be, Mrs Mudge's presence would cast a gloom over it. A skeleton at a banquet would be the 'life and soul of the party' compared with Mrs Mudge. Horror of horrors, Mr Mudge announced that he was only waiting for one lady.

It flashed through Harding's mind that it might be possible to say that he had suddenly been called to Scotland, or to state on oath that he was dead, or to tell some other monstrous lie and leave the building.

Then it was that the thing happened.

Sumptuously gowned, magnificently jewelled, a figure glided across the red velvet carpet. Her hair of deep brown was arranged in the French fashion, which on an English woman generally produces the effect of an over-elaborately dressed head, but was particularly becoming to her. Her profile was almost Greek, her violet eyes shone bewitchingly under long eyelashes. But the greatest beauty she possessed was her wonderful complexion like peaches and cream; it was daintily tinted, obviously caressing to the touch. Harding noticed that her figure was in keeping with her other gifts. She walked with all the grace and confidence of an American woman, and she could not be—well, she could not be more than twenty. Oh, if only he was to dine with her!

To his surprise she approached Mr Mudge. This marvel of grace and beauty deliberately went up to the old man with the snow-white Father Christmas beard—a polar beaver of the first water, to be technical—and said:

'Mr Mudge, I think. Mr Mudge, I'm sure.'

'May I introduce my wife . . . Miss Clive. Mr Harding . . . Miss Clive.'

When the introduction was effected the old man asked:

'But how did you recognise me?'

'Ask yourself, Mr Mudge,' she replied, smiling.

'Look round this room. Are there any other solicitors here? Obviously you are the only eminent family solicitor present. And you are clearly . . . oh, so clearly Mr Mudge.'

This little speech had revealed to Harding the additional fact that she was possessed of beautiful teeth. Was the woman in all things perfect? Perhaps she would turn out to be stupid.

He shuddered at the thought. How terrible! What ignominy to fall in love at first sight with a woman who was a dolt!

During dinner he became convinced of two things, one that she was a brilliant woman, and the other that Mr Mudge did not know how to order a meal.

On all subjects she talked, and on all subjects she talked well. Her mind, indeed, seemed to be filled with information that as a rule can only be acquired by personal experience.

He, himself, made every effort to interest her. He even made a sacrifice very uncommon in a barrister. He forbore to tell her anecdotes indicative of his forensic acumen.

The Mudge beard worked hard. He ate heartily and spoke little. Mrs Mudge, after the *entrée*, had practically ceased to be present.

Harding and Miss Clive performed a conversational duet. Her face mesmerised him. He absorbed it with his eyes. And strangely enough, although he realised he had never in his life seen any woman so beautiful as she, yet there was about her face something not unfamiliar. Was there any truth in the theory of the transmigration of souls? Had he, in a previous existence, wooed and won this marvellous woman? If he had seen her before in this life, he would certainly have remembered her. There were many men at the Savoy, dining at tables near, who stared at her. He was quite convinced that no one of those, if he met her again, would think he met her for the first time. Why was memory playing him such a strange trick? He, who always prided himself upon the fact that he never forgot names or faces, could not shake off the idea that he had seen her before.

He put the question to her:

'I can't help thinking, Miss Clive, that I have met you somewhere. Do you remember ever having seen *me*?'

'Your name,' she answered laughing, 'is very familiar to me, but I have completely forgotten your face.'

As he handed her into her motor, he said:

'May I come and see you?'

She smiled graciously.

'Certainly, Mr Harding. I shall be delighted.'

'On what day?'

'I am often in about tea-time.'

'But what day?' he persisted.

Pouting her lips into a rose-bud, whilst her eyes twinkled, she answered:

'Oh, please, won't you take your chance, or am I asking too much? Besides, I am on the telephone. 2835 Mayfair.'

'2835 Mayfair is the most beautiful telephone number in the world. But what is your address?'

'Sixty-nine Pembroke Street.'

Then the motor glided off.

She was living in Clifford Oakleigh's house.

CHAPTER VIII

2835 MAYFAIR

HE went back to Mudge, whose duties as a host, so far as the speeding of the parting guest was concerned, he had usurped.

The solicitor, while an attendant helped him with his great-coat, was being told by his wife on no account to neglect putting on his muffler. He extricated his huge beard from his coat and draped it satisfactorily over the muffler.

'What a charming woman!' exclaimed Harding.

'I'm delighted to have met her.'

He was intent on extracting particulars. Throughout dinner she had given him no hint as to her circumstances. Beyond the facts that she was Miss Clive, that she was extraordinarily beautiful and fascinating, and that he was hopelessly in love with her, he knew nothing. And yet he did not like to put definite questions to Mudge. He felt that any curiosity exhibited by him would reveal the state of his affections.

'Is she by any chance the daughter of Frederick Clive—in the wool business?' he asked, nonchalantly.

He knew of no Frederick Clive in the wool business; he knew of nobody in the wool business; he had but a vague idea of what the wool business was. But the question served its purpose.

'No,' replied the solicitor, 'her father is not alive: neither of the girl's parents is alive. I'm glad you like her,' he added, 'I fancy she takes an interest in you.'

'You flatter me,' Harding answered gallantly.

At that moment the lumbering Mudge landau drew up at the door. The shapeless Mudge footman, in the ill-fitting Mudge livery, opened the door and the Mudges entered. Much to his annoyance they did not ask him whether they could give him a lift. He was athirst for information as to Miss Clive. But the landau drove off into the Strand, leaving him alone on the pavement.

However, he knew that her telephone number was 2835 Mayfair.

When he reached his home, he took up a Court Guide and searched the 'Clives' for a hint of elucidation. He had faint hope that he would trace her. He found that there existed two Captain Clives; there was also a General Clive; and a Mrs Clive lived in Campden Hill Gardens. They might or might not be related to the only woman in the world.

He felt an irresistible desire to ring her up on the telephone. Irresistible though the desire was, he resisted it.

Heavens! he thought, he must be phenomenally in love to think even for a minute of making himself so ridiculous. Even if he were to ring her up and announce that he had broken his leg, or changed his religion, or grown a beard, such a proceeding would not fail to be regarded as an intolerable impertinence. To summon her to the telephone and say, 'Are you Miss Clive? I have a shrewd suspicion that your house is on fire. A well-wisher,' was a course that actually suggested itself to him. He would love to hear her voice. After all, he was in love with her. She was bound to find out that he was in love with her. It would be the object of his life to tell her that he was in love with her. Why should he not let her suspect at once the condition of his feelings?

Although it is idiotic to fall in love at first sight, it is not an unpleasant occurrence to be fallen in love with at first sight. At any rate, she could not take offence. He would zealously lay siege to her heart.

Suddenly he seized his courage in both hands and went to the telephone.

'2835 Mayfair, please.'

. . .

'Are you 2835 Mayfair? Can I speak to Miss Clive?'

. . .

'Oh, you *are* Miss Clive?'

His face broke into a smile.

'I hope you won't think I'm awfully rude. I know I have no business to wake you up.'

. . .

'Oh, you have only just got into bed. So you have your telephone by your bedside. How very convenient!'

He noticed that she had not asked who he was. Could it be—obviously it must be—that she had recognised his voice? How delightfully intimate was the knowledge that she was talking to him from her bed! How marvellously beautiful she must look in bed!

'Oh, you know who I am. Yes, I am Mr Harding. George Harding. And I rang you up because I am most anxious to know whether you will be in between four and five tomorrow. I am very methodical,' he added, by way of explanation, 'and I never like to go to bed without knowing exactly what I am going to do the next day.'

But her answer displeased him.

A shade of disappointment passed over his face.

'Well, on Monday?'

To this query the reply was satisfactory.

'Good-night. I am so sorry to have disturbed you.'

He glanced at his watch.

Twelve o'clock. Good Heavens, there were forty hours to get through before four o'clock on Monday!

He looked at his engagement book. It was good to know that he was lunching out with some cheery friends. The afternoon he would spend in paying calls, and in the evening he was dining with 'The Beavers' at the Ritz. He was sure of a delightful evening at the best of all London dining clubs. 'The Beavers' would not break up until well after twelve: there would be delightful conversation and merry jests. And on Monday he would be busy in the morning and afternoon in Court.

Yes, he thought, it would be quite possible to live through those forty hours.

Picturing to himself the huge joy of the forty-first he undressed and went to bed.

Sunday passed far less tediously than he had dared to hope.

On Monday morning the papers were full of the disappearance of Mingey's daughter. Disappearances, apparently, were the order of the day; tunnel murders were no longer in fashion. In two papers which he read there were leaders on the subject. These journals were seriously alarmed. It appeared that no one was safe. Anybody, the most unlikely person for choice, might vanish at any moment. The *Morning Star* maintained that Parliament ought to interfere. The *Morning Star* always believed in the omnipotence of Parliament, mainly because it was against the Government. If the weather was bad for crops—which the weather always is—if a church was struck by lightning, the *Morning Star* tried to rouse the legislature from its lethargy. At the first symptom of the end of the world the *Morning Star* would certainly urge the Government to take strenuous action to frustrate the peril.

The facts given were exactly as Mingey had described them. There were no new details. The girl had left her humble home in the Monmouth Road, Bayswater, and she had not yet returned. The parents were disconsolate and could suggest no clue. The *Morning Star* gave a portrait, a wood block, that made the heroine so painfully unattractive that any suggestion of an amorous solution of the matter appeared impossible. As he walked along Piccadilly on his way to the Temple, most of the contents bills bore the legend:

MYSTERIOUS DISAPPEARANCE OF A BAYSWATER GIRL

However mysterious the disappearance of this girl might be, he reflected, it was not so mysterious as the appearance of Miss Clive in his life.

Miss Clive! He did not even know her Christian name. He ran through a list of names suitable for beautiful women, but he could not fix upon one which seemed suitable for her. She required a stately name, a beautiful name.

Gwendolen was possible but not adequate. Katherine would not be out of the question. He dismissed contemptuously Winifred and Hilda and Margaret and Maud. Mary was, perhaps, of all names the most beautiful, chiefly in a measure owing to its sentiment. He would not be disappointed if her name was Mary. It would be the right name; the only possible name. As she was perfect in figure and in face, there would be no jarring note in her name.

It could not be that she would answer to the name of Muriel or of Nellie.

He shuddered at the thought.

CHAPTER IX

69 PEMBROKE STREET

THAT afternoon, when he rang the bell at 69 Pembroke Street, he was in an ecstasy of happiness. So triumphant was he, that no fear lest she should not be at home crossed his mind.

And she was at home.

A dignified butler showed him to the drawing-room, which was furnished entirely in the fashion of Louis XV. Every piece of furniture in the room was genuine. Each ornament was a veritable specimen of the period.

He felt that he was out of place, angular, awkward, hideously modern in these beautiful antique surroundings. She, on the other hand, though dressed in the height of the fashion of the day, seemed perfectly in the picture. All beautiful things are, as has been well said, of the same period.

'How good of you to be in, Miss Clive!'

'How good of you,' she corrected, 'to keep your word!'

As he looked at her it seemed to him that she was genuinely pleased at his arrival.

'I hope you have forgiven me for ringing you up in such an unmannerly way. But I was very, very anxious to see you again.'

'You were, really?' she asked, her eyes looking straight into his.

'Really,' he replied.

He felt that he was making headway. But still it seemed absurd to be in love with a woman of whose character and of whose antecedents he knew nothing. He hoped that she would enlighten him in the course of the conversation.

Vainly, however, did he strive to make her talk about herself. Of all women she appeared to be the least egotistical. She was

as sensible as a man. She showed no sign of desiring to talk
about ailments that occurred to the body. If a body is not in
good condition it is not a matter to be mentioned in polite
society. Either one is well or one is not well. The condition
of ill-health is not suitable for discussion.

During tea, he mentioned the fact that she had taken the
house belonging to a friend of his.

'Do you know Sir Clifford Oakleigh?' he inquired.

'I have never seen him,' she answered, 'but I understand
that he is a great friend of yours.'

'He is my greatest friend, or rather . . .' he was on the point
of adding, 'he was my greatest friend.'

For an instant it seemed to him that it was disloyal to his
love not to tell her the mystery of the little house in King
Street: he felt also that he had been disloyal to his friend in
not going to find out if Reggie had any more information.
On the whole, there was no object in telling Miss Clive of
the strange events of Friday night. What interest would she
take in a landlord whom she had never seen?

'It is a very beautiful house,' he commented.

'Yes,' she said, 'I think it is a perfect little house. All the
rooms are as charming as this.'

'But £2000 is a preposterous rent.'

'I don't think so,' she answered, shrugging her shoulders
and speaking as one to whom money is of very slight importance. 'It's the most perfect house . . . of its kind . . . in
London, and one must pay for perfection.'

Deeply in love though Harding was, he felt considerable
pleasure in this evidence of Miss Clive's wealth.

He remained talking to her for half an hour and then
reluctantly rose to leave.

'A few friends of mine are coming to dinner on Friday at
a quarter past eight at the Carlton. I should be delighted if
you would come too.'

She thought for a moment, and then said:

'On Friday, let me see. What day is this? This is Monday. Oh, yes, I shall be delighted. Thank you very much.'

Then he went away and reflected on the question of which of his friends deserved the privilege of meeting Miss Clive. Clifford Oakleigh should have headed the list.

The thought called to his mind his nearness to King Street. He would go and see Reggie and ascertain if there were any news.

Reggie opened the door and received him with enthusiasm.

'It's all right, my dear Harding,' he said. 'He's alive, at any rate.'

Harding mistrusted him.

'I won't believe it on your evidence alone.'

'Here's the evidence of his own handwriting,' said Reggie, and he produced from his pocket an envelope containing a plain sheet of notepaper. 'I found it in the letter-box this morning.'

Harding looked at it curiously.

'Yes,' he said, as he examined the envelope, 'it is his hand-writing. But do you know it seems to me to lack a certain amount of vigour. It is not so strong, not so bold as his handwriting used to be. Am I to read the letter?'

'Yes, certainly.'

This is what he read:

'*Monday*.
'Shall be back tomorrow. Say nothing to anybody.
'CLIFFORD OAKLEIGH.'

'Well, that's all right,' said Harding, with a sigh of relief. 'At any rate, he is safe. We know he is alive. But beyond question, his handwriting has altered. I should say he must be ill: it is certainly very feeble, for him. And how did the letter come?'

'It was dropped in the letter-box. I heard a ring.'

'You know, Reggie,' said Harding, thoughtfully, 'this makes the matter even more mysterious than it was before.'

'You don't think,' answered Reggie, 'that it is possible that this letter is a forgery. That it was done to prevent my going to the police?'

'I don't think so,' the other replied; 'a forger would have copied the writing exactly or would have made mistakes here and there. This note is clearly written by our friend, but written under circumstances which are unusual. He has never, to my knowledge, had a day's illness in his life. I'm afraid he is ill now.'

Reggie might have suggested that his master was recovering from a very serious drinking bout. But he made no such suggestion.

The K.C., with a great weight off his mind, but with a far more astonishing problem on his brain, went out of the house.

At ten o'clock the next morning Reggie heard the sound of a latchkey in the door.

With bated breath he listened and darted into the hall.

The door opened and Clifford Oakleigh entered.

A man in the prime of life, strenuous and active, obviously in the most robust health.

The theory of drunkenness fell to the ground.

He closed the door. He nodded to Reggie.

'Good-morning.'

'Good-morning, sir.' answered the valet, every inch a valet.

'You got my note, eh?'

'Yes, sir.'

'By the by, what time did you come in from the Covent Garden Ball on Friday night?'

'I didn't go to the ball, sir.'

Sir Clifford looked keenly at him.

'What did you do? When did you get in?'

'Soon after ten.'

The eminent physician was on the point of putting a question to him, but he stopped, as though suddenly realising that he knew the answer to the question.

'Pardell,' he said, speaking very seriously, 'I am paying you £500 a year not so much for your services as for your silence. You can never ensure, no matter what price you pay, the silence of a real servant. But a gentleman ought to know how to hold his tongue if you buy him a golden gag.'

'I thought you were dead, murdered perhaps. I found you lying on the floor,' stammered Reggie.

'I don't know what had happened. I was at my wits' end.'

Clifford's black eyes glittered.

'I told you when I engaged you that you were never to tell anybody what happened in this house.'

'I am very, very sorry, sir, I only told one person.'

'The dickens you did! And who was it?'

Nervously Reggie answered:

'I really thought you were dead. I thought there would be an inquest. And so I told Harding—I beg your pardon, sir, Mr Harding.'

Oakleigh whistled.

'Well, I tell you what you've got to do now. You've got to go and tell him that the whole thing was an illusion. No, wait a minute. I'll do it. I'll tell him that you're suffering from a serious nervous ailment, and that I am, out of my old friendship, keeping you here in the hope of effecting a cure. You know, Reggie,' he added kindly, 'you've led such a devil of a life that such an ailment would be but a very slight punishment for your misdeeds. Yes, if everybody had their rights, old chap, you would be dead.'

'By the by, sir,' said Reggie, delighted at the good humour with which his master treated his indiscretion, 'the young person next door who is employed as a housemaid tells me that she saw you in a hopeless condition being put into a four-wheeler by a woman.'

'The deuce she does, does she?' answered Clifford.

'Well, it doesn't matter what she says. I don't want you to say anything to her or to anybody else.'

'All right, sir.'

'Now help me off with my coat.'

As Reggie removed it, he noticed that the dress suit was uncrumpled, that the shirt and white waistcoat were entirely fresh; the collar and tie were in perfect condition. These were not the clothes of a man who, in a drunken state, had been bundled into a cab by a woman.

But upon his face was three days' growth of beard. His cheeks were like the wheel of a musical box. It struck Reggie as an astounding thing that the inventor of 'Baldo' should not take the trouble to remove this repulsive growth. Ever since he had known him Clifford Oakleigh had always been exact in his habits.

Why, in Heaven's name, had he not taken the trouble to remove his surplus fittings?

CHAPTER X

THE MINGEY MYSTERY

'THE disappearance of Miss Mingey' occupied a large portion of the papers. Every possible and impossible hypothesis was suggested to account for it. Mr Mingey was interviewed; Mrs Mingey was interviewed; pictures of the Mingey home were reproduced in the press. A verse, not altogether in the best taste, was sung at one of the musical comedy theatres. One enterprising journal offered a prize of a life's subscription to that journal for the most probable solution sent in by one of its readers on a detachable coupon.

The police also helped the press to elucidate the mystery. Everybody talked about the matter. Some people even went so far as to buy Mingey postcards embellished with the portrait of 'The latest vanishing lady'.

From the details furnished with regard to the inner life of the Mingey home there were those who maintained that in all probability the unfortunate Sarah, bored to death by her dull, drab surroundings, her funereal father, her entirely uninteresting mother, and the pseudo-religious atmosphere in which she lived, had committed suicide. Several men, presumably not remarkable for the robustness of their intellect wrote her letters proposing—in the event of her not being dead—that she should become their wives. Some of these letters came from Scotland. One was from an upholsterer in Aberdeen. He stated that his name was MacTavish (which in all probability was only too true): he affirmed that his business was in a flourishing condition, and stated that he had fallen in love with her picture at first sight. He would dearly like to meet her and make her his. At the same time, he protected himself in a postscript wherein he reserved the right of withdrawing his offer in the event of the explanation of her disappearance not being satisfactory to his 'mither'.

In this way Mingey acquired a certain amount of fame. He was spoken of by the other clerks in the Temple as the father of the vanishing lady.

This was not a subject suitable for chaff, but the melancholy and austere demeanour of Mingey had made him unpopular in the neighbourhood of the Law Courts. The feeling among his brethren was that, whatever had happened to his daughter, her present position could not be anything but an improvement on her life in the Mingey home circle.

Harding, obsessed by his great love, only gave his clerk perfunctory sympathy.

On Wednesday he telephoned to Pembroke Street. In his mind he had only the vaguest idea of what he would say to the lady. But he received a reply, presumably from a servant, to the effect that she was out of town.

'When would she be back?' he had asked.

But he received no definite answer.

The situation was intolerable to him. Desperately in love, he naturally felt an intense yearning for the society of the girl. He regarded it as a personal slight that she should have left town suddenly. He spent his entire time in thinking about her. But beyond her own personality he had little scope for reflection. As to her mode of life, or indeed her social status, he knew nothing. She was simply the ideal woman, that was all. And indeed the only question that remained for solution was 'Would she regard him as the ideal man?' He knew he was not the ideal man. No reasonable man could possibly maintain that he himself could be the ideal man in the eyes of any reasonable woman. But he devoutly hoped that, with luck and tact, he might behave in such a manner as to present to her imagination a colourable imitation of ideality.

That same evening he dined at the Gridiron with a view to picking up some cheery companion who would accompany him to a theatre or a music-hall.

Greatly to his annoyance, he found that at the long table there was no one who would afford agreeable companionship under the tension from which he suffered. There was Colonel Cazanova, a popular favourite, puffy, adipose and alcoholic, an authority on no subjects except the causes which were sending the Service to the dogs. There was Peplowe-Price, one of the leading non-actors of our day, always eager to explain to an uninterested public the faults in other people's Hamlets. And the rest were worse.

He had just finished his oysters when he found himself patted on the back.

He looked up.

Beaming down upon him was Clifford Oakleigh. In his surprise he dropped his glass.

Then Clifford sat down by his side. A smile of amusement played about his lips.

'My dear George, you're suffering from nerves, eh?'

Harding had no answer ready. He simply stared vaguely at the newcomer.

Then Oakleigh burst out laughing.

'My dear chap,' he said, 'you are the limit, the absolute limit! Did you actually think I was dead? I believe you did. Looking at your face now, you are expressing that surprise which one would expect to see on the face of a man who saw, or thought he saw, a ghost. I suppose, really, you barristers can believe in any old thing. When a man has schooled himself to believe in the law, any other feat of credulity is child's play, isn't it?'

'My dear Clifford,' protested Harding.

But the other would not allow him to proceed.

'Say no more about it,' he said. 'I admit that you have insulted me grossly. I can imagine no more terrible insult than to assume a man is dead, except perhaps to meet the man and behave as though he was a ghost. You are an eminent K.C. Good heavens, old chap, to think that on the evidence of Reggie Pardell you came to the conclusion that I was dead! I can forgive a man anything except the presumption that I am dead. Great Scott! if the idea got about among my patients it would do me a deuce of a lot of harm. There is one thing a doctor can't be. and that is dead.'

Harding justified himself. He described his interview with Reggie. He described it with great accuracy and the other listened keenly. At the conclusion he said:

'There it is. I have told you exactly what occurred. Is Reggie mad, or is he not? How much of this is true and how much is invention?'

'In the first place,' Clifford replied, 'I am not dead. That is clear. Mind you, I can't prove that I'm not dead. And I won't labour the point. You must form your own conclusion. My own idea is that I am not dead. But, after all, we know so little about death that it is quite probable that when we are absolutely defunct we shall not be able to grasp the fact. Perhaps that is the explanation of ghosts. It may well be that it will take some time before people become convinced that they are extinct. As a rule, ghosts are more or less contemporary. At most, they have only been dead two or three hundred years. You never hear nowadays of the appearance of a ghost dating from the time of the Caesars. I expect that a man of ordinary intelligence after ten years of decease takes the knock—if I may use the expression—with regard to so serious a matter. He gives up trying to behave as a living man.'

Harding was nonplussed at his levity.

'Don't you worry,' he said, 'you are not a ghost. If you were a ghost, it would be almost impossible to account for the disappearance of the steak which you are eating with such intense rapidity. A ghost never eats, or, indeed, does anything useful. Joking apart,' he added, 'was all this an hallucination of Reggie's? Mind you, he swore to me that he had seen you lying dead on the floor in King Street. He told me that he had touched your face and it was cold. What are you going to do about it?'

'Do about it? Why, nothing! What can one do about it? Is it worth while doing anything about it?'

'Perhaps not, but what about Reggie? If he gets into the habit of making these statements, he will be a deuce of a nuisance, won't he? Anyhow, if he is liable to see corpses on carpets, there must be something awfully wrong with him. You, a physician, an expert in nerve diseases, must grasp the fact that his is a very bad case.'

Slowly the great physician answered him.

'Do you know that a man who is only insane on one subject is the exception? Most of us are mad on half a dozen subjects. Some of us are so devoid of all sense of proportion that we are mad about practically everything. Of course, Reggie's brain is not normal. He has led a devil of a life, a much worse life than mine. I have been able to stand it. He has not. But mind you, I don't think he will come to any evil owing to his trouble. It doesn't matter what he says about me. I shan't bring an action for slander against him. And on all other points he is completely sane. But with regard to me he can't tell the truth; his vision is distorted; he sees everything wrong. When you meet him again, old chap, it will be better not to mention the matter, because he has probably forgotten all about it by now. Of course, he has forgotten all about it by now.'

He gave a low chuckle.

'Really, one ought not to laugh at this sort of thing, but I suppose one gets case-hardened. And when all is said and done, this is not serious at all. Anyhow, I am looking after him properly.'

'And he is actually your valet?' asked Harding.

'Is that true?'

'Yes, that's true. He is perfectly safe under my care.'

'And you pay him £500 a year?'

'Yes, poor chap.'

'You're a devilish good fellow, Clifford.'

'Oh, yes I am,' remarked the other, 'and I'm not only a devilish good fellow but I'm having a devilish good time. I doubt whether anybody in the world is having such a devilish good time as I am.'

'If you are not doing anything tonight, Clifford, what do you say to going to a music-hall?'

The physician shook his head.

'My dear sir, I'm having such a devilish good time that I'm not going to waste a minute on a music-hall. I am going home.'

'Stop. This is a singularly curious thing about my clerk's daughter, Sarah Mingey, that I sent to you.'

Clifford thought for a moment.

'Yes, yes. There was nothing much the matter with her. I had no trouble with her. I cured her at once.'

'You cured her so thoroughly that she's vanished off the face of the earth.'

Clifford laughed.

'That is, indeed, a complete cure for all mortal ills.'

CHAPTER XI

'PURE BROMPTON ROAD'

'BEFORE you go home,' said Harding, in his voice a trace of nervousness, 'I want to ask you one or two questions.'

Graciously Clifford nodded permission.

'I met an awfully charming woman on Saturday night at the Savoy. I dined with old Mudge. The girl was a Miss Clive. It seems that she has taken your house in Pembroke Street. By the by, why did you keep the fact that you had a house in Pembroke Street and, for the matter of that, a house in King Street, a complete secret from your friends?'

The other's eyes twinkled.

'I say, George, did you ever hear the story of the man who made a large sum of money . . . by attending to his own business?'

Harding affected not to grasp the personal allusion.

'Yes,' he said. 'I have heard the story, but I never believed a word of it. Now about Miss Clive?'

Clifford looked at him sideways.

'So you take an interest, eh?'

'I don't take . . . an interest.'

'Then you are only asking out of curiosity?'

'Out of interested curiosity,' he replied.

Mischievously the other spoke.

'What do *I* think about Miss Clive, eh? Well, nothing. This is what I have heard. If the girl were not so stupid and so plain, she would be quite a pleasant creature. But, in addition, the poor thing has got no figure, no style. In fact, she is pure Brompton Road. No, not quite that. She's a Kensington girl with a Bayswater manner—a West Kensington girl with a North Bayswater manner, to be exact.'

Harding gave him the lie.

'Nothing of the sort. She is one of the most beautiful girls I have ever seen, and one of the most charming. Her figure is superb. Kensington, indeed! Bayswater, forsooth!'

Clifford looked at him. He seemed on the point of bursting into laughter, but he controlled himself.

'I think you've taken a fancy to her, you know.'

'My dear chap,' protested the K.C., 'I've only seen her once.'

'Twice,' corrected Clifford. 'You know you have seen her twice.'

Surprised, he answered, 'Yes, I have seen her twice. But how did you know? Did she tell you? She couldn't have told you?'

'No, she didn't tell me, but I . . . know.'

'I don't understand how you know that I called upon her.'

'My dear George, there are many things that even a man of your great intellect will go to his tomb without understanding. Have you ever understood a woman yet?'

'I have never wanted to, until now.'

'May I take it, George,' he inquired very seriously, but with more of a suggestion of mockery in his seriousness, 'that you are anxious to understand Miss Clive?'

The barrister made no definite reply.

'I am anxious,' he said, 'for you to tell me anything you know about your tenant.'

'Whether good or evil?'

'Whether good or evil.'

Clifford spoke deliberately.

'I don't know that I can tell you much. She has taken my house and she pays me £2000 a year—a quarter in advance. Therefore I gather that she is wealthy. From your behaviour I assume that she is beautiful.'

'Marvellous!' exclaimed the K.C., 'wonderfully beautiful! Do you mean to say you have never seen her?'

'No, I have never . . . actually . . . seen her.'

Harding sincerely hoped that he never would. Clifford was obviously a handsomer man than he, . and he had a far more effective manner of dealing with women. Besides, Clifford had led a romantic life in London. Hundreds of women had been at his feet, and it was marvellous that his reputation as a breaker of women's hearts had not interfered with his practice. A less skilful specialist would have been ruined had one fourth of the stories that were told about Clifford collected round his name.

'Perhaps, if ever you ask her to dinner, you might ask me. But I daresay I'm asking too much.'

Harding's hand was forced.

He affected enthusiasm. 'My dear fellow, delighted! She's dining with me at the Carlton on Friday. *Do* come.'

Much to his relief the physician replied:

'Thanks very much, but Friday is impossible.' With a queer look in his eyes, he added: 'If she is as beautiful as you say, it would not be at all a bad idea for me to call on her. I suppose it wouldn't be a breach of etiquette for a landlord to call on his tenant—especially on such a good tenant?'

Harding shrugged his shoulders, as though it were a moot point.

'Or I might get Mudge to ask me to meet her, as he asked you to meet her.'

'Now why do you suppose he did that?'

'Would you really like to know, George? Well, I asked him to.'

'*You* did!'

'Certainly. Mind you, I settled the whole thing with her by correspondence. She gave me to understand that she knew nobody in London. I don't know whether it was her handwriting that inspired confidence, but when she paid the £500 down there was no room for doubt. However, I was interested in the woman in a vague sort of way: so I arranged with her and Mudge that she should dine with him and that you should be asked. I wanted to have two expert opinions on my tenant. Thus it was that you met her the day after she took possession of 69 Pembroke Street. I am glad,' he said, 'that you and Mudge are favourably impressed. I think you are more favourably impressed than Mudge. But then Mudge is Mudge, and married to Mrs Mudge. How rarely it happens, George, that other men's wives are as unattractive as Mrs Mudge.'

Harding stared into his eyes.

'Would you mind telling me precisely how much of this rigmarole is a lie?'

Clifford laughed:

'Do you know, old chap, if I were to tell you the truth, the whole truth and nothing but the truth, it would sound infinitely falser than what I have said? I have told you something that is not altogether plausible. But, making a certain allowance for eccentricity on my part, and perhaps on the part of the lady you so much admire, the story is quite probable. If I were you, I should accept it as truth. You and I, George, are old friends. You know that it has been my object in life to get out of life all that life holds. I am in love with life, but life does not satisfy me. Perhaps I want more in life than there is. It may be that I want a miracle. It may be that I can effect a miracle. But even if I can, even if I have, I doubt whether I shall ever be satisfied. You may take it from me, old chap, that I have not sought for a new sensation at your expense. I am telling you all that you need know about Miss Clive. I am telling you probably infinitely more than she will ever tell you. You are an expert cross-examiner. In the Law Courts you can rob souls of their secrets. But I doubt whether you will extract any statement from Miss Clive beyond "I am Miss Clive of 69 Pembroke Street". Sixty-nine! Curious numerals.'

'Do you think she will be reticent as to her Christian name?'

'Oh, I myself will tell you that! Her Christian name is Miriam. Strangely enough it is my favourite name.'

A gleam of enthusiasm shot from the lawyer's eyes.

'It is the most beautiful name in all the world!'

Her name seemed to him, if possible, even more beautiful than her telephone number, which was saying much.

CHAPTER XII

On returning to his house he, not without deep thought, wrote six notes.

Each contained an invitation to the Carlton to dinner at a quarter past eight on the following Friday. Each was written to a charming man or a beautiful woman. He felt that only the most attractive people of his acquaintance were worthy to meet Miss Clive, and he doubted, in his heart, if even they were worthy.

Love is the most selfish of all pursuits. Even now, he felt a sensation of jealousy. These extra six persons would be playing unnecessary parts in the drama of his life.

Though they were unnecessary to the drama of his life, yet they were indispensable to convention. It would be fitting that the supers should be the most agreeable that he could muster.

As he looked at the names on the envelopes, he felt confident that Miriam would be pleased with his guests. They would do him honour as guests. It is not every man who can, at three days' notice, obtain the attendance at dinner of three eminent men and three beautiful women.

A shade of fear came over him as he reflected that it was entirely possible that they might all be engaged. If the worst came to the worst, he would be able to find adequate substitutes.

The servants had gone to bed; so he, himself, went to the pillar-box and posted the notes.

Before sleep came to his eyelids, he had spent much time in picturing the dinner.

It would be a perfect dinner. He would go to the Carlton on his way back from the Temple the next afternoon; he would consult with M. Jacques and with Auguste Shurin: the three of them would produce a masterpiece of culinary art on Friday next.

Suddenly an idea struck him.

Suppose she were a Roman Catholic! The menu would be all wrong!

Though he, like most men, practised no form of religion, and was only content to do what was right in the world's eyes and to obey the world's rules, he considered that the mystical rites of the Catholic creed threw an additional charm over a woman. To all the senses the Catholic religion appealed. It gratified the eye with the miracles of the painter's and the sculptor's art. The intoxicating perfume of incense penetrated to the innermost cells of the brain and floated there. The mysterious and voluptuous music played havoc with the heart. The religion had all the charms of love. A woman nurtured in that creed had been rehearsing for the advent of passion. If she were, in fact, a Catholic, he knew that she would be devout where the regulations of her faith were concerned.

He turned on the electric light and looked at his watch.

It was twelve o'clock.

He would ring her up and ask her whether she were a Roman Catholic.

It would be a great joy to him to hear from her lips at midnight that this was her faith.

He pictured her in bed, around her neck, hanging in a tiny bag, a model of the Virgin.

'Confound it,' he said suddenly, 'I am insane with love. I know she is out of town.'

He turned out the light and fell into a troubled sleep. Every now and again he awoke, always with a feeling of deep oppression. Time was not passing, Friday would never come.

The eventful day came and he found himself in the Palm Court at the Carlton, seated on a green wicker chair. . . . Mr William Gillett was in the offing.

On his right-hand side was Lady Griselda Oakshott, who, in spite of being a Christian scientist, had retained her looks, and in most things her power of judgment. To her was talking Sir Findlay Jackson, the only unmarried Judge on the Bench, a man who in addition to this distinction was never a buffoon in office hours; his duller colleagues on the Bench maintained that he had no sense of humour. Lord Lashbridge, remarkable for a note of asceticism in his appearance, chatted to the beautiful Mrs Tudway, our leading living authority on toques. She it was who made strenuous pilgrimages to Paris four times a year, and, on her return to London, solved for the benefit of her less erudite sisters the great toque question. All that could be known about hats she knew. Anything that could be called a hat without exactly looking like a hat (in the eyes of a man) she could wear. So svelte was her figure, so dignified without being repellent was her bearing, that she could give the cachet of the inevitable to the most improbable toque.

Harding turned to Mrs Onslow-Parker, a beautiful widowette.

'I'm awfully sorry,' he said, 'that Sir Clifford Oakleigh couldn't come. I know you like him.'

She raised her lashes.

'Everybody likes him—except his patients.'

Harding's eyes questioned her.

'I don't know what he has been doing lately,' she answered. 'He appears to be so busy that he can't do any work.'

'How do you mean?'

'I happen to know one or two people who have been anxious to see him lately and he has not been able to give them an appointment. You know nowadays, no self-respecting woman ever has an illness that is not supervised by him. They would rather die under Clifford than recover under anybody else. Well, my friends have tried to make appointments and he has declined to fix a day. He has made some absurd excuse. And,

do you know, I am afraid my unfortunate friends will get well
. . . perhaps they won't even have an operation at all.'

He smiled.

'I know that there is nothing more unfashionable than
robust health.'

She babbled on:

'My dear Mr Harding, everything that is difficult is unfashionable. It is vulgar to be well: it is bad taste to be rich: it
is odd to be honest. In fact, we are in for a boom of the
negative virtues.'

'I suppose,' he answered, 'negative virtues are positive vices,
aren't they?'

'I don't know,' she smiled, 'one gets so mixed up with
virtues and vices nowadays. What is one man's vice is another
man's virtue.'

'And what is one woman's virtue?' he asked.

'Good Heavens!' she replied, 'I don't think that virtue has
ever got thoroughly acclimatised in this wicked world of ours.'

He looked nervously at his watch. It was twenty minutes
past eight.

'Who are you waiting for?' she inquired.

'A Miss Clive.'

She fanned herself with mock petulance.

'Well, one doesn't wait long for an unmarried girl, I trust.
One should never wait for an unmarried girl. For a married
woman you can wait ten minutes—never a minute more.'

'And for a widow?' he inquired.

'Almost as long as for an actor.'

'Oh, if you are foolish enough to ask an actor to a meal
you deserve that he shouldn't come . . . which he probably
wouldn't. No self-respecting actor would ever dream of being
. . . punctual . . .'

Then she broke off:

'Is she very beautiful, this Miss Clive? Do you know, Mr
Harding, that for a K.C. you seem singularly ill at ease. You

look almost as though you expected to be cross-examined yourself.'

There was a mischievous twinkle in her eyes.

'You look as though someone would suddenly come into the hall and expose the secrets of your hideous past before us all.'

He hardly heard her. He made a spontaneous movement towards the door.

Miss Clive entered.

The eyes of everybody in the Palm Court turned towards her.

A few ladies ceased staring at Mr William Gillett.

In some cases, men nudged women; in others, women nudged men.

Instantly Harding knew that his appreciation of Miriam was shared by everybody present. Clearly he was justified in having fallen in love at first sight.

More radiant in her beauty than ever, she glided towards him.

'My dear chap,' she said, 'I'm devilish late.'

Then she seemed to remember herself and added:

'Oh, I beg your pardon, Mr Harding, I don't know what I was thinking of!'

CHAPTER XIII

A LITTLE DINNER

A GLANCE at Shurin proved to Harding that his guests found favour in the sight of that most eminent of *maîtres d'hôtel*.

As the little party seated itself at a round table it was evident that they had caused a flutter of interest. Harding could see that men were inquiring of women, and women of men, as to the identity of Miss Clive.

She was in high spirits and talked brilliantly. In fact, she absorbed more than her share of the conversation. On all subjects she spoke as one having authority. She talked with a confidence unusual in a young girl. Without the aggressive self-assurance of a blue-stocking, she yet seemed extraordinarily confident in her own knowledge. She corrected Lord Lashbridge on a detail connected with yellow fever in Sierra Leone. She appeared entirely conversant with the leading cases that had been tried by Sir Findlay Jackson. Further, she knew by sight, at any rate, the distinguished and fashionable people in the room. About many of them she told amusing and intimate anecdotes.

Lashbridge evidently took an interest in her. He was puzzled, and every now and again threw inquiring glances at his host.

The conversation drifted on to the subject of the disappearance of Miss Mingey.

Sir Findlay Jackson thought that it might be a case of dual identity. Such things, he said, had frequently occurred. It was perfectly possible for a person to forget suddenly his or her identity and to become, for a space of time, an entirely different individual.

'One of the strangest cases of the sort I ever heard of,' said Miss Clive, 'was that of a Congregational minister in New York. The Rev. Mr Briggs his name was. One morning he went out from his home, stating that he would return for dinner. He went to the bank and withdrew £100 to pay for a piece of land he had bought. He was seen to enter a tramcar, and that was the last of him for the time being. Now, what do you think was the sequel?'

No one was prepared with an answer.

The girl continued:

'He appeared suddenly in a town in one of the Southern States, a thousand miles from his home, under the name of Gibbs. He rented a small shop and set up in business as a grocer. One day he suddenly rushed into the shop next door and asked what the name of the town was. The man had no knowledge of how he had got to his present surroundings. He could not understand why he was a grocer. He had never had any desire to be a grocer. He had no particular talent for selling groceries. He stated that he was a Congregational minister. People maintained that he was mad. But he was not. However, on being hypnotised, his recollection came back to him and he was able to recall the circumstances under which he left home.'

'That's most extraordinary,' said the Judge. 'In my own profession it has often struck me as entirely inexplicable why people, who have hitherto led irreproachable lives, should suddenly commit crimes which can in no possible way benefit them.'

Miss Clive told him that the dual identity theory afforded a satisfactory solution.

But the Judge would not hear of it.

'Then we should have no criminals!' he exclaimed, a condition of things which he apparently deprecated.

'My dear Sir Findlay,' said the girl, earnestly, 'it would be quite possible for you, on your way home tonight, to forget that you are a judge of the High Court and to believe yourself to be a stockbroker.'

'Good Heavens!' he protested. 'How horrible!'

'A curious thing occurred in 1903,' she continued. 'A workman left King's Cross at 6.45 on Monday morning to go to his work in Wardour Street. He looked at the clock at the Euston Hotel as he passed it at 6.50. Then five and a half days were cut out of his life. Of what occurred on those days he remembers nothing. But at 4 p.m. on Saturday he found himself in a strange town. On inquiring of a policeman, he ascertained that he was in Leighton Buzzard: he had never been in Leighton Buzzard before; he had never heard of Leighton Buzzard; he did not know there was such a place as Leighton Buzzard. The condition of his boots and his blistered feet indicated that he had walked all the way. Really, Sir Findlay, even the best of us have no security for our future good behaviour. Only last year, a barrister in Paris, a man of very great ability; with a big practice and entirely devoted to his wife, a man of the highest moral character, suddenly had a quarrel with his stepfather, the result of which was a complete loss of memory. He left home and plunged into the most terrible dissipation for three weeks.'

The Judge laughed.

'I'm afraid he had great difficulty in persuading his wife that he had not lost his memory on purpose.'

He rather resented the behaviour of this beautiful girl who deliberately told him fairy tales.

'Do you know, Miss Clive, I've heard a lot of stories of that sort from my friend, Sir Clifford Oakleigh. He believes firmly in the possibility of a dual identity. I fancy he would like to be two people, but I doubt whether even two identities would satisfy him.'

'He ought surely to be content with being Sir Clifford Oakleigh,' said Mrs Onslow-Parker, 'I can imagine no more delightful position than his. Enormously successful, very rich, hugely popular, and unmarried. What does a man want more?'

Harding replied:

'Clifford wants everything. I don't think he will ever be satisfied. You see, it is impossible in this world to be Pope of Rome and also Emperor of Germany.'

'On the contrary,' said Miss Clive. 'Sir Clifford Oakleigh is an absolutely contented man . . . a perfectly contented person.'

'You know him?' inquired Harding.

'Only by reputation,' she answered quickly, 'and, of course, I have seen pictures of him. That man *must* be perfectly happy.'

The Judge interposed:

'My dear young lady, no man in this world with a gleam of intelligence can be perfectly happy. In every house there is a skeleton in the cupboard: the handsomer the cupboard the more terrible is the skeleton.'

'I'll tell you a very curious thing about Clifford,' said Harding. 'You know I have known him all his life . . . pretty well, that is. I knew his people when he was a boy, and I knew him at Oxford. Well, you wouldn't say there is anything effeminate about him, would you?'

'Good heavens, no!' answered the Judge.

'As a matter of fact,' continued the barrister,

'he was intensely athletic at Oxford: good at all games, keen on all sports. And yet he has told me not once, but twenty times, that he always regretted that he wasn't a woman, for he held that women occupy the best position both in life and in love.'

'What an extraordinary thing to regret,' sighed Mrs Onslow-Parker. 'Being a woman is bad luck. No, it is even worse than that. Being a woman is a curse. Have you ever come across a woman, a sensible woman, not the ordinary ridiculous creature who spends her entire life in talking about appendicitis and kitchen-maids, who would not give her soul to be a man? No, no, there is no fun in being a woman: it is simply bad luck.'

Lashbridge expressed surprise at what Harding had said. 'You see, Oakleigh is so very fond of women, has had such wonderful success with them, that he must know them well enough to understand that being a woman is not . . . well, not worth while. You really ought to meet him, Miss Clive. Will you come to lunch with me on Sunday week at my house and I will ask him to meet you?'

'On Sunday week,' she reflected. 'Where are we now? Oh, this is Friday. I'm afraid,' she said slowly, 'that I shall be out of town on Sunday week.'

'Miss Clive,' interrupted Harding, 'is always out of town. She has only just returned. By the way, Miss Clive, where have you been to?'

'I have been staying with friends,' she answered in a tone that prevented him from pursuing the matter further.

'Some other day,' persisted Lashbridge. 'May I drop you a line?'

'By all means,' she smiled.

Harding felt jealous. What did Lashbridge mean by admiring her? It was obvious that he did admire her. And he was a Peer. The barrister scented danger. However, as he put her into her motor-car, he fancied that she returned the pressure of his hand.

In the hall his other guests plied him with questions. Who was Miss Clive? Where did she come from?

But it irritated him considerably to be unable to supply any particulars beyond the fact that she had taken Sir Clifford Oakleigh's house in Pembroke Street, and that she did not know her landlord to speak to.

CHAPTER XIV

THE EVIDENCE OF NELLIE

ONE evening as Reggie was leaving No. 34 he heard a low whistle, and, on turning round, saw Nellie, the under-housemaid, in the next door area. She was dressed for 'going out' and ran rapidly up the steps.

'Hi, you mister,' she cried, 'I want a word with you.'

'Well, you can't have it,' he answered brusquely, 'I'm busy.'

'You look it,' she replied, 'you look dressed for being busy. I never see such a walking-out kit on any valet as you've got. Why, bless my heart,' she added, as she stared him up and down from the top of his shiny hat to the tips of his brilliant boots,

'I never see such a toff in all my born days. And we receive good company next door, in spite of the fact that master is only a stockbroker. But missus did come of a good family, and she don't let us forget it, even when she forgets it herself.'

'Really, the manners and customs of one's neighbours are of no particular interest.'

'Oh, ain't they?' she chipped in. 'The manners and customs of *your* house axe the talk of every servants' hall in the street.'

'I don't wish to talk about them,' he said coldly, attempting to close the episode.

But she persisted.

'I suppose you *can* walk a yard or two, in spite of your boots,' she sneered, 'or perhaps my lord has to take a cab, has he?'

Several times Reggie had noticed that the girl had tried to get into conversation with him. Evidently she had something to say that she obviously would find an opportunity of saying. He was not conceited enough to imagine that she had fallen in love with him, although, in very truth, were he to give her the slightest encouragement, Nellie's heart would have been at his feet . . . or anywhere he needed it. Was he not the Prince of Valets? Had he not the softest of all jobs? On the whole, it would be better to let her say what she had to say and have done with it.

'I'm in a great hurry, my dear young lady. But as you seem anxious to have a talk I can spare you a few minutes.'

'My word!' she exclaimed, 'this is the proudest day of my life. The footman at No. 37 saw us through the dining-room blinds. It will be all over the street that you and me are walking out.'

She threw a leering glance up at his face. 'I hope I haven't turned your head.'

'No,' he replied, 'what have you got to say?'

'I take an interest in you,' she began. 'Oh, no, mister, not in you only so much as in No. 34.'

'No. 34?' he queried.

'No. 34 King Street,' she said definitely. 'No. 34 King Street, May fair. Everything that goes on in No. 34 King Street inter-ests me and interests all the other girls. You've got hold of the rummest job I've ever heard of.'

'What,' he asked angrily, 'has No. 34 King Street got to do with you?'

'Rightly speaking,' she replied, 'it ain't got nothing to do with me. But, as a human being and not a cabbage, I natu-rally take an interest in next door. It wouldn't be neighbourly not to.'

'Oh, don't you worry about being neighbourly,' said Reggie. 'You do your duty in your menial capacity . . .'

She hitched up her face at the words 'menial capacity.'

'Menial or no menial,' she snapped, 'it's better than being valet to a mystery. "The Mayfair Mystery" we call No. 34.'

Reggie tried to awe her by stating sententiously:

'You are not good at giving nicknames above your station. You've been reading a penny novelette; that's what you've been doing.'

She was quick in her retort:

'Your home beats any penny novelette I've ever struck. What do you make of a gentleman—Sir Clifford Oakleigh, oh, yes, I know his name; there ain't so many Sir Cliffords about but what by putting two and two together one can find out who he is—well, what do you make of a gentleman who keeps only one servant, and that servant himself a gentleman, or I don't know what I'm talking about, which I do, and has a charwoman in by the day, and sometimes never leaves the house for a week?'

She stopped to take breath. Then she continued:

'What do you make of a gentleman who sometimes comes in when he has never gone out?'

Reggie stared at her in astonishment.

'Why the dickens don't you attend to your own business?' he inquired. His eyes nervously sought the faces of the passers-by. It would be an awkward thing if anybody saw him walking out with a palpable housemaid.

That was what he was doing . . . 'walking out'.

'Oh, I intend to mind my own business right enough,' she replied, 'and this may be business that will mean money for little Nellie, and a pretty tidy sum. Now, look here,' she added, fumbling with a small imitation Russian leather bag which she carried in her hand. She produced a newspaper cutting. 'Come here and look at this.'

Standing under a lamp in Mount Street she held up a somewhat crude woodcut representing a young girl in spectacles.

'Ever seen her?' she asked, looking curiously at Reggie.

His face was a blank.

'Never,' he answered, 'and I don't know that I should pay any very large sum for the privilege.'

'Give over,' she said, nudging him, a process which he resented.

'Well, *I've* seen her,' she continued very firmly.

'My dear girl,' he answered, shrugging his shoulders, 'I can't help your troubles.'

'There's no trouble about this, leastways, not for me. This is a stroke of good luck for me. There's £50 offered for any information about this young girl. This young girl is Miss Mingey, what's disappeared.'

'That's just the sort of girl who might disappear and whose disappearance wouldn't be regretted. I have rarely seen such an unnecessary-looking girl in my life.'

'Oh, chuck it,' she rejoined, in no little irritation. 'This cutting is out of the *Weekly Dispatch* of last Sunday, and there is £50 reward offered for any information leading to the discovery of this Miss Mingey. Well,' she continued impressively, 'I've seen her, and, what is more, so have you. At any rate, she has been in No. 34.'

'Nonsense.'

'None o' your lip. I see her coming out. She was the creature who helped your governor into a four-wheeler the night he was toxy.'

'I really can't listen to any more of this rubbish.'

'It's not rubbish,' she cried indignantly, 'it's gospel truth, and I can swear to it. And if you was not such a fool of a gent who has sunk down, no doubt owing to being a disgrace to his people or the fool of the family or what not, you would say to me, "Nellie," you would say, "come into the Running Footman and have a glass of fruity port, and we'll talk things over." That's what you'd say.'

'I can't imagine,' he replied, in a chilly tone, 'my making any such proposition.'

'Oh, you're a chump-head,' she sneered, 'you know more about it than I do, and if we was to go to the police-station together we could bust up the mystery in No. 34 and get fifty of the brightest and best to divide.'

He did not know what manner to assume. He impersonated the heroic servant.

'If there was anything I knew against my governor, do you think that I should give him away?'

'Oh, stop it, mister. You're fresh and soft, aren't you!'

He pleaded guilty.

'Well, I'm not. Look here, come into the Running Footman and stand me a glass of fruity port, and we'll talk a bit.'

There was something in the girl's demeanour that convinced him of her earnestness. She evidently believed that the picture in the *Weekly Dispatch* represented the girl—or creature, as she had called her—who had helped Clifford into the four-wheeler on the night of the mysterious occurrence.

Hastily looking up and down the street to see that there was no one of his acquaintance in the neighbourhood, he took her by the arm and drew her into the saloon bar of the Running Footman. There he gave her a glass of fruity port. So pleased was she with its fruitiness that she consumed another. The wine made her talkative, and he hoped for further details. He plied her with all sorts of questions and affected to disbelieve her tale.

'Look here, my girl,' he said, 'how can you swear that these two are one and the same? One dowdy girl in spectacles looks very much like another dowdy girl in spectacles.'

Nellie nodded her head.

'Oh, no, that's just it. She wasn't wearing spectacles when she put him into the cab. It makes it all the more remarkable, doesn't it, my recognising her?'

'Very much more remarkable. So remarkable that it's almost incredible.'

Then suddenly he remembered the pair of woman's spectacles that Harding had discovered on the mantelpiece.

He whistled softly to himself.

'That's curious,' he said, 'devilish curious.'

CHAPTER XV

INSPECTOR JOHNSON

As the result of his interview with Nellie, Reggie was more puzzled than ever. He had thought of going to Harding and consulting him on the matter, but on reflection it seemed to him that the wisest course would be to place the whole story before Clifford Oakleigh.

He walked down to Arthur's, spent an hour or two playing Bridge, and then returned to King Street.

Soon after his arrival, he heard the eminent physician's key in the door. He went out into the hall to receive him.

'May I have a few words with you, sir?'

'Come into the sitting-room.' Clifford smiled.

'You're not going to give notice, I hope?'

'No, sir, I'm not going to give notice, but I have just heard something that I think you ought to know.'

Clifford shot a keen glance at him.

'Who did you hear it from?'

'From Nellie, the under-housemaid next door.' His master smiled.

'Ah, Pardell, Pardell,' he said with mock gravity,

'I can't have you flirting with the neighbours' servants. What is it?'

Reggie told him the story of his meeting with Nellie, the episode of the fruity port and the account which she had given of the mysterious visitor.

The other listened attentively. Then he suddenly dropped, as he very often did, the relation of master and servant.

'Sit down, old fellow,' he said.

The two sat opposite one another by the fireside.

Reggie lighted a cigarette and began.

'The whole thing's devilish odd . . .'

'I admit that. But the precise degree of oddity that the affair has reached would surprise even you. I don't say it's the oddest thing that has ever occurred. But it's one of the oddest. That I can say without improper pride.'

'My dear chap,' replied Reggie, 'the affair is so odd that it's on the point of being brought to the notice of the police. You see, this is a very peculiar position for me. You are doing something extraordinary. You always were an extraordinary man, and obviously I seem to be mixed up in it. But what am I mixed up in? That's what I want to know.'

Very gravely the other replied.

'That's what you never will know. It's not necessary for you to know it.'

'But look here, my dear Clifford, of course, you and I have always been pals, and you've given me a devilish good job over this matter. But I think I'm entitled to some information as to what the game is. Here are you, one of the leading physicians of the day. You build a house in King Street; you furnish a small portion of it. You employ, I think I may say without undue conceit, a gentleman, at any rate an ex-gentleman, to act as your valet. You keep no other servant in the house. You vanish mysteriously for three days. You take away no clothes. You, the inventor of "Baldo", return in evening-dress, wearing the same shirt that you went out in, and the shirt is perfectly clean. But you have a three days' growth of beard. That's peculiar enough in all conscience. Still, that is only a drop in the bucket. A girl mysteriously disappears. The day of her disappearance she is seen helping you, who are blind to the world, into a four-wheeler. You have always been an intensely temperate man, and yet you, in a hopeless state of intoxication, are helped into a four-wheeler by a girl for whom all London is looking.'

'Not so fast, Reggie,' interposed Clifford. 'The girl is identi-fied by a servant, an under-servant, from a rough woodcut in a weekly paper. A rough woodcut in a weekly paper as a rule looks like anybody except the person for whom it is intended, if it looks like anything at all.'

'Yes, I admit that,' answered Reggie, 'but there is one very curious thing about this girl. In the picture she wore spectacles. On the mantelpiece in this room on that night Harding and I found a pair of woman's spectacles. They seem to have been hastily put down, as though the owner had just taken them off.'

Clifford smiled at him:

'How on earth could you tell that they were a woman's spectacles?'

'Harding thought so, from the size. They were smaller than a man's.'

'Smaller than a small man's?' inquired the physician.

'Oh, I don't know.'

The query baffled Reggie, but he pursued the matter.

'Anyhow, they were made of plain glass. It's an extraordinary thing that anyone should wear spectacles of plain glass, except, of course, for purposes of disguise.'

'That knocks your theory on the head,' replied Clifford. 'Miss Mingey, apparently, was always in the habit of wearing spectacles. Do you assume that she was always in the habit of being disguised?' Reggie shrugged his shoulders.

'I can only place the facts before you and ask you to give me, in a spirit of ordinary fairness, some information as to the business.'

Clifford rose.

'Pardell,' he said, immediately becoming the master, 'if you wish to give notice, you can.'

Reggie got up from his seat, placed his cigarette in an ash tray and became Pardell.

'Oh, no, sir,' he replied hastily.

'You are satisfied with your situation?'

'Yes, sir.'

'And with your wages?'

'Yes, sir.'

'I should think so! But I'm not satisfied with your curiosity. There's too much of it. You have used the word police. I presume, therefore, that you think I have committed some crime, that I have stolen a pair of plain glass spectacles, or perpetrated some other infamy. You are entitled to your opinions so long as you don't express them. But I forbid you to gossip with the girl next door.'

'Yes, sir. But supposing she goes to the police with her story?'

'Let her go to the devil with her story. Or, if you are anxious to prevent her doing so, why don't you marry her and close her mouth?'

Reggie made no reply to the proposal.

The master continued.

'I'm going out in a few minutes. I shall not be back for three days.'

'Will you take any luggage, sir?'

'No.'

'You're going in evening-dress?'

'Yes. You can go to bed. Good-night.'

'Good-night, sir.'

Reggie went down to the basement, where he slept, and listened attentively for the departure of his master.

At three o'clock, when he fell asleep, he had heard no sound of a closing door.

In the morning he got up, went to the hall, and to his surprise found Clifford's hat and coat hanging on a peg.

He came to the conclusion that a man who leaves his house in the small hours of the morning without hat, coat or luggage must be mentally deranged.

At about twelve o'clock there was a ring at the bell.

On opening the door he saw two determined-looking gentlemen.

'I'm Detective-Inspector Johnson of Vine Street,' said one, 'can I see Sir Clifford Oakleigh?'

Reggie knew in an instant what had occurred. Nellie had made a dash for the £50.

'I'm afraid you can't,' he said.

'He's out, is he?'

'He is out.'

'When will he be in?'

'I can't say.'

'When did he go out?'

'Early this morning.'

The Inspector glanced sternly at Reggie. Then he said to his assistant, one P. Barlow, 'Come in.'

P. Barlow, a man whose chief characteristic was his admiration for his Chief, closed the door.

Then Johnson turned on Reggie.

'It won't help either you or your master for you to tell lies.'

Angrily Reggie retorted:

'What the dickens do you mean by talking to me like that?'

The indignation he showed was unlike the indignation of a servant. His tones were not those of a domestic.

The Inspector was for an instant baffled.

'What are you?' he said. 'Are you a friend of Sir Clifford Oakleigh's?'

'Certainly I am. Oh, no . . . I am his valet.'

'Take that down,' said the Inspector to P. Barlow, and P. Barlow obediently jotted down something—probably something entirely incorrect—in a note-book.

'You noticed that the servant was confused in his reply?'

P. Barlow had noticed it. He invariably noticed anything that Johnson told him he had noticed.

'What is your name?'

'Pardell.'

'Put that down.'

P. Barlow wrote down Parnell.

'Your first name?'

'Reginald.'

Reginald was not a usual name for a servant. In all his experience Johnson did not recollect having interviewed a single Reginald who followed that calling.

'What are you?' he inquired.

'I am Sir Clifford Oakleigh's valet.'

'How long have you been in his service?'

'Oh, a deuce of a short time.'

'How short?'

Quickly Reggie replied:

'Two or three weeks.'

'And where were you before?'

'Oh, I was in . . . all sorts of places before.'

'As a valet?'

'No, confound it,' he said, losing his patience.

'What were you?'

'Look here, I'm not going to be cross-examined by an infernal policeman. If you want to know, I was in the army,' he added, hoping that this would satisfy the Inspector.

'What regiment?'

'The Cape Mounted Beavers.'

'Private?'

'No, damn you.'

'What then?'

'I was a subaltern.'

'And now you are a valet?' inquired the other incredulously, while P. Barlow took the answers down all wrong.

'And why not, pray? We don't always remain what we start. I daresay you were an intelligent man once. Now you're a policeman.'

'Sauce won't do you any good. Will you kindly tell Sir Clifford Oakleigh that I should like to see him?'

'I have already told you that he went out early this morning.'

Suddenly the Inspector burst upon him.

'This house was watched all night, and he never went out.'

'Well, you know best,' answered Reggie, shrugging his shoulders. 'If he has not gone out, he's here. Search the house.'

Johnson communicated in a whisper with P. Barlow. As a result he became more amicable with Reggie. Said he:

'I suppose you haven't the slightest objection to our looking over the premises . . . as though we were possible tenants?'

'I have no objection. If you want to look round, you can look round.'

Johnson winked at him:

'You are naturally anxious about your master. We will help you to find out if he's concealed anywhere.'

'You can do what you jolly well please,' was the reply, 'but I tell you he went out some time after three o'clock this morning.'

The detective looked incredulously at him.

'Well, then, go and search,' said Reggie.

They searched, and they searched in vain.

Disappointed, Johnson showed Reggie a photograph of Miss Mingey.

'Have you ever seen this lady?' he inquired.

'Never,' he answered deliberately,

'Quite sure?'

'Absolutely.'

The detectives were on the point of leaving. Unconsciously, after the manner of a gentleman dealing with the police, Reggie slipped half-a-crown into the hand of the Inspector.

This proceeding, coming from a valet, struck Johnson as being extraordinary. However, he made no comment. But as he stepped out into the street he said gravely to P. Barlow,

'The plain clothes man who was on duty last night must have been asleep.'

CHAPTER XVI

'UNCLE GUSSIE'

MR AUGUSTUS PARKER was a power in the land.

He had invented for himself a position in Society of an eminence without parallel. No ball was complete without his presence, and on any dinner-party he shed lustre. Many, indeed, believed that a Society wedding without Mr Parker was illegal. Not particularly handsome, not particularly rich, not particularly amiable, he held a phenomenal position among swift people. If he danced with a girl, that graceful act was far more important than her presentation. It set upon her a cachet that was invaluable.

Enterprising mothers would give him untold dinners, conscientious fathers offered him as much hunting and shooting as he cared for . . . if only he would dance with their daughters. Often, indeed, it had occurred that a hesitating suitor had, immediately after he had seen his quasi-inamorata whirling round in the arms of Mr Parker, offered his hand and heart.

Mr Parker himself was not married. Any alliance that he might contract could not, of course, be other than a mesalliance. There was not, at the time, an unmarried Queen in Europe.

Mr Parker sat in the study of his comfortable little flat in Down Street. Mr Parker was baffled. He tugged at his long white walrus moustache and rubbed his right hand over his clean-shaven chin. On the table in front of him lay the cause of his bewilderment.

It was a letter, written in a somewhat masculine-feminine hand. It was dated from 69 Pembroke Street, and it stated definitely that Miss Clive would have the pleasure of calling upon Mr Augustus Parker at ten-thirty in the morning of this very day. It was now on the point of ten-thirty.

Mr Parker had never heard of Miss Clive, and anybody of whom Mr Parker had not heard had, in his opinion, and in the opinion of most people who were anybody, no physical existence.

During the interval between the receipt of the missive and this morning he had made inquiries. But they had been futile. No one of his acquaintance knew anything about the lady. He had even gone so far as to inspect, surreptitiously, the exterior of 69 Pembroke Street, and the house had found favour in his sight.

But the impertinence of the lady had come as a great shock to this social autocrat. Indeed, he had been in two minds as to whether or no he should receive her. He was still in two minds. In order to decide one way or the other he walked to the window and there hid behind a blind and waited to inspect this singularly audacious person. Should she be of unattractive demeanour, should she come on foot, he would instruct his man to state that he was engaged.

Precisely at ten-thirty a motor-car, which he roughly valued at between £800 and £900, drew up.

He was pleased with the motor-car. It was a motor-car in which he himself would not hesitate to drive; and from it alighted a woman of radiant beauty. He was pleased with the woman. He would not hesitate to drive in that motor-car with that woman. In fact, he would like to.

He walked away from the window and assumed an easy attitude, nonchalantly toying with a coroneted envelope.

His man announced Miss Clive.

He behaved with extraordinary dignity, with such dignity, indeed, that he gave one the impression that he had been acquired by the nation at his own valuation, and that in his opinion the nation had made a very good bargain.

'To what do I owe the honour . . .?' he began.

But he got no further.

Miss Clive took a seat, and in a very business-like manner made her statement. .

'Mr Parker,' she said, and as she spoke the musical notes in her voice appealed to this eminent expert in women, 'I have come to make an extraordinary proposal.'

He assumed the air of one to whom extraordinary proposals were the ordinary events of life.

'Proceed,' he said, with quasi-regal dignity. Was he not the Dictator of Dowagers? Of course he was. Yet this young girl did not seem overawed.

'I am anxious to get into Society,' she said.

'You, Mr Parker, can get me into Society.'

He winced at her bluntness.

'I am asking you a great favour,' she continued.

'Anything in the nature of a favour that I can do by way of return it will be a pleasure for me to do.'

He saw that she was expensively dressed, that her clothes were the work of first-rate artists; the motor-car and the servants on the motor-car were indicative of wealth. However, he temporised.

'Such a proposal is unheard of,' he said.

'Oh, no,' she answered smiling, 'one has often heard of such a proposal; one has also heard of such a proposal being accepted. Of course, in return for some such payment as £1000.'

'I know to whom you allude.' But he had the tact not to mention a well-known but inferior rival of his own.

'I wonder if you do know,' she laughed. 'I was for the moment thinking of the case of the pretty Miss Bottlebaum, a somewhat rich Jewess.'

Her eyes were fixed upon him, and a slight quick movement that he made did not escape her. Also, he knew that she had noticed.

'I think £1000 was the sum in her case. No, I am wrong. It was a thousand guineas. It the case of Miss Nasalheimer of Westborne Terrace that you were content with £1000.'

It was incredible to him that any woman should dare to come to him and make these statements. But there was something in this girl's demeanour that kept him completely under control. She was more like a barrister stating facts, crude, bald facts of whose truth he was entirely satisfied, than a *débutante* who desired to get into Society. And she was approaching the great and only Augustus Parker. How had she obtained this exact knowledge? He knew that there were in circulation rumours to the effect that he accepted payment for launching girls on the high seas of Society. But here were two definite charges succinctly made against him by a girl who did not hesitate to come and see him alone in the morning. He smiled a sickly smile.

'My dear lady,' he said, 'you shouldn't believe all you hear.'

'Oh, I don't,' she answered with a rippling laugh, 'I only believe what I know. You may rely upon me, Mr Parker, for absolute secrecy. I will give you a cheque for £500 today and £500 at the end of the season. That was the course pursued by Mr Nasalheimer, who is a business man.' Here again was a fact. The girl seemed to him uncanny. If he could actually rely upon her discretion he would be willing to accept her proposal. It flashed across his mind that her interview was intended as a joke, or that, horror of horrors! she was a journalist. He would require more particulars. She seemed to read his thoughts.

'Mine is a very extraordinary case,' she said.

'I am absolutely alone in the world. I have no relatives at all. I have a beautiful house—I think I may say that without pride—in Pembroke Street, the fashionable side of Pembroke Street, which I have taken from Sir Clifford Oakleigh.'

Here was light at last. He knew Clifford Oakleigh. He would go and see him.

'I have an income,' she pursued, 'of, roughly speaking, £20,000 a year. Really,' she laughed, 'it seems very egotistical to talk like this but I have been well educated. As a matter of fact, I am far better educated than most women. I can hold my own with most men on politics, science or history.'

'You are indeed a paragon,' he interposed, and she did not know whether there was a sneer inside the word.

'No,' she added, 'I have one fault. I can't hold my own with women about dress.'

'That is a fault,' he replied, 'which is almost a virtue. But you must admit that all this is very mysterious.'

'I do admit it.'

'When did your parents die?'

'With regard to my parents I can give you no information. You must look upon me as though I had suddenly sprung from nowhere.'

'But that is very hard to do,' he muttered.

'You must try and do it.'

'When did you spring from nowhere?'

'To tell you the truth, I sprung from nowhere, well, within the last few days.'

'Don't you know anybody in London?'

'Scarcely anybody except my solicitor, Mr Mudge; and Mr George Harding, the K.C., is a friend of mine.'

'An old friend?'

A shade of irritation passed over her forehead.

'I have no old friends.'

The mention of Mr Mudge and the K.C. was very much in her favour. They were people who, though not, of course, in Society from Mr Parker's point of view, were solid people.

'If only you could get . . .' 'References' was on the tip of his tongue, and she knew it.

She laughed her silvery laugh.

'Oh, that would be too absurd, wouldn't it? You wouldn't like me to go to Mr Harding and say, "Mr Harding, will you kindly write out a testimonial to the effect that I am a fit person to be introduced into Society by Mr Parker for the sum of £1000." I couldn't go very well, hat in hand . . .' She stopped abruptly. He was lost in thought, so she continued: 'It would be ridiculous for me to go to Mr Mudge and ask him if I might refer you to him. No, Mr Parker, you must trust me as I trust you. It would be no more to my interest to say that I had got into Society through subsidising you than for you to spread abroad a similar report.'

He shook his head.

'But women do talk.'

Impatiently she said, 'But I'm not a woman . . . of that sort.'

'That may be, that may be,' he muttered half to himself as he moved uneasily about the room.

'By the by,' she said firmly, 'there is one privilege that you have accorded to *débutantes* which I don't bargain for, and that is driving in your brougham.'

She was standing erect, her hands on her breast, in a manner suggestive of the way in which a barrister in cross-examination holds his gown.

Mr Parker shot a quick glance at her. The glance said very clearly, 'What do you mean?'

Very slowly she spoke, with half-closed eyes.

'Do you remember dining at a house in Grosvenor Gardens? Do you remember taking a girl on in your brougham to a dance at the Grafton Galleries?'

'Such a thing has often occurred,' he replied.

'Do you remember that when the bicycle was first introduced and people used to annoy cyclists, riders often used to carry ammonia squirts? They used them to squirt at the eyes of offensive people. The girl in the brougham, Aggie Craven-Hill . . .'

'That was not her name,' he snapped, foolishly taken off his guard by his delight in finding her out in an inaccuracy.

She shook her head and laughed.

'You're quite right, Mr Parker. Aggie Craven-Hill was not the girl who used the ammonia squirt on you in the brougham. That girl's name was Gwendolen Oakleigh, a niece of Sir Clifford Oakleigh's. Aggie Craven-Hill it was who found that your brougham took an hour to drive from Hill Street to Grosvenor Square. I'm afraid she never really cared for you, Mr Parker, but she seems to have cared for Gwendolen. That is why she warned her of the extraordinary method of transit you sometimes employed. Hence, also, we have the ammonia squirt.'

A sinister smile, almost concealed by his large white moustache, played about his lips.

'Considering that you have come from nowhere within the last few days, you have heard a lot of scandal.'

'I don't think we need go into that,' she answered. Then, after a pause, 'Is it a bargain, Mr Parker?'

More or less cowed by the influence of her personality, he answered:

'It is a bargain.'

'Good,' she replied, holding out her hand, which he shook. From her gold vanity-bag, studded with emeralds, she produced a cheque.

'I have made it payable to self. I thought it would be the more discreet course.'

'Thank you,' he said as he took it.

'Now, then,' she said in a business-like way,

'let us get to business. I've got to be introduced as somebody.'

'Well, you can't be introduced as a miracle: a woman from nowhere would hardly be accepted anywhere, and of course it would be impossible—even for me—to get you presented unless you were prepared to state something more definite about your parents.'

'I don't really care about being presented,' she replied. 'You see, I expect to entertain a great deal.'

'But,' he interrupted, 'you must have a chaperon. You can't live alone at 69 Pembroke Street.'

'That's just what I must do,' was her answer.

'I don't propose to have a woman in the house.'

'That makes it very difficult,' he rejoined.

'I know it's very difficult. But you, Mr Parker, can do it.'

Vaguely he threw out, 'If only we could get hold of some sort of story to account for you. You see, you must be accounted for. Here you are, enormously rich, aristocratic in appearance—if you will allow me to say so—and, besides that, beautiful. How on earth I'm to explain you I don't know.'

'I suppose I couldn't be a member of your own family?'

'I have no family,' he answered, almost brusquely.

'Oh, my dear Mr Parker, why forget your sister who married a veterinary surgeon at Chipping-Sodbury?'

'You know that, too!' he gasped.

'I know that too.'

'At any rate,' he replied, 'I have no family—to speak of.'

'I can quite understand a man in your position not caring to speak of a sister who married a dog-doctor. Now, wait a minute, Mr Parker. You have got one sister whom Society knows nothing of. I notice that the papers never chronicle the fact that among those walking in the Park at Church Parade were Mr Augustus Parker and his sister-in-law, Mrs Lindo, the wife of the well-known Chipping-Sodbury vet. No one knows of Mrs Lindo. Why not invent a sister? Why not let this sister be the wife of a man who has made a large sum of money in Australia? So many people have made large sums of money in Australia. While we are about it, let us invent Mr Clive, who, of course, is now dead, and Mrs Clive, who is no longer with us, my father and mother. Why not make Mr Clive a kind of a crank? A really rich man is entitled to be somewhat of a crank. Under the terms of my poor father's will—your brother-in-law's will—I was to be educated by governesses in London. I was to come of age at nineteen, which age I have just reached. Then you, Mr Parker, are to introduce me to modern Babylon, as Mr Sims, the Hair-restorer King, so aptly styles the metropolis. Where is that story weak?'

Each of them took the story and found flaws. They added details to conceal the flaws. After an hour's conversation, each felt that the genesis of Miss Clive might be placed before the world without fear of a catastrophe.

'That's all right,' she said, rising at length, 'Uncle Gussie.'

He shuddered. No one had ever dared to address him as Gussie. A Crowned Head had once alluded to him as Augustus and had ever afterwards regretted the familiarity. But Gussie! Never, never, never. However, she was so extraordinarily beautiful that he succeeded in pardoning her.

Holding her hands in his he looked straight into her eyes. There was a twitching movement of his moustache.

She drew back.

'No, Uncle Gussie, that's not included in the bargain.'

CHAPTER XVII

A PROPOSAL OF MARRIAGE

PARKER'S niece became the success of the season. Very deftly the elderly gentleman had introduced her to the right people. Her beauty and talent and wealth carried all before them. She gave the most exquisite little dinners and lunches in Pembroke Street. Indeed, she received within a short time no less than three quite reasonable proposals of marriage. Parker, also, reported to her that he had been approached by several people, either on their own behalf or on behalf of their sons. But he, himself, did not appear anxious to marry her off. There was no cloud upon the sky. True, one or two old gentlemen expressed surprise that Parker had never mentioned the existence of his beautiful and affluent niece. But Parker, who acted as her press-agent, successfully disseminated the story that the two of them had concocted. Her *dossier*, accompanied by pictures of herself, was described in so many papers that it met with universal credence. It was a little strange, perhaps, but it was credible, and in a sceptical age it is a great satisfaction to be able to believe anything at all.

The new turn of things, however, did not particularly please Harding. He had to be at work through a great part of the day, during which Miss Clive was always in the company of swift young men at Ranelagh, Hurlingham or Sandown. Often he met her in the evenings. Indeed, he went to dances again in order to be more in her company. But he could not tell whether or not she was flirting with him.

One night, at a dance given by Lady Brinsley, the beautiful wife of the eminent Sir Septimus, in her somewhat florid house in Park Lane, the two found themselves together in the seclusion of the conservatory. Max Boulestein's intoxicating waltz, *Une Plage d'Amour*, set his nerves a-quiver. Never in his life had he seen a more beautiful creature. As he bent over her he felt that he must risk his fate.

Her hands toyed with her fan, and she appeared to be trying to think of something which she wished to talk about.

'My dear Miss Clive . . .'

'Ah, I've got it,' she said with a sudden movement. 'I know what I wanted to speak to you about. Look here, George—I beg your pardon. How silly of me! Mr Harding . . .' She laughed.

'I haven't the slightest antipathy to being called George.'

'No, no, of course not,' she answered, apparently taking no interest in the matter. 'How did you get on in that Probate case the other day?'

Why, he asked himself, should she take the slightest interest in a Probate case? The idea flashed through his mind that she was, indeed, so interested in him, that even the details of his professional life appealed to her. If only that were so! But he doubted it.

'Which case do you mean?' he said, at length.

'Why, Lawson and Lawson. I see that you lost the case, but I must say that I think the decision was wrong. In my own mind I am perfectly convinced that it was a case of undue influence. And I will tell you why.'

To his astonishment, this girl rattled off her views on this complicated case. She seemed, even to his acute mind, to possess an extraordinary knowledge of medical jurisprudence. Never in his Chambers, when discussing these matters with the most eminent physicians, had he been so impressed as he was by this beautiful girl's knowledge of the subject.

'Precisely,' he said, 'I entirely agree with you. We ought to have won, and we should have won, if only Clifford Oakleigh had been called as a witness. But he treated me most abominably about it. I wrote him, as a personal friend, asking him to give evidence, because I knew it was a subject in which he would have taken an interest. In fact, his views would in all probability have been very much like those that you have expressed. Still, mind you, I wired to him, I sent messengers, I called upon him. But I could get no answer. Of course, this does not interest you. You don't know him. But he is my oldest and my dearest friend. I was very disappointed.'

She threw him a side glance.

'Something very extraordinary has happened to him lately. What it is I can't guess. He seems to be giving up his practice. He only attends at Harley Street about three days in the week, and not on any definite days. Everybody is talking about it.'

'Yes,' she answered, fanning herself absently,

'I have heard it commented on. Everybody seems extraordinarily interested in him.' With an arch movement of the eyebrows she continued, 'I should so like to meet him.'

On the whole George was not particularly anxious that she should meet Clifford. It did not seem necessary. The more he saw of her the less anxious was he that she should meet the fascinating medical man.

'Still,' he added, 'it's rather curious that you've never seen your own landlord.'

'Ah,' she replied, 'I've a perfect horror of landlords. Landlord is a dull word. There is nothing more unromantic than a landlord.'

'Are you romantic?' he inquired.

She tossed her head.

'Good Heavens, no! I believe that some men are easier to get on with than others, and some women are harder to get on with than others. I believe that with a little tact it is possible for almost any man to get on reasonably with almost any woman.'

'Then you think,' he asked, 'that "getting on" is the apex of happiness?'

'I do.'

'And love? What of love?'

'Oh, love,' she answered, 'is a term invented to account for the idiotic actions of people who are as a rule sane.'

'You don't think it would be possible that you should ever commit any actions that might warrant the use of that term?'

She looked at him frankly.

'I like you better than anybody else in the world, and I . . .' (and here came the surprise) 'always have.'

The blood surged to his cheeks. A little disconcerted he was, perhaps, at the lack of modesty in her statement. But she was totally unlike anybody else. She had given him the hint, and really, when all was said and done, it seemed a very sensible thing to do. He held out his hands towards her.

'Miriam,' he said, 'I worship you. Will you be my wife?'

She looked straight in his eyes. A smile played about her face.

'No,' she answered very firmly. 'Not that.'

'But you said . . .'

'I know.'

'You said you liked me better than anybody else in the world.'

'So I do.'

'But surely, liking . . . to that extent . . . borders on love?'

'I admit it,' she laughed. It seemed to him that she was playing a comedy. 'It does border on love.'

'But,' he persisted, 'how do you know that it is not past the border? If you have never been in love, you don't know what love is like. Many people say that it's very disappointing.'

He waited for her to speak.

She searched his face with her eyes and then said:

'Do you find it disappointing?'

'Oh, no,' he replied, 'I don't. Very far from it. I liked it enormously until just now. I thought it was the finest thing in the world until just now, when you refused to marry me.'

Her eyes were full of mischief.

'I don't think you have ever proposed in your life before.'

'What makes you think that?'

'You propose so awkwardly.'

'No,' he answered, 'I have never proposed . . . marriage before.'

'Is it wise,' she queried, 'for you to alter your habits, well, in middle life?'

Her question completely mystified him.

At that moment Frederick Robinson came into the conservatory, nodded to Harding, and went up to Miriam.

'My dance, I think, Miss Clive?'

She nodded an affirmative. And then with complete nonchalance she turned to the K.C. with a smile of pure friendliness that was not in itself a denial of love.

'When shall I see you again?' he asked in a low voice. 'I must see you again soon.'

Hastily she replied:

'Oh, we're dining together tomorrow night.'

'Oh, no,' he said, 'I'm dining with Clifford Oakleigh. You've made a mistake.'

'So I have,' she answered. 'Good-night.'

'A very curious mistake to make,' he reflected,

'to think that you're dining with a person you don't know. Confound it, she is a wonderfully fascinating girl. Rough luck to have to dance with Frederick Robinson!'

CHAPTER XVIII

JOHNSON AND BARLOW

THE long table at the Gridiron Club was full. At one end sat
Harding, on his face an unmistakable expression of gloom.
On either side of him were Sir Algernon Spiers and Frederick
Robinson, the latter unnecessarily talkative.

'By the by,' said the architect, who had just finished
his supper of devilled bones and whisky and Perrier, 'it's
an extraordinary thing that disappearance of your clerk's
daughter, Harding. Is there any news at all?'

'Nothing of importance,' replied the barrister, shortly. 'The
case is in the hands of Inspector Johnson.'

'Then nothing will come of it,' commented Robinson,
toying with his inverted eyebrow of a moustache. 'Johnson
is no earthly good. Did I ever tell you chaps how he dealt
with an affair of mine when I lost an opal pin?'

'Yes,' snapped Harding, who did not want to hear the story.

'I'm sure I never told you.'

'From your assumption I assume we are in for the worst,'
replied Sir Algernon.

Several men in the middle of the table urged Robinson to
tell the story. They were men with whom the architect was
not personally popular.

'I'll tell you the story,' said Robinson, 'not in order to give
you the slightest satisfaction but because my experience
of Johnson will prove to our friend Harding that the mere
fact that he has undertaken the case makes it absolutely
hopeless. No, don't go, my dear Harding, I'm doing this
for your own good.'

The members of the Gridiron prepared to listen to the

philanthropic exercise which the novelist was taking for the benefit of the barrister.

In a somewhat staccato voice Robinson spoke.

'To me this opal was a precious thing, not so much on account of its intrinsic and artistic value as by reason of its general utility. For the recognised province of the opal is to ensure the efficacy of prayer; and if it is surrounded with diamonds the wearer has the additional advantage of being invisible in pitched battles. So an opal-and-diamond pin is a particularly handy asset for a man who is religiously minded and doesn't get on very well with his own sister.

'But my sister never liked the pin. Alice hated the opal, called it the clown among precious stones. She hated it for itself alone. Also, she doubted its powers in the prayer line. Further, she maintained that whether I were invisible or not in pitched battles, nobody was likely to hire me for military purposes. Indeed, I am one of Nature's non-combatants.

'Alice left for Monte Carlo on the Monday morning. Immediately after her departure I returned from the station to my house in Albemarle Street.

'My idea was to put on the pin. I had no particular occasion for the offering of prayer. My sister had gone, and the world looked sunny for me. Nor was there any pressing need for invisibility. Still, I had a wish to wear the jewel. What was the good of keeping a thirty-guinea opal tie-pin eating its head off in my jewel-case? No good. If Alice didn't like it, I shouldn't wear it in her presence. It is well to yield to one's sister with regard to small matters.

'In my bedroom I found a window-cleaner—that is, his feet were in the room, the major portion of him was out of doors.

'The opal pin was not in the jewel-case. All my other pins, rings and studs were there, but the opal was gone!

'On close inspection, the window-cleaner turned out to be larger than I had at first thought. In fact, he was one of the largest window-cleaners that I had ever met. I realised that, without my diamonds, I was visible to the naked eye. Without my opal, any prayer for signal success in a contest with that large man would not do me any real good.

'I had only myself to rely on. True, the amethyst that I wore in a ring would drive away the fumes of wine; but it wouldn't drive away an irritated window-cleaner accused of theft.

'So I sent the butler round to Vine Street police-station to state the case and to bring back an inspector.

'As my message was urgent, Inspector Johnson came punctually—the next day. With him was a sort of assistant—P. Barlow.

'Johnson said he was a detective-inspector.

'I told him that I didn't want a man who only inspected detectives. I wanted a man who could overhaul window-cleaners and make them confess their guilt.

'Johnson said he would overhaul the window-cleaner immediately. If he made any confession of guilt Barlow would take it down in writing, alter it, overhaul it, and use it against him at the trial. That sounded well.

'But the window-cleaner spoilt it all. He had left.

'P. Barlow said this was a suspicious circumstance.

'Johnson said not.

'He pointed out that window-cleaners were engaged by the job, like hansom cabs, not by the week, like seaside lodgings.

'I took to Johnson at once. He was a shrewd man who had evidently seen much of life. At his request I told him the story of my loss. P. Barlow took it down in writing—all wrong; read it over in a clear voice, and said, "Everything points to one thing."

'Johnson said not.

'Then he added: "I don't want you, sir, to go away with the idea that I have formed an opinion. I may or may not have formed an opinion. But I can tell you something. Your pin is, beyond all question, missing."

'That of course was so.

"'Further,' he said, "I favour the theory that the pin has been stolen by one person."

"'Indeed! Which one?" I asked intelligently.

"'When I say 'one person', I do not specify any particular person. But I mean the theft is not the work of a syndicate—a gang of Continental thieves, for example."

'Johnson always talked sound sense. He did not theorise. The obvious was good enough for him.

'Then he stated that with the assistance of Barlow—what assistance Barlow could ever be to anybody was a mystery to me—he would examine the servants.

'One by one, each of them was questioned in the dining-room.

'After about three hours, Barlow came and told me that I might join Johnson.

'I availed myself of his permission.

'Johnson told me that the matter was far more serious than he or Barlow had ever supposed.

"'In what way?" I asked succinctly.

"'Your butler has been with you for ten years. Have you ever had any suspicion of him?"

"'Never."

"'Such confidence in a butler, Mr Robinson, is certain to warp his character. You have destroyed that butler as a butler. Your footman has been with you only a month."

"'He is absolutely honest."

"'How can you guarantee the honesty of a servant who has been with you only a month?"

'The great detective paused. "Your cook has been in your service sixteen years?"

"'That is so," I admitted (to my shame).

"'Is she a good cook?"

"'Excellent."

"'Do you think that any good cook would remain in the same situation for sixteen years unless she was making a fortune out of secret commissions and perquisites?"

'And so with my entire executive. According to Johnson—and Barlow entirely shared his view—I was living in a den of thieves: old criminals of ten years' standing, like my butler and my cook; youngsters just stepping into the abyss of crime, like my footman and Ada, the "between-maid"—whatever that condition of life may mean.

'I was staggered. Johnson, with great presence of mind, offered me a brandy-and-soda. He drank whisky, and smoked some of my cigars to pull me together. When they were satisfied that I was quite pulled together, they went away, promising, however, to return at any moment.

'The butler was the first to give notice. He suggested that I had employed hirelings to call him a thief, and he insisted on going at once. The cook adopted the same view. She wouldn't stay another minute in a house where she was accused of stealing things which weren't any part of her business anyway. She'd go there and then—blessed if she didn't. And she did. By seven o'clock there wasn't a servant in the house. My home was depopulated. Johnson had driven my servants out of my house more quickly than St Patrick had solved the Irish snake question.

'That night I dined at the Club, and wrote letters to all the registry-offices I knew of, ordering complete staffs of servants to be sent to me at once.

'Then I went home and protected my property. I barricaded the doors, and packed my jewellery and certificate of birth in a biscuit-tin, which I put on top of my wardrobe.

'The Wednesday was an eventful day in my life. I collected a vile breakfast of cold cheese-straws (five or six), fag end of mutton (the part that "careful cooks" are advised to make into beef-tea by ladies' papers), lemon sponge (a fragment), and a bottle of Bass. It was like being besieged, but much duller.

'After breakfast I tried to make myself useful about the house. By the twelve o'clock post the insulting letters from the registry-offices began to arrive. All sorts of things were said about me. It was urged that I should employ only detectives for domestic duties.

'Grave doubt was expressed as to any English servants ever entering my employment again. Chinese labour was suggested. "Mrs Blunt presents her compliments to Mr Robinson, and begs to state that she does not supply criminals to private houses." Several people presented the same sort of compliments, and begged to state similar matters. For lunch I had tinned tongue and Waw-waw sauce and a pint of champagne.

'At two o'clock I opened the door to Johnson and P. Barlow. Johnson is perhaps my favourite detective. In fact, he is more like a friend than a detective.

'When I told him of the departure of my servants, he was genuinely grieved, but not astonished.

'P. Barlow was astonished, but not grieved. Johnson corrected him. I don't see the use of Barlow anyway. He is always wrong on all points. In that respect he is consistent; which is something, though not much. But Johnson helps him out and bears with him. I suppose I must be good to Barlow for Johnson's sake. I suggested that it was suspicious that all my servants had left suddenly.

'Barlow said it was.

'Johnson corrected him and explained that there were thieves *and* thieves. The more I see of Johnson, the more I like him. He takes you into his confidence; he gives you the benefit of his experience; he tells you all he knows; I think my sister would like Johnson.

'Also, he had found out that Harper's Stores had employed the National Window-Cleaning Association to clean my windows. They had sublet the contract to the House-to-House Supply Company, which concern, having too much business on hand, had transferred the work to the Boy Helpers' Corporation. The Boy Helpers' Corporation being in bankruptcy, the cleaning of my windows had been taken on by a recently-started company called Distressed London Ladies, Limited. The Distressed London Ladies, not feeling up to the contract themselves, had transferred their window-cleaning department to a jobbing-builder in Battersea. He had been ordered to Bournemouth owing to some lung trouble, and his son-in-law, a plumber and glazier, was giving an eye to the business. Johnson had found this all out himself, and Barlow had taken it all down—wrong. But even this sketchy version shows the extraordinary ramifications of England's window-cleaning trade today. The man who had cleaned my windows had not, of course, been traced. But, Johnson said that was not to be expected. Barlow was in two minds. He weighed the pros and cons, as he said. If I were Johnson, I wouldn't let him do that sort of thing.

'I am quite convinced that Johnson liked and respected me.

'The empty bottle gave him an idea. He said that Barlow was not really strong. Barlow had been doing too much; it might be well to pick him up. I didn't see the point of picking up Barlow. However, it is always a pleasure to oblige Johnson. I opened a bottle of champagne; and then it turned out that Barlow was a teetotaller. Johnson, happily, was not. Barlow's stupidity will stand in Johnson's way. This I hinted to Johnson, but he said "No," and kindly explained to me that Barlow was not stupid; in fact, he was one of the greatest thinkers of our time. That accounted for my mistake. Barlow's appearance of crass stupidity caused people to blurt out the truth to him, whereas, he (Johnson), owing to his (Johnson's) analytical physiognomy, was mistrusted by our entire criminal community. No one regretted it more than he (Johnson), but these were the conditions under which he had to detect. More honour to him (Johnson) that he invariably succeeded, he said.

'During the afternoon the detectives began to arrive in earnest.

'Harper's Stores sent their leading man. The Distressed London Ladies, Limited, were represented by ex-Inspector McQuisker. The young plumber and glazier, who had married the daughter of the jobbing builder in Battersea, felt that he was somehow mixed up in the matter of my pin, and arranged with a private detective to look after his "rights". The Boy Helpers' Corporation contributed a sort of Jaggers, who had an incipient talent for detecting things. By four o'clock I had admitted twenty-three persons who professed to represent guilds, corporations, leagues, syndicates, jobbing experts, and others who had not actually cleaned my windows. All of them were anti-teetotal, except the Boy Helper. He made up for that trouble by smoking cigarettes (sold in packets containing photographs of our brainiest boy burglars and hooligans). On the entrance of each detective I had, of course, explained that the matter was in the hands of Inspector Johnson. They all said that he was a very able man, and expressed their willing-ness to work with him and help him. Johnson didn't mind how much help he got. So they all sat down in the dining-room and worked with him and helped him generally. Two or three miscellaneous detectives came later. They were expert Continental thief-catchers, and fancied that the robbery might have been done by a gang which had the week before ransacked an hotel in Nijni Novgorod. I didn't see why the gang should leave rural Russia simply to come over here and take my pin. Perhaps they couldn't pronounce Nijni properly.

'But I let them help. A man came from the Discharged Prisoners' Association to assure me that the affair was not the work of any of his "clients". He held a sort of watching brief for our leading criminals. But he helped, too, in his way. An unintelligible alien, giving an address in Budapest, suspected that the robbery was the work of an Austro-Hungarian thief—I think he said a relative of his by marriage. But I'm not sure. He proposed to help a little. But I can't see that he was of any real use.

'I was; or should have been, but for Barlow.

'The scarf-pin I was wearing at the time was a meloceus— the only stone that discovers thieves. Its properties are perfected by the blood of kids. I explained this at some length to Johnson, who admitted that the system was new to him.

'I asked him if he was familiar with Alphonso's *Clericalis Disciplina*, or that convenient handbook of Marbodius, Bishop of Rennes in the eleventh century, called *De Lapidibus Enchiridion*, or the celebrated treatise on precious stones by Onamakritus.

'He said he wasn't.

'Barlow thanked God he wasn't, and asked how many kids I required.

'I told him, rather severely, that Onamakritus was a Greek author whose knowledge of the practical utility of gems had been endorsed by Ovid in the *Metamorphoses*. He had written a poetical treatise on jewels—not a cookery-book.

'But Barlow regarded the invaluable meloceus as a blackleg in his profession.

'Even if the meloceus could discover thefts, he said, no stipendiary would accept its evidence. You couldn't take it down in writing and alter it and use it against anybody at his trial. How could Sir Charles Mathews cross-examine a meloceus?

'On this point Johnson became pro-Barlow.

'By five o'clock my house became a mass-meeting of detectives; European, American, Asiatic and Irish. Oddly enough, there was not a Japanese detective present. I commented on this, and asked Boswell—I mean Barlow—if that wasn't suspicious. He thought it was, Johnson maintained not. He told me that he had never heard of a Japanese burglar stealing an opal pin. Japanese burglars were rare anyway, he said. In fact, he had their names at his fingers' ends. He told me them. They were like Welsh villages, only worse.

'The detectives finished helping Johnson by about six o'clock, and went away, promising to come back next day and do some more work.

'I had not been alone ten minutes when there was a ring. I opened the door.

'The new arrival wore a full set of red whiskers, but was otherwise a gentleman.

'"Too late," I said, "the meeting is adjourned for today. You can come round in the morning and help the others to help Johnson if you like."

'He said he didn't want to help Johnson; didn't know Johnson: knew some Johnsons, but not one that he wanted to help.

'"Well, what is your idea? Do you want to carry on an independent investigation?"

'Yes, he did. He wanted to examine my gas fixtures.

'"But you can't trace criminals by examining gas fixtures."

'"No, certainly not. Why should I?"

'"Well, then?' I answered, clinching the matter. He said it would be a great advantage for me, as a householder, to know if my gas fixtures were in good order.

'"Then you don't want to detect anything?"

'"If there was an escape of gas anywhere, I shall certainly detect it."

'"You'll be satisfied with that. On your word of honour, that's all you want to detect?"

'He said that would do for him.

'"Well, you may come in. I don't burn much gas here. I use electric light. But if you take your pleasure that way, you may examine the gas fixtures."

'So he came in.

'I asked him frankly: "Are you doing this for your own selfish amusement, or out of a mistaken wish to please me? And, if so, which pays?"

'He wagged his whiskers sadly and explained that it was the duty of all householders to have their gas fixtures examined. He helped them to perform that duty. In fact, he was a sort of guardian angel for gas-fittings. Anyhow, he wasn't a detective.

'I had begun to tire of moving solely in detective circles.

'So I humoured him and let him see my fittings. He was a pleasant, conscientious fellow, and examined everything. When I told him that I had lost all my servants, he didn't sympathise much. He said servants were a nuisance. But I never saw a man so pained as he was when I told him I'd been burgled. I feared he would weep. But I cheered him up by saying that the loss was slight.

'He complimented me on my gas fixtures. They were the best he'd handled in a private house for some years. He praised me very much for having them. And altogether he seemed to think more highly of me than any of the detectives—except, perhaps, Johnson.

'He was genuinely pleased to hear that I had learned a lesson from my loss. I told him that I had put all my jewellery in an oval thin Captain biscuit-box on top of my wardrobe, and gave him permission to recommend that course to any of his clients who were afraid of being burgled.

'He said that was a great scheme, because it was hardly probable that any burglar would burgle in Mayfair for oval thin Captains.

'He made no charge for all he'd done, and said that he wouldn't detain me if I was going out. I told him that I intended to dine at the club.

'He remarked that, as I'd had a tiring day, he would advise me to get to bed early.

'I said that I never went to bed before three when my sister was away, because I was very fond of playing Bridge. Besides, all the men at the club would want me to tell them about the robbery. Anyhow, I *should* tell them.

'He was a nice man, but his whiskers were too red for ordinary wear.

'He didn't say that he would call again, but he repeated that it was a pleasure to meet fittings like mine.

CHAPTER XIX

THE DETECTIVES

'When I came home next morning, the house had been ransacked. The servants' beds, some cane chairs, a refrigerator, and the fire-escape remained. Otherwise my home had ceased to be. The place had given up being a house. It was merely an architectural feature. A tramp in a small way of business might have consented to live there for a day or two; but he would not have taken his wife there—if he loved her.

'When the detectives congregated, they detected the change at once. The man who held the watching brief was really astounded at the completeness of the removal. The Austro-Hungarian was nonplussed.

'Johnson preserved his calm. Barlow said that he felt sure Johnson expected it all along.

'Johnson corrected him.

'The meeting of detectives was more complete than yesterday's. It seemed to me a full house.

'In all human probability my collection was complete; I had examples of every known brand. There were detectives who looked like archdeacons, detectives who ate like British workmen defying German competition, detectives who drank like lords, policemen disguised as detectives, detectives disguised as policemen. It was a full hand.

'It was unique.

'I had made a corner in detectives.

'Had I possessed any financial ability, I should have floated the population of my house as 'Detection, Limited', joined the board after allotment, and sold the goodwill of the entire concern to a composition of leading British criminals.

'Even in the scullery there were men whose reputations were world-wide for the detection of robbery from the person with violence. Any quieter form of robbery could have been detected with despatch by equally prominent practitioners. I had amongst my guests a specialist in riot and unlawful assembly. If anybody had shown a tendency to riot the least bit in the world, or to assemble in an indiscreet manner, he would have been dealt with then and there. Loiterers with felonious intent, or people without visible means of subsistence, would not have dared to show their faces in my house, even if there had been room.

'No "person or persons unknown" "about to commit felonies" showed any wish to practise in Albemarle Street. My box-room was occupied by a select committee of detectives, whose special talent lay in apprehending persons suspected of being about to demand money with menaces. Every brand of criminal, or ex-criminal, or criminal *in posse*, seemed to be catered for.

'I asked myself this question: "What would happen if a member of the criminal classes, or some bright young mind who had never got beyond the stage of being 'about to commit a felony', were to blow up my house and destroy the flower of our detective force?"

'I got no answer.

'So I asked Johnson.

'Hastily he changed the subject, and addressed the meeting which hung upon his words.

'"There has been a burglary here," he said, with absolute frankness.

'One could have heard a pin drop—and some of the men present would have detected the man who had dropped it.

'Again Johnson spoke: 'This burglary is not the work of a single man.'

'Accustomed as I was to the statements of this master mind, I gasped:

"'Do you mean to say that you have discovered a clue which proves that this is the work of a married burglar? Can you say for certain that he is not a widower? Are you convinced that the culprit is not—say—a burglar who has obtained a judicial separation, with the custody of the children?"

"'When I use the word 'single' I do not speak matrimonially. I speak numerically. No one man could, unaided, have removed your grand piano, your billiard-table, and your bound volumes of *Punch*. No man could possibly have lifted any one of these things without assistance, mechanical or otherwise."

'A murmur of admiration ran round the room.

'He spoke again: "You don't think it could have been done by a club friend out of petty spite?"

"'Petty spite!" I cried. "Why, it looks as though two impis of Zulus had gone through the place!"

"'That is impossible,' said Johnson. "If there were only one impi of Zulus in Mayfair, the police would certainly hear of it. Even the Intelligence Department of the War Office would get to know of a foreign invasion of the Metropolis."

'Then they all helped one another and worked. I got tired of watching them work. My home—or, rather, the place where I used to live—looked as though an auction had been held there.

'The detectives remained all day. I helped them —as much as a layman could—by going out and getting tinned meat and cheese, and whatever other food they thought they could detect on best. In fact, I became a sort of handyman to the Force. One young detective to whom I hadn't been introduced took me for the caretaker and spoke rather harshly about my incivility. My friend Johnson corrected him. He is really the best all-round detective that I have met. Though the house was packed with people, more continued to come in. I opened tin door to a young man who said he wanted to enlist, and thought that this was a Yeomanry recruiting-office.

'I said I was hanged if it was. It used to be an Englishman's castle; but now it was a home for lost detectives. He said he'd just as soon be a detective as a Yeoman. So I let him in. I daresay he helped.

'When I got time, I, too, helped. For example, I asked my friend Johnson if he knew of any recently-married burglar who owned a refrigerator.

'Johnson went through Barlow's list, but couldn't find one. He said that, as a class, burglars did not buy refrigerators.

'My idea was that some young burglar who had just married, and had got a refrigerator as a wedding present, had completed the rest of his furnishing arrangements by removing my stock.

'Barlow said there was nothing in the idea.

'Johnson was with him. There are moments when Johnson is positively Barlowesque. So I didn't think it prudent to say anything about the gentlemanlike person with red whiskers. It was my burglary, and I had a right to express my views, but I reserved that right.

'Later Johnson said: "The thing to do is this. I will call the officer who was on point duty outside the house last night. He is one of the cleverest men in the Force. Your goods were removed last night, because I saw them here myself at five-thirty-seven." Barlow made a note of it at my direction. "And your goods are not here now. Make a note of it, Barlow; they are not here now. Assume my hypothesis to be correct, and that your goods were removed in the night, an intelligent officer who is on duty outside your door must have noticed something. I don't say what, I say *something*; possibly the removal of your goods."

'The officer was sent for.

'He knew all about it and readily described the whole occurrence.

'At half-past ten the night before, three furniture-vans had driven up to the door, and, having been filled with the things that I used to own, had been driven in the direction of the North of London, or the North of England—he couldn't say which.

'Johnson complimented the officer upon his intelligence and accuracy.

"'Did you notice anything about one of the men?" I blurted out. "Was he wearing whiskers at all—red ones?"

'Johnson said that burglars never wore highly-coloured whiskers. They would attract observation.

"'Did anyone connected with this removal speak to you?" asked Johnson.

"'One of the men said it was a fine night," the officer answered.

"'Was it a fine night?"

"'It was, sir. So the remark did not excite my suspicion."

"'Didn't it seem to you suspicious that I should have my furniture removed in the middle of the night?" I asked.

"'No, sir. I knew that you were well-to-do and kept your carriages and what-not, and paid all the tradesmen regular and the servants liberal. No, sir. I didn't suspect you, sir, I'm bound to say."

'The more I looked at the idiot the more mysterious did his face seem to me. I am rather a judge of physiognomy, and I should say that the policeman was intended by nature for a window-cleaner—or, at any rate, that he had window-cleaning instincts.

'Of course, this might have been accounted for by atavism.

"'Besides, sir," he added, "the man said that you had been suddenly called away to go salmon-fishing in Norway."

"'Oh! Do you think that I go salmon-fishing in Norway with a grand piano and a billiard-table?"

'Johnson corrected me kindly but firmly.

"'It is," he said, "no part of the duty of a constable on point duty to pry into the habits of respectable householders. We do not countenance the Continental system of espionage in 'Merrie England'."

'Everybody murmured applause (except the Austro-Hungarian investigator).

'The house sat till a late hour that night.

'Next day I received a black pearl and diamond scarf-pin. It came by post, anonymously. Presumably it was the gift of some woman sympathiser who knew that my sister was out of town.

'Black pearls enable the wearer to penetrate the most secret mysteries. This one didn't help me one per cent, with my burglary. But, somehow, my wearing it helped my sister. She came home from Monte Carlo in a bad temper, and got all the servants back, made me apologise to them, re-furnished the house out of the burglary insurance money, and caused the cook to confess that she was engaged to marry the intelligent policeman on point duty, who hated being in the Force, and remained in it only because she liked to see him in uniform, but cleaned windows better than anyone in England, he being, as you might say, born and bred in the profession, his father having cleaned windows at Buckingham Palace itself with his own hands, which she would have told before only nobody hadn't asked her, and she gave him the job when off duty, as the saying is, the Window Cleaning Company only sending people to break windows and not to clean them, in a manner of speaking.

'Of course, Alice meant well when she arranged, by way of a surprise, to have the black pearl substituted for the opal in my scarf-pin. She says that it is not manly to rely on outside help to ensure the efficacy of one's prayers, and that an opal is a vulgar stone, whereas a black pearl is deep mourning.

'It certainly does clear up hidden mysteries in a business-like way. But it doesn't explain why my sister doesn't like Johnson, nor what that man did with his whiskers when he removed my furniture on that singularly fine night. Still, you now thoroughly understand the futility of trusting to Messrs Johnson and Barlow.'

CHAPTER XX

JOHNSON BECOMES BRIGHTER

WHEN he had finished, the house was against him. Said Sir Algernon:

'You only told that infernally rotten story in order to introduce the subject of whiskers. You're mad about whiskers!'

'Good heavens!' replied the novelist, 'we're all mad about something; and whiskers are quite the sanest things to be mad about. At any rate, it is better to talk about them than to wear them. You, Sir Algernon, are always wearing them: I'm not *always* talking about them.'

Several voices from the middle of the table:

'For Heaven's sake, shut up about whiskers.'

With intense politeness Robinson turned to Harding:

'My dear Harding, this instructive anecdote will, I trust, completely prove to you the futility of believing in Johnson. Even without Barlow, I doubt whether Johnson would be of the slightest use.'

The K.C. answered:

'You may be surprised to hear that, as a matter of act, Johnson is on the track of this girl.'

He had, in the days when a Junior at the Old Bailey, had a very considerable experience of Johnson. He did not consider Johnson by any means a fool. Still, of Johnson's efforts in the Mingey case he would not have spoken at the Gridiron Club but for Robinson's attack upon that eminent detective. That very morning, certain events had occurred which he described in detail to the listening members.

This is what had happened.

Harding was sitting in his chambers at nine-thirty, as usual engrossed in his work, when Mingey entered with wild, staring eyes. Since his daughter's disappearance, he had grown infinitely more cadaverous. His hands were shaking. In a quivering voice he said:

'Oh, sir, there's news of my daughter! She has been seen.'

The K.C. expressed his delight.

'Then she is alive! That's good hearing. But, excuse me, Mingey, I've got this case to get up. We will talk about that afterwards.'

'If you could do me a great favour, sir, I should like you to see Inspector Johnson, who is here. Besides, we shall not be on in Court 5 before the adjournment. It would be doing me a great kindness, sir.'

Mingey had been a faithful servant. It was a matter of vital importance to the clerk.

'Let the Inspector be shown in.'

The detective entered, bustling and business-like.

He explained that he was anxious to place the facts which had come to his notice before the K.C.

'You, sir, have had a great deal of experience in criminal matters, and owing to your friendship for a gentleman whose name figures in this case you may be able to throw some light upon it.'

'I will do anything I can, Johnson. Is Mingey to stay or to go?'

'Oh, let him stay, if you please, sir.'

Then Johnson told his story.

He told of how Nellie, the servant-girl, had gone to Vine Street police-station, how he had interviewed her, and how she had identified the photograph of Miss Mingey with the woman who had helped Sir Clifford Oakleigh, while in a drunken condition, into a cab. He repeated from P. Barlow's notes his conversation with Sir Clifford's valet. He stated that he had used every effort to see the celebrated physician

but had failed. He added that the movements of Sir Clifford
Oakleigh were extraordinary. 'He comes and goes in a most
mysterious manner. I don't know whether he bribes my men
who are on the watch or not, but, at any rate, he enters and
leaves the house without their seeing him.'

'Really!' exclaimed Harding, 'you don't mean to say that
you suggest Sir Clifford Oakleigh has anything to do with
the disappearance of Miss Mingey?'

'The moment has not yet arrived for me to draw any conclusion. I am completely baffled. But you know Sir Clifford
Oakleigh well?'

'I know him well enough to know,' said the other hotly,
'that his character is beyond reproach.'

The clerk interposed.

'My daughter was very grateful to him for what he did
for her. You know, Johnson, he completely cured her of a
nervous trouble.'

'Look here, Johnson,' said the K.C., 'I haven't lately done
much in the way of criminal work, but years ago I used to see
a great deal of you at the Central Criminal Court, and also at
the North London Sessions, and it always struck me that you
were a discreet officer. It is not discreet to make a fantastic
charge against a man who is at the head of his profession.'

'I repeat, sir, I make no charges.'

'But the innuendo!' cried Harding. 'Undoubtedly you are
making an innuendo, and it's the most remarkable innuendo
that I've ever heard. A doctor, one of the most respected doctors
in the land, is connected—with all respect to Mingey, who is the
best fellow in the world—by a girl who is not of his own class.
In an incredibly short time their acquaintance ripens to such an
extent that he becomes intensely alcoholic in her company, and
she takes him off, Heaven knows where, in a four-wheel cab.'

'Ah,' said the detective, 'but we *do* know where she took
him. We have traced the cabman. Cabmen, as a rule, are very
hard to trace, but we've got this man.'

'Where was it?' exclaimed Mingey.

'To No. 69 Pembroke Street, Mayfair.'

'Good Heavens!'

Johnson supplemented: 'That house belongs to Sir Clifford Oakleigh.'

'But he has let it to Miss Clive,' interposed Harding.

'Do you know Miss Clive, sir?'

'Certainly I do.'

'Well, the fact remains that he and Miss Mingey went there that night.'

'That isn't possible,' answered Harding. 'Miss Clive doesn't know Sir Clifford Oakleigh. Although she is his tenant, she has never met him. It's extraordinary, I admit, but it *is* so.'

The detective smiled incredulously.

'Do you know that for a fact, sir?'

'I had it from her own lips. She has never met him.'

'I will make a note of that. That is what the lady herself said.'

Harding struck the table in annoyance.

'You don't mean to say that you've been poking your nose into her house.' Here indeed was infernal impertinence. Why should the woman of women be annoyed by the police?

Apologetically Johnson said that he had only made 'ordinary inquiries.'

'Yes, but, Johnson, don't you understand that ordinary inquiries are extraordinary to a young girl? You surely don't suspect that she had anything to do with it? You will never make head or tail of anything, Johnson, if you believe the evidence of cabmen and servant-girls.'

'Well, sir, we can't get our evidence from Prime Ministers and Archbishops.'

'What is your evidence now you've got it? To me, it amounts to nothing. It is more than likely that these two people were mistaken. There is a reward offered, and anybody will make up some cock-and-bull story for the sake of a reward. This is the most cock-and-bull story I have ever heard. Cock-and-bull! Why, it's a farmyard and ranch story! And to make it at all possible you have to invent a theory that a man in the position of Sir Clifford Oakleigh bribes your plain-clothes men in order to move about surreptitiously with a patient whom he has only seen once or twice!'

Very gravely Mingey interrupted.

'No, Johnson,' he said, putting his hand firmly on the Inspector's shoulder, and there were tears in the red rims of his eyes, 'my daughter is not that sort. She has never galli-vanted. She was always took up with her reading and her Sunday School. Neither my wife nor I hold with putting a lot of fal-lals on a girl. But ever since she has disappeared, my wife has often said to me, not once nor twice but twenty times, "If Sarah had taken more trouble with her dress, she would have been a pretty girl," but she did her hair nohow, and that's the truth. Not that it would have mattered a bit if she had made herself look pretty. She would have disappeared all the same, only more so.'

'I take your meaning,' replied Harding, with a nod.

Though pressed by the detective, neither by reason of his own criminal knowledge nor his knowledge of Clifford Oakleigh, could he throw any light on the matter. He could not help, and the interview terminated.

These facts he placed succinctly before the listening members of the Gridiron. Around the table were seated two Treasury Counsel, the leading expert in medical jurisprudence, and a writer of detective novels whose fame is world-wide.

'Can any of you men help?' he asked.

For two hours they discussed all possible theories, but when they parted no satisfactory conclusion had been reached.

CHAPTER XXI

NEWS OF SARAH

'I DON'T know what has happened to you, Mingey,' said Harding, 'you seem to have lost your memory. I told you to watch Appeal Court II this afternoon, and you were not there.'

The shambling clerk expressed his regret.

'Oh, that's all very well, but these things are important. You knew that I could leave the King's Bench whenever I was wanted. What's the matter, man?'

Mingey made no answer, but rubbed his thin hands together.

'I make every allowance for what you've gone through,' said the K.C., 'but believe me, the only way to escape from a sorrow is by attending to one's work.'

'I'm very sorry, sir.'

'I'm sure you are.'

But he could see that the clerk was desirous of saying something to him. He sat down at his table, threw a cursory glance over the briefs that lay upon it, untied the red tape that surrounded one of them. Then, without looking at Mingey, he asked, in an apparently offhand tone:

'Is there any news about Sarah?'

'Yes, sir, there is. That's what it is. I've seen her.'

'Seen her?' But he did not look up from his papers.

'I saw her last night, sir.'

Harding dropped the blue pencil with which he had prepared to mark the brief, and leaned back in his chair.

'Last night!'

Mingey took a step forward.

'Last night, sir, as I'm a sinner: last night, sir, as I'm a Christian, I saw her with my own eyes.'

'Where? Where?'

With wide-open, sightless eyes the clerk answered:

'Coming out of the Prince of Wales' theatre.'

Harding looked in astonishment at him.

'You in the neighbourhood of a theatre!'

Mingey explained.

'I had come from a meeting of the Particular Strict Baptist Benefit Society, and I was walking to a 'bus. I was just outside the Prince of Wales' Theatre when the audience was coming out. It was raining. I hadn't got an umbrella so I stopped for a minute under the portico. And I saw her. She was with a gentleman and a lady. She was laughing and talking. You won't believe me, sir, but I tell you this, she seemed a sort of glorified version of my Sarah. She was splendidly dressed, silks and laces and diamonds, and her hair all waved.'

Then he staggered to a chair and buried his face.

'Oh, my God, my God,' he sobbed, 'that she should have come to this!'

Harding rose, and tried to console him. He patted the quivering old man on the back. But he sought in vain for words of comfort. The best thing he could find to say was, 'Well, after all, it's a great thing to know that she's still alive.'

The lean, lank man sprang up erect.

'A comfort!' he cried, 'to know that my daughter is a gay woman! That's what she is, a gay woman. A comfort! Oh, sir, I have served you all these years. I have been faithful to you. And this has happened to me in my old age. She was a girl I would have trusted . . . as I trust you, sir.'

He presented a deplorable figure of sorrow, this anaemic old man with thin hair, red eyes, and a semi-clerical frock-coat. Tragedy in the make-up of Farce.

Harding walked towards the window, it seemed to him impossible that the colourless daughter of the grotesque Mingey could ever hope to embark successfully on the career of a 'gay woman'. After a slight pause, he said:

'What did you say to her?'

'I'll tell you what I said, sir. First of all, I went directly up to her. I stood in front of her. She looked at me, and I said, "Sarah!" That is all I said, and I held out my arms. And she looked at me: she looked right through me. She didn't seem to see me, and I said "Sarah," I said, "if only you will come back, I will forgive all." The gentleman who was by her side heard my words. He looked at me. He seemed astonished, and, of course, he would be astonished at hearing a man like me saying what I did say. I didn't care how he looked. But what killed me was the way she looked. As God is in Heaven, she didn't seem to remember me. And she was my Sarah. There wasn't any doubt about it. And just so sure as I recognised her, she must have recognised me. No matter how low a daughter has sunk, she can't forget her father . . . in less than a month.'

'What did she say?'

'She said, in a voice that sent the chills through me, "I have really no idea who you are." I shall never forget those words. Then a motor-car man comes up and salutes. The gentleman who is with her says to me, "Will you kindly get out of the way," and bustles her, all silks and finery, into a motor-car.'

Harding walked up to his clerk. He stood looking at him for a second or so; then he said:

'Did your daughter absolutely decline to recognise you? How did she behave?'

'Well, if you ask me, sir,' he answered, 'anybody who didn't know that I was her father would have thought that she'd really forgotten me. She didn't seem to know me, not from Adam, but,' he said, with tight-clenched teeth, 'that's play-acting. When a girl has sunk to what she has sunk to, I don't suppose it's any trouble to be a play-actress. There's no sort of iniquity that she can't sink to.'

'But look here, Mingey, are you quite sure you haven't made some mistake? Are you absolutely convinced that this was your daughter?'

It struck him as an extraordinary thing that the drab figure whose photograph he had seen—a bespectacled, blousy, untidy, though possibly attractive, woman—should suddenly have found favour in the sight of a man to an extent that enabled her to drive about in a motor-car with a groom. 'Motorman' he took to mean groom.

The clerk negatived the possibility of doubt.

'That's not a thing, sir, you *could* be mistaken about. She was very much changed. Oh! so changed!'

'For the better?'

'For the better and the worse. She looked happy. She was beautifully dressed. I never saw a woman so beautifully dressed, not to speak to, outside the Divorce Court. But for the worse. Oh, my God, for the worse! It will kill her mother.'

'What type of man was she with? What sort of man put her into the motor-car?'

'He was more or less a young man, sir, with a shiny hat and white gloves, and a strange sort of white waistcoat. But I noticed that he had a moustache. It was only a sort of half moustache.'

'Was she covered with jewels?'

'No, sir, she was not covered with jewels, but she, well, I don't know how to say it, but she gave you the idea of being very expensive. Everything that she had seemed to me to be the sort of thing which—God help me for saying it—a respectable girl oughtn't to have. Besides that, there were lots of things in her hair.'

'Look here, Mingey,' answered Harding, 'I'm afraid that you've come across a mare's nest. I sincerely hope, of course, that your daughter is alive, but I think you've made a mistake. You have shown me a photograph of Miss Mingey, and I can scarcely credit that a girl whose appearance was practically a guarantee of her virtue, and who also wore spectacles, which are a sort of moral chastity belt, could have become what you call a gay woman. You call these people gay women, Mingey, because you know nothing about them. Believe me, there is very little of gaiety in their lives. But I am of opinion that no daughter of yours would ever dream of adopting this terrible career. I think you are over-worried, Mingey, I think you've made a great mistake.'

'It was she, it was she, it was she!' he cried.

'She hadn't got on spectacles, but I couldn't make a mistake. How could a father make a mistake about his own daughter?'

Earnestly the clerk stared at him.

His eyes were starting out from their sockets. He spoke in a whisper.

'There is more behind it than you think, sir. Last night, at the conclusion of our meeting, the members present, knowing of the distress I was in, proceeded to prayer on my account. It was silent prayer. But suddenly Brother James Potter, one of our greatest lights, rose from his knees and said, "Our brother Mingey will find his lost lamb tonight."'

'Brother Potter really said that, did he?'

'As true as I'm standing here, sir.'

'Well,' commented Harding, 'that settles it.'

In his own mind the matter which the observation that Brother Potter had settled was that he (Harding) would have to get a new clerk.

CHAPTER XXII

THE CURE FOR CANCER

THAT night Harding, having been to the Opera with a friend, went to the Gridiron. There had been a first night at His Majesty's Theatre, and the Club room was full. The leitmotiv of the conversation was Clifford Oakleigh.

'What has Clifford been doing now?' he inquired of Lord Lashbridge as he ordered his supper.

'You lawyers never seem to know anything! You live in a groove. You divide all humanity into plaintiffs and defendants, into petitioners, respondents and co-respondents. But really, really, George, I thought that you occasionally read the newspapers.'

'I always read eight papers a day.'

'Oh, no, nonsense,' replied the other. 'I believe you are getting into training for your approaching elevation to the Bench. You want to make a corner in universal ignorance. You want to be able to look down on some unfortunate junior and wither him with the question, "What is the *Daily Mail*?" or "Is Radium a breakfast food?"'

Harding sat down by the side of Lashbridge.

'Joking apart,' he asked, 'what has Clifford done now?'

Lashbridge, imitating the intonation of a toastmaster, tapped the table with his knife and said:

'My Lords and Gentlemen, pray silence for your Chairman. Mr George Harding, King's Counsel. Mr George Harding has not heard that Sir Clifford Oakleigh has discovered a cure for cancer.'

Everybody laughed.

'What do you mean, Lashbridge?' asked the K.C., testily.

Lashbridge explained.

Clifford Oakleigh had lately been treating two certified cases of incurable cancer at Guy's Hospital. Today, the physicians appointed to report upon the patients had pronounced them completely cured.

The men present had listened in silence to Lashbridge's statement. Then a babel of chatter ensued. Clifford Oakleigh was the greatest man of the age. There had never been a man like Clifford Oakleigh. Something must be done for Clifford Oakleigh. Everything must be done for Clifford Oakleigh. They were all proud to know Clifford Oakleigh. A somewhat alcoholic sculptor suggested a public subscription for the erection of a statue of Clifford Oakleigh in the act of discovering the cure for cancer. Clifford Oakleigh. Clifford Oakleigh. Clifford Oakleigh.

There was but one discordant note. That came from Frederick Robinson.

He suggested that hypnotism had played a large part in the alleged cures.

'Why,' he asked, 'had Oakleigh's treatment been kept secret?' Oakleigh was notoriously addicted to the practice of hypnotism.

'And why not?' came as a chorus.

'Because,' he answered, 'all hypnotists are charlatans.'

'Oh, stop it,' cried Harding, 'you believe in nothing except whiskers.'

'Good Heavens!' he answered, 'I don't believe in whiskers—that is in the utility of whiskers. I know they exist as a fact, or as facts, but I don't believe they serve any useful purpose.'

Shouts of 'Turn him out!'

But Robinson sat firm.

For at least an hour Clifford Oakleigh was the sole topic of conversation. Nearly everybody had some item of news in connection with him. One said that, having made his discovery, he intended to retire from practice. Another contradicted him, having heard on good authority that Oakleigh intended to devote himself almost entirely to patients suffering from this terrible disease, and that he would treat them gratuitously at Guy's Hospital. A third maintained that so curious was the great man's character that it would give him great pleasure, having proved beyond question that he could cure cancer, to take his secret to the grave. When a man has suddenly become the topic of the moment, no story about him is too absurd to receive credence. For years Oakleigh had been regarded as one of the most striking figures in London. His marvellous cures, his multitudinous love-affairs, had caused him to loom large in the public eye. True, many people had regarded him as a quack. But in every walk of life, in art, literature or science, the successful man is liable to be accused of quackery. With regard to every man, however great, there is a pessimistic opinion. In the case of Oakleigh his avowed use of hypnotism had found little favour with many of the older members of the Faculty.

He had never sought advertisement of any sort. But his intense vitality, his strenuous enjoyment of the good things of life, had taken him into many different strata of Society. Every man or woman whom he met was interested in him and talked of him and told anecdotes of him. In this way he multiplied his personality a thousand times. The ordinary Harley Street practitioner, the most ordinarily eminent Harley Street practitioner, is known, perhaps, to some few members of the Athenaeum Club and to the Royal Society and to the Royal College of Physicians and to certain moribund patients. That is all. He is an uninteresting individual, who sits in his consulting-room surrounded by his whiskers. In him, as a man, the public takes no interest. Clifford Oakleigh had always been a prominent figure. He was known by sight almost as well as a leading actor, infinitely better than most Cabinet Ministers.

Now he had discovered the cure for cancer, a fact that was established, and it is scarcely exaggeration to say that on this day there was scarcely a household in the country where

Clifford Oakleigh was not being energetically discussed. The strange stories that had been in circulation with regard to his mysterious disappearances were now accounted for. He could not attend his private patients because he was perfecting his great humanitarian discovery. All honour to him!

There is always in the air some sort of telepathy whereby one feels instinctively that something of surpassing interest is occurring.

Each man's head turned towards the door. Clifford Oakleigh had entered.

Members of the Gridiron felt that it was a great compliment to themselves that this genius—that was the word that sprang to their minds—had in the moment of his triumph come to their club.

Although the members of the Gridiron are the least demonstrative of men, each considered that the occasion should be marked, if not in a suitable way, at any rate in a way as suitable as possible.

He walked down the room with an air of triumphant modesty. He appeared ignorant of the silence that his entry had caused. His bright eyes were flashing with the vigour of health and a smile of perfect contentment played about his mouth. One could see that his goal was the empty seat by Harding's side.

Suddenly Lashbridge rose, a glass in his hand.

'Gentlemen,' he said, 'I know I'm doing a thing that somebody ought to do, and I know that it's the sort of thing that ought to be superbly done, or not done at all. But, however badly I do it, I shall be proud to have done it. I give you the health of Sir Clifford Oakleigh, the greatest man in the world!'

Everybody rose and held their glasses in the direction of the physician.

His face paled, and in contrast to his pallor his eyes shone more brightly.

Evidently he was completely taken aback. After a pause he spoke, and his voice was vibrant with emotion.

'I thank you,' he said, 'I thank you a thousand times. . . . Such a thing has never happened in the Gridiron. . . . I thank you from the bottom of my heart. . . . One does what one can. That is all one can do. . . . But that is the least one can do.'

Then he sat down by Harding's side. And as he did so he pressed the K.C.'s hand.

The members of the club gazed proudly upon him as he talked to his old friend. Each felt that he had been present at an historical occasion, as though he had assisted at the supper given toast. George after the slaughter of the Dragon.

Again there came a discordant note from Robinson. He, of course, found it necessary to interfere.

'By the by, Sir Clifford,' he said, 'a curious thing happened last night. I had a box at the Prince of Wales'—a small theatre party—"Babs" Barton and Guy Jebb, and your tenant, Miss Clive. As we were coming out an extraordinary man, all wet and dripping, like an aquatic undertaker, suddenly came up to Miss Clive, called her Sarah, and said that if she came home, all would be forgiven. Deuced funny, wasn't it? How could one possibly forgive *anything* to a woman who was called Sarah?'

Neither Oakleigh nor Harding seemed interested in Robinson's query.

He stroked his lank hair and closed his eyes.

'Sarah, Sarah,' he repeated. 'No one is ever called Sarah nowadays. Yet there has been a Sarah talked about a good deal in the papers lately.'

He seemed to be racking his brains.

'Yes, yes,' he said suddenly, 'I've got it. I say, Harding, your clerk's daughter who disappeared was called Sarah Mingey, wasn't she?'

'Yes,' said Harding. His eyes were fixed on the ceiling and he was blowing a cloud of cigar smoke from his mouth.

CHAPTER XXIII

THE MYSTERIOUS BEHAVIOUR OF SIR CLIFFORD OAKLEIGH

BEYOND question, Clifford Oakleigh was the man of the moment. Every newspaper in the kingdom published paeans of praise. Throughout Europe and the United States he created an immense sensation. His consulting-rooms in Harley Street were besieged. Not only did sufferers from cancer seek his advice. Thinking that a man who could baffle this terrible disease could therefore cope with any other ailment, all sufferers sought an interview. Telegrams came from all parts of the world. His own secretary was powerless to cope with them. He could have fixed up appointments for the next three years without intermission. Immense offers were cabled from New York, from San Francisco, from Boston, from Philadelphia, if only the great doctor would go to the States. From his point of view money had lost all value. A thousand guineas meant nothing. He was the twentieth-century miracle-worker. And who shall assess the market-price of a miracle?

It was impossible to answer the letters that flowed in upon him, even with the help of Reggie Pardell, who had been summoned to Harley Street to perform clerical functions. Reggie had to be on duty at eight-thirty in the morning: and from that time till midnight, with scanty intervals for meals, Clifford Oakleigh received patients . . . for three days.

The cures that he effected were marvellous. People went into his consulting-room moribund wrecks and they emerged completely restored to health.

But so great was the strain upon him that he maintained that he could not work for more than three days a week.

Still, in those three days he reaped a golden—nay, a diamond—harvest. Yet there was somewhat of an outcry. There were many who complained that his charges were excessive, and indeed Reggie had started a sort of sliding scale. A shrewd judge of character, a man with a very considerable knowledge of the higher class of Society, he knew the maximum sum which could be wrung from a patient. . . . And he got that sum.

Violent letters were written to the newspapers accusing Oakleigh of greed: in fact, a considerable newspaper war raged around him. Many claimed that a man who had been gifted with quasi-omnipotence in the healing of disease should not exact the uttermost farthing from the sufferer.

One or two ungrateful patients actually wrote to the *Times* giving their experiences.

'Paterfamilias' complained that, on the authority of a well-known physician, he was suffering from an incurable form of diabetes. He had gone to Sir Clifford Oakleigh, he had been shown into the presence of that worthy by a secretary to whom he had paid a hundred guineas, he had entered into conversation with Sir Clifford Oakleigh. Clifford Oakleigh had asked him one or two questions. Within twenty minutes of his entry into the consulting-room he was shown out of it. Sir Clifford Oakleigh had said nothing to him of any great interest. He had certainly done nothing to him. He could not, in fact, recall accurately the details of his visit. The result, however, was that he had been completely cured of an incurable form of diabetes. Still, he maintained that the charge was excessive.

Many people wrote to various journals in a like strain. Their cures had been so simple. They had not been compelled to spend large sums of money in foreign hotels. They had merely come into the consulting-room in Harley Street suffering from various ailments, and they had left entirely cured. They seemed to regard this as not being correct. They wanted to have value for their money. If you suffer, they argued, from a serious disease, you must be cured seriously or not at all.

These were the carpers. They, however, stood in a vast minority.

The bulk of Sir Clifford Oakleigh's patients were delighted at the astonishing rapidity of his cures. They did not resent the fact that he did not give them medicine, that he did not send them to take 'cures'. But one thing all resented, and that was the fact that they could never recall the method of his treatment. Any man or woman who at a dinner-party could have described the precise manner in which he or she had been healed would have been in great demand.

Of course, there were many cases in which Sir Clifford did not effect cures. A patient would often come, attended by his or her medical attendant, and after the doctor had heard a complete description of the matter in hand he would state frankly that he could not deal with it. He, unlike the great majority of medical men, did not take a fee for acknowledging his inability to produce beneficial results.

This course of conduct caused many practitioners in the Harley Street and Cavendish Square district to fall foul of him. The major portion of their incomes was due to cases which they left *in statu quo*.

'Good Heavens!' they exclaimed, 'if a man is going to state baldly that he can do no good to a patient (and not to make a charge for same) what, in the name of the Pharmacopoeia, is the profession coming to?' They took umbrage also at the fact that he only worked three days a week. They called him a charlatan. 'If a man could work three days a week,' said they, 'he could work six.' That was their point of view. Yet he was working too much as it was. His success was a severe blow to almost all other medical men. Everybody wanted to see Clifford Oakleigh. No one wanted to see any other doctor.

'Surely,' said sensible people—and even in the twentieth century in Merrie England there exists a large number of sensible people—'it is infinitely better to pay a hundred guineas and be cured in half an hour than to pay Heaven knows how many sums of two guineas to consume the devil knows what preparations and to be sent the dickens knows where to drink waters for the term of one's natural life without any appreciable difference in one's health.'

Anything, however, that the medical profession could allege against him was seized with avidity.

Had the editor of the *Stethoscope* thought that an attack on him for his three-days-a-week system would compel him to work longer hours, he certainly would not have penned it. But the article was written with intense skill. Between the lines could be read a sinister innuendo. So delicately was the insinuation conveyed that an action for libel would not have succeeded. But everybody who read this number of the *Stethoscope* with intelligence—and nobody paid sixpence for the *Stethoscope* who had not the ability to read it with intelligence—understood the point of the attack. Clifford Oakleigh was a morpho-maniac. That was the innuendo. When under the influence of the drug, he acquired marvellous hypnotic powers. But after three days there came a collapse.

Still, during the three days that he worked, and sometimes these three days included a Sunday, he worked with astonishing vigour . . . for astonishing fees.

A man writing from an address in the East-end, under the name of J. H. Nelson, had procured an appointment. He had arrived ragged and unkempt. He had said to Reggie that with the greatest difficulty, assisted by kind friends, he had scraped together the sum of two guineas. Reggie had looked him up and down.

'Nelson,' said he, 'is a well-known name. It's a name well known and respected. It is a terrible thing to think that a man of that name should be hard up for a couple of guineas. I'm quite sure that Sir Clifford Oakleigh would willingly treat a man called Nelson for nothing.'

Mr Nelson flung his arms wide in delight.

'You tink so, mein friend?' he queried eagerly.

'You tink dat he will cure me of cancer for noding?'

'Oh, no, not *you*,' answered Reggie, 'you are Mr Hans Nasalheimer of Park Lane. I don't think he will cure *you* of anything . . . *for* anything. Out you go.'

At last, the stress of his labours began to tell on Clifford.

At six o'clock one evening he said that he could see no more patients that day, no matter who was waiting: no matter though appointments had been arranged up till midnight. Telegrams must be despatched: telephone messages must be sent.

But this arbitrary decision of his to stop work caused a great deal of inconvenience. If a man had expected to be cured of cancer at half-past ten, it drove him well-nigh mad to be told at six-thirty that his appointment was postponed *sine die*.

One day, when he had suddenly applied the closure at seven o'clock, he said to Reggie:

'Do you know, I'm sick of the whole thing. I'm absolutely tired. There is no amusement in it.'

'Amusement?' queried Reggie.

'In all genuine amusements,' he replied, 'there must be something of the gambling element. The only charm in loving a woman is in knowing that she may be unfaithful to you. You can't imagine how tedious it is, Reggie, for me to see a stream of complete strangers: unsympathetic people, tedious people, impossible people. And to cure them. There's no trouble about it. I either cure them or I don't undertake their cases. But I am beginning to hate them all. Most of them are not worth curing.'

But Reggie protested.

'It must be a marvellous thing to exercise this power. To know that you can do what no one has ever been able to do.'

'No, it's not,' he replied wearily, 'that is, it isn't . . . now. When I cured my first patient it was the most marvellous sensation in the world. To discover the North Pole can be nothing compared with the discovery of the cure for cancer. The North Pole was there all the time. We have always known that it was there. But we didn't know whether or not there was a cure for cancer. Now, the whole thing is so commonplace, so stale, so flat, so unprofitable.'

'Unprofitable?' interposed the other.

'My dear chap, I don't require money. I've got all the money I want. What I want is sensation.' Here a sudden smile played about his lips. 'I am getting almost all the sensations I need.'

At that moment, the door opened and his secretary entered with a lengthy telegram.

'Oh, don't worry me now,' said Clifford.

'But this is very important, sir, very important indeed.'

He took the telegram and glanced at it.

Then he gave a whistle.

'The Emperor Augustus has summoned me to Badschwerin at once. It seems he is in a very bad way.'

'Well, that's a sensation, isn't it?' said Reggie, 'that's a new sensation, isn't it? To go to Badschwerin to cure an emperor?'

Dropping the telegraph-form to the ground he answered:

'Yes, it would be a new sensation . . . to go. But . . . I'm not going.'

CHAPTER XXIV

UNPOPULARITY

The announcement that Clifford Oakleigh had refused to go to Badschwerin and attend the Emperor produced a very bad impression. Every man's tongue was against him; every man's pen commented adversely on his conduct.

Here was a physician of intense affluence to whom an Emperor had turned for succour. It might well be that even a great European monarch would not offer him terms which would compensate him for the loss of his London practice during such few days as he would be compelled to absent himself from England. True, we have pleaded guilty to being a nation of shopkeepers, but even a shopkeeper should be a patriot. It is not necessary that the shopkeeper should remain eternally at home. Where indeed would the insular shopkeeper be without commercial travellers?

The Emperor Augustus was in sore straits. The brilliant physicians of his capital, men who had for years taken the lead in medical science, were powerless to deal with his case. It was a national compliment to us that he should have asked an Englishman to come to his rescue. Should he, a notoriously hostile potentate, be cured by the skill of an Englishman, that Englishman's skill would probably form a potent factor in the direction of peace.

To everybody it was incredible that Clifford Oakleigh should decline so brilliant an offer. Could it be, urged some, that he had so little confidence in his own powers that he hesitated to face the practitioners of Badschwerin? Might it not be that he was only a charlatan after all, and that he dreaded the fierce light which the most eminent medical men in Europe would throw on his treatment of a Crowned Head?

There is for the public no greater pleasure than to place a man on a pinnacle for one day and then to drag him into the gutter the next. Such a procedure gives them two immense sensations. To discover a god is a delightful emotion, but to find that he has feet of clay is a pleasure that is infinitely more acute. In this case the pleasure that the public took in attacking Clifford Oakleigh was unbounded. Everybody felt that he was behaving in an unpatriotic manner. Either he was ... well, almost a traitor, or he was a quack. Were it in his power to save the life of the Emperor, England would have a sort of moral lien upon that Sovereign's good-will. If an Englishman saved his life, surely, surely he would not devote that life to the subjugation of England?

To all questions there are, as a rule, two sides. But as to Clifford Oakleigh's conduct in this matter there was but one opinion. Everybody expressed opinions that were firmly anti-Oakleigh. Even Harding, when approached by friends, failed to invent any satisfactory explanation of the physician's conduct. The matter worried him hideously. The only thing to do would be to interview the man himself. Therefore he went round one afternoon about five o'clock to Harley Street.

The pompous butler informed him that Sir Clifford Oakleigh was out of town.

Harding moved aggressively into the hall.

'Look here, Odgers,' he said, 'I want to know where Sir Clifford Oakleigh is.'

'I don't know, sir.'

'I want to see him on a matter of the greatest possible importance.'

'Yes, sir.'

'How can I communicate with him?'

'I can't say, sir.'

'When will he be back?'

'I don't know, sir.'

'Good Heavens!' exclaimed Harding, losing his patience, 'do you mean to say that you don't know? . . . or do you mean to say that your instructions are not to tell?'

Stolidly the butler replied:

'I don't know when he will return, sir . . . I think tomorrow.'

'You think tomorrow, do you?'

As though weighing his words, Odgers answered:

'I don't think, sir, I have no reason for thinking, no definite reason for thinking, but judging from . . . well, judging generally, if one may say so, sir, I think he will come back tomorrow.'

'Are there appointments for tomorrow?'

'I think not, sir. The first appointment that I know of is for eight o'clock in the morning . . . the day after tomorrow.'

'Then he will be coming back some time tomorrow night?'

'Some time tomorrow, sir, I've no doubt.'

Before the stolid, treble-chinned face of the adipose butler Harding stood motionless for a second or two. He looked curiously at the deep-set black eyes, honest in spite of their smallness. He felt convinced that Odgers was an entirely faithful servant to his master. Though Odgers knew well that Harding and Oakleigh were great friends, Odgers would be firmly pro-Oakleigh in all matters. Harding could go to the deuce for all he cared.

The K.C. tried a different tack. He became confidential.

'Look here, Odgers,' he said, 'I am particularly anxious to see your master. I think he is making a very, very grave mistake. Of course you've heard of the fuss that all the papers are making about his refusal to attend the Emperor.'

'Yes, sir.'

'Well,' continued Harding, 'I'm sure that he is very ill advised. If it ever became known that he is . . . out of town . . . for purposes of his own when he might perform a great national service, it is quite on the cards that he may have his windows broken.'

'Yes, sir.'

'You don't think by any chance that he is at King Street, do you?'

The question came quickly, suddenly, craftily. He sprang upon Odgers his knowledge of that mysterious house. He had no conception whether or not Odgers knew of its existence. The stolid, muffin-like face of the butler was illegible. Harding could read neither knowledge nor ignorance. The eyes blinked: that was all.

'Beg pardon, sir?' he inquired.

The barrister repeated the question.

'Don't know, I'm sure, sir. I understood he was going out of town.'

He would try King Street. He jumped into a hansom and drove there.

The door was opened by Reggie.

'Clifford in?' he asked.

'No.'

'I suppose I can come in and have a smoke?'

'Right you are, certainly.'

The two passed into the study.

'Have a cigar?' asked Reggie, producing his case, 'I've got some excellent Cortina Moras.'

But somehow the idea of smoking even a bogus valet's cigars did not appeal to Harding.

'Thanks very much,' he answered, 'but I'm smoking cigarettes these days.' And he lighted a Mimbroso, a new brand of Turkish cigarette which had just been placed upon the market, and which would be excellent for three months and would then become a mixture of hay-seed and horsehair . . . after the ordinary manner of the fashionable cigarette.

'Look here, Reggie,' he said, settling himself on a sofa, 'what has really happened to Clifford?'

The other did not look him in the face. He watched the smoke come from his cigar.

'In what way?'

'Why, about the Emperor.'

'He has declined to attend the Emperor, that's all.'

'Yes, but why? Why, in the name of common sense?'

'I don't know at all,' replied Reggie. 'How should I know? Supposing he made a failure of the Emperor's case, what then? You see he has everything to lose and not very much to gain.'

'Not very much to gain!' exclaimed Harding.

'Why, what can he gain?'

'Well, he can gain a peerage. It's all over the town that the highest influence has been brought to bear on him to go.'

Reggie closed his eyes.

'It has, has it?'

'Why, man, don't you see what the position is? Here is Clifford, who has discovered a cure for cancer. The Emperor Augustus is notoriously antipathetic to this country. The Emperor Augustus is dying of cancer. An English physician has it in his power—this fact has been certified by the Faculty—to effect a cure. The English physician declines to go to Badschwerin to see His Majesty. What is the inference? The inference is that it is the desire of the British Government that the Emperor should not survive. You know that the wildest statements are in circulation. There are people who maintain that he has been offered a peerage to cure the Emperor Augustus. There are others who state that if he declines to go to Badschwerin he will be made a peer.'

Reggie nodded.

'I read the papers and I read between the lines.'

'Damn it!' cried Harding, 'I've not come here to find out any views that you may have gathered from the papers. I've come here to find out the truth from you.'

He rose and walked up to the other.

'I want to find out from you where Clifford actually is.'

Slowly the other spoke:

'My dear chap, if I knew where he was, I shouldn't tell you. I'm perfectly frank with you about the matter. I am Sir Clifford Oakleigh's servant. I am also Oakleigh's friend. I am a servant first and a friend after.' He smiled. 'I'm not giving you the chronological order, but I'm trying to give you some idea of my dual position and the order in which I am influenced.'

'Confound your dual position! Can't you talk sense?'

'My dear George, I *am* talking sense. I should be talking nonsense if I pretended to understand why he declined to attend on the Emperor. Clifford is a big man, a deuced big man, let me tell you. They say that no man is a hero to his own valet. I am not really a valet, and it may well be that he is not really a hero. But he is a big man. In the twentieth century we don't have heroes, but we have big men: few of them, I admit, but when one does come across a big man one regards him as a deuced sight better than a hero.'

Then he burst out laughing, and his laughter was inexplicable to Harding.

'You must excuse me, old chap, if I'm loyal to my master.'

Perfunctorily the K.C. replied, 'Oh, yes, yes.'

'Don't imagine, George, that I'm underrating your abilities when I say that I don't think Clifford really requires anybody's advice with regard to the conduct of his own affairs.'

'The devil you don't,' said Harding, as he moved to the door. 'Well, I wash my hands of the whole matter.'

Reggie smiled at him.

'My dear George, your hands have never been near the matter at all.'

Harding banged the door.

CHAPTER XXV

'I LOVE YOU'

FINDING himself so near Pembroke Street he decided to call on Miriam.

As he walked along the street, his resentment burned deep against Clifford. It seemed to him intolerable that his oldest friend should have committed so grave an error without consulting him. True, he was no medical man, but he flattered himself—or rather he did not flatter himself; he only did himself justice—in thinking that he was a man of the world. He could have given Clifford shrewd counsel, and the shrewd counsel which he would have given him seemed so obvious, that the doctor's refusal to attend the Emperor struck him almost as an act of lunacy.

Mentally he attempted to wipe Clifford out of his life. Though the two had for years been inseparable, each devoted to the other, it seemed to him that his old Eton pal had committed an action in its egregious folly fatal to friendship. Automatically he would have strained every nerve on behalf of his friend had the necessity arisen.

But, somehow, as he stood in front of the door of 69 Pembroke Street, the question of whether the landlord of that house cured the Emperor of cancer mattered little in comparison with the question of whether or not Miriam Clive was in.

She was.

Lying on a sofa in her boudoir, a delicate vision of pink and white, caressingly begowned, she received him, and to his annoyance she immediately embarked upon the topic of the moment.

'What do you think of Clifford Oakleigh? Oh, I beg your pardon, will you have some tea? William, some tea, please.'

When the footman had left the room she continued:

'By the by, George . . . oh, I beg your pardon, I oughtn't to call you that.'

His eyes flashed. 'Pray do.'

'May I?' she asked.

'Of course you may.'

'Well, George, you have your hand on the pulse of the public, do you think this is a very grave mistake of his?'

'Why do you take an interest?' he inquired.

'One naturally takes an interest in the mistakes of one's landlord.'

'If you ask me,' he answered, seating himself in a chair of gold and satin, 'I think he has made an almost disastrous mistake. He is, perhaps, the most unpopular man in England today, and mind you, it takes a great deal to cause an Englishman to hate. Hatred is a lost art. We have not practised it in northern climates since the seventeenth century. We know how to praise but we don't know how to blame. We don't even know how to punish the guilty—that is the guilty whose offences are not dealt with by the Criminal Law. The morally guilty we can't condemn, we haven't the strength to condemn them. A man to whose incompetence is due the slaughter of 10,000 English soldiers secures promotion. Look at the position of Clifford Oakleigh! By going to Badschwerin he could, beyond question, secure the peace of Europe. But he doesn't go.'

'What do you think he deserves?' she asked, leaning forward and staring into his eyes. 'What do you think he deserves?'

'It is not for me to condemn him,' he answered.

'But you are condemning him.'

'I suppose I am.'

'Yes,' she persisted, 'to what?'

'His case is unusual,' he replied.

'But can't you pronounce an unusual sentence? Should he be imprisoned in a fortress for life?'

'Frankly,' he answered, 'I think he ought to be tarred and feathered. He's my greatest friend, but that's what I say.'

She leant back on the sofa and watched him. From head to feet it seemed to him that her eyes took an inventory of him.

When tea was served and the butler and footman had left the room she said:

'I think you are quite right Mr . . .'

'George.'

'George,' she smiled, 'I think you are quite right, George. But of course, it's quite possible that he can't go to Badschwerin.'

'Why not?' he asked sternly.

'It may be that he has engagements here. That's quite possible.'

Impatiently he rose from his chair.

'Engagements of what sort? I'm not trying to make you jealous because you don't know him. But what do you suppose are the engagements of a busy man, of a man of high repute, who vanishes for three days in the week and never lets anyone know where?'

'What do I suppose?' she queried.

'What do you suppose?' he repeated, 'a woman!'

She laughed an almost boisterous laugh.

'Do you know I'm sure you're right.'

'Well, it's a damnable thing,' he answered.

She looked at him earnestly.

'George, I'm afraid you are extremely lacking in sentiment. A woman means nothing to you.'

'You forget,' he answered, 'that I asked you to be my wife.'

'Oh, I remember that,' she replied. 'I've got a list of all the men who have asked me to be their wives: I have written their names down. And I also remember the names of the men who . . . didn't ask me to be their wives. I don't find it necessary to write their names down. They were most ridiculous people. I think you would laugh if I told you. Someday, perhaps, I will tell you.'

He flashed indignation.

'If I know them, I hope you won't tell me their names.'

She lay back on the sofa. Her hands were behind her head. He could see two dainty white leather shoes with paste buckles and a suggestion of open-work stocking.

'What beautiful feet you have,' he said. devouring them with his eyes.

'Beautiful shoes,' she corrected.

He drew his chair towards her. She made no movement of prohibition.

Looking deep down into her eyes he asked:

'The more I see of you, the less I understand you. Will you tell me why you have refused to be my wife?'

A smile played about her lips.

'Do you want to know the truth?'

'You have sentenced me to death,' he answered.

'I should like to know my offence.'

'I'll tell you the truth,' she replied. 'I'm not going to marry you because. . . . No, I'm not going to tell you the truth. But I'm going to tell you something, George,' and a tiny conical hand set with a cabochon emerald stole towards him.

Instinctively he seized the hand and covered it with kisses. He felt that a tremor ran through her frame. He felt that his presence, his physical contact, filled her with emotion. Her eyes closed. With a spasmodic movement she threw her head back. In a whisper she said, 'I can't marry you . . . I love you.'

So low were her tones that he could not grasp whether she had said, 'I can't marry you because I love you.' He did not care. She had said 'I love you.'

Instantly he threw his arms around her. He smothered her lips with kisses. He caressed her face with his lips. Her breast was heaving. 'Oh, my darling, my darling, my darling!'

In a paroxysm of passion he gripped her to him and pressed his lips upon her eyes. Then her lips sought his in an ecstasy of delight. Her flesh was the most exquisite he had ever felt, of the texture of satin marvellously perfumed with the scent of health.

She placed no obstacle against the tide of his passion.

He stood by the fireplace, his shoulders hunched, staring with burning eyes at her limp figure. She turned languidly towards him and opened her eyes. Around them were deep black rims. A spasm shook her figure.

'My dear George, what are you thinking about?'

He did not tell her what he was thinking about.

In his mind had appeared a problem very hard of solution.

Many of us lead complex lives. We are this today and that tomorrow. But did Nature ever involve a maiden who was also a Phryne?

'What are you thinking about?' she repeated.

'Are you thinking it is strange that you are the only man I have ever loved?'

'Something of that sort,' he answered.

CHAPTER XXVI

'UNCLE GUSSIE' IS NONPLUSSED

SCARCELY had he left Pembroke Street when the neat, one-horse brougham of Mr Augustus Parker drove up. Very dapper he was and spruce. Having dressed himself with extraordinary care, he fancied that he had taken ten years off his past. In this supposition he erred, but he looked quite five years younger than his actual age.

In spite of that, he did not give one the idea he intended to convey, namely, that of a possible bridegroom for a young girl.

He waited a quarter of an hour in Miriam's boudoir. During this time he walked nervously up and down the room, or rather up and down so much of the room as commanded a view of the mirror over the chimney-piece. Egotist though he was, he could not conceal from himself the fact that of late his influence had waned. There were many people who regarded him as a joke. In various papers he had been twitted for a tuft-hunter. It was obviously necessary that he should do something, what did not much matter, but something of importance if he were to regain his glorious position.

Miriam entered. The usual sparkle was absent from her eyes, there was a tired, bored expression on her face as she held out her hand to welcome him. She gave him one of those welcomes which are scarcely distinguishable from good-byes. He held her hand in his a little longer than was necessary. She took it away with almost a jerk and dropped down upon the sofa.

'Tea . . . uncle?'

'No, thank you very much. I have come here,' he answered, 'for something more important than tea.' Then reflectively he added, 'Our little arrangement has worked very well.'

'Admirably.'

'No one has suspected that we are not actually uncle and niece. You have been, my dear Miriam, a very great Society success.'

'Thanks to your tact,' she replied. 'But what is the business? Our financial arrangements are settled.'

'I have come to speak to you, Miriam, about something more important than finance.'

'Is there anything in the world more important than finance?'

From a gold cigarette case she took a cigarette and lighted it.

'Oh, yes,' he answered. 'There is, at any rate, one thing more important.'

'Religion?' she inquired.

'Yes, yes, of course, religion, but I was thinking of love.'

She was tired of the old man. She wanted him to go. There was a note of rudeness in her voice as well as more than a touch of rudeness in her words.

'You are always unselfish. For whom are you thinking about love now?'

'For you,' he replied.

'For me!' she exclaimed. 'Oh, don't you worry about that.'

In a voice that he intended to be impressive he stated, 'I am thinking about love, also, for myself.'

She opened eyes wide with astonishment.

'You know I have never married, Miriam.'

'And,' she said, 'I have always understood the reason. That Dowager Duchesses were too old for you, and that other Duchesses were, of course, married. Princesses of the Royal blood never marry commoners, even such eminent commoners as you, dear uncle.'

On the defensive, he urged, 'You have omitted to mention the fact that I have never been in love.' She laughed. 'I thought that I hinted at something of the sort when I called on you for the first time. You remember we had a little chat about a girl . . . and a brougham.'

'Oh, that,' he protested, 'was nothing.'

'The girl took a different view.'

'That was a mere *affaire*. I am talking of a great passion.'

'Whose?' she queried with uplifted eyebrows.

'Mine.'

'For whom?'

He took three steps towards her. 'You.'

She sat up suddenly on the sofa, her hands fell on her knees. With something of a masculine attitude she threw back her head and roared with laughter.

He flushed an unbecoming purple.

When she had sufficiently recovered herself, she inquired:

'Since when has it been the fashion for Society leaders to marry their nieces?'

'My dear Miriam,' he said, a little flustered,

'I've thought out the whole matter, and it's possible. Will you listen to me?'

She accorded him a bored permission.

'I can explain the whole thing as a whim. I can tell people, of course, in a very tactful way, that we have been engaged for a long time, and that I introduced you into Society as my niece simply to save you from the jealousy which you would have aroused had it been known that you were actually my fiancée. I don't understand what you are laughing at,' he added testily.

'I am laughing,' she explained, so soon as she could explain anything, 'at the infernal fool that you would make of yourself.'

Indignantly he cried:

'Have I ever made a fool of myself? I am Augustus Parker. You don't seem to realise that I am Augustus Parker.'

'Oh, yes, I realise it fully, but I think you overestimate the credulity of Society. They have believed that I was your niece, because we both said that I was your niece. But I don't think that you will be able to persuade them that I am your fiancée if I deny it, and persist in stating that I am your niece.'

He rose from the chair, tottered for a second, and then gasped.

'Do I understand that you refuse . . . me?'

She nodded an affirmative.

He seemed bewildered.

'Am I to understand that I, Augustus Parker, have been refused by a girl from nowhere?'

Again came the nod. The world was tottering. This way and that his brain turned in search of an argument that would bring her to reason. With his hands outstretched, he stared blankly at her.

'My dear girl, you don't seem to understand what an advertisement it would be for you to be married to me.'

Her patience was at an end.

'Don't be a fool,' she replied. 'I'm not going to marry as an advertisement. I'm not going to marry at all. So let us leave it at that.'

Her determined attitude towards her celibacy softened the blow, but hardly to an appreciable degree.

'After all, lots of girls have said that, Miriam.'

'But they have not meant it. I mean it.'

'I trust to your honour not to tell anybody that I have offered my hand to you and been refused.'

She was anxious for him to go.

'Is it likely that I should state that my uncle had gone mad and proposed marriage?'

'I quite see that,' he answered, somewhat reassured. But he was bitterly disappointed at the failure of the first of his two schemes for the booming of Mr Augustus Parker.

CHAPTER XXVII

AT THE SAVOY

A LIMP and dejected man, he got into his brougham, having told the coachman to drive to Clifford Oakleigh's house in Harley Street. On the way, he concentrated his mind on his second scheme. If he could use his influence with this erratic physician to go to Badschwerin, he would become little short of a popular hero. Being a popular hero he had always regarded as somewhat vulgar, but in his present precarious position he felt that the affection, the esteem and the regard of the masses, and the delightful personal articles in praise of him which would appear in the papers, could not fail perhaps even to gain him an admission to Court circles, which he had always coveted, and which he had, at length, been compelled to regard as out of the question.

His name would be advertised all over Europe. Mr Augustus Parker would be the man who had established an *Entente Cordiale* between a British Monarch and the Emperor. Mr!— no, surely not. *Sir* Augustus Parker. How could a man who had done such things be refused a baronetcy, which he had so richly earned already by introducing dancing men into the homes of Duchesses?

He was roused from his reflections by the sudden stoppage of the carriage. It was not opposite Clifford Oakleigh's house. In surprise, he put out his head. The coachman turned to him, saying:

'I beg pardon, sir, but I can't drive any further. There's a regular mob outside the house.'

And the coachman spoke true words.

A seething crowd had surrounded Clifford Oakleigh's

consulting-rooms. Stones were being thrown; windows were being broken. Cautiously Augustus Parker alighted. He addressed a man of the costermonger type in mufti, with that offensive courtesy of a superior to an inferior.

'What's all this about, my good man?'

'Not so much of your my good man,' replied the other in a surly voice. 'Oo are yer talking to, yer bloomin' white walrus?'

Mr Parker's face expressed surprise at the appellation.

The man explained for the benefit of another loiterer in the same walk of life.

'This 'ere bloke don't know as 'ow 'e's a bloomin' white walrus. 'Ere, Bill, the old geyser grows 'is moustache to imitate the tusks of a walrus. Blime! 'E's a rum 'un, 'e is.' Then he added in a gruff tone, 'And 'e don't 'esitate to call me, me 'oo 'e don't know, Bill, "my good man".'

His friend took a different line. He was ingratiating to Mr Parker.

'Don't you listen to none o' Jim's lip. What can I do for you, guv'nor? I got one or two stones, if yer want to 'ave a chuck. A bob a time, mister. Goin', goin', gone! The perlice will be 'ere d'rec'ly.'

Mr Parker declined to do a deal in missiles.

Suddenly someone in the crowd shouted out,

'Three groans for Clifford Oakleigh,' a suggestion that was received with enthusiasm. Then the crowd swayed, as though impelled from the opposite direction, and Augustus Parker was almost carried off his feet. Jim and Bill, however, protected him.

'It's all right, guv'nor,' said one of them. 'We'll look after yer. This ain't no place for an elderly walrus. Besides, there won't be no more fun. 'Ere's the perlice, and the bloomin' doctor isn't in the 'ouse, anyway.'

Mr Parker shook himself free of his protectors and darted into his carriage.

Bill put his head through the window.

'Give us a tanner, guv'nor, and I'll tell the coachman where to go.'

Repelled by the man's huge grimy face, Mr Parker thrust his head out of the other window and commanded 'Home.'

'That's all right, coachman,' shouted Bill. 'Take 'im to the Zoo—walrus department.' Then he grinned into the carriage through the window again. 'Give us a tanner, guv'nor, I ain't got nothink o' yours. It's Jim as got your gent's gold watch and chain.'

With that he was gone.

'Confound it,' said Mr Parker, fingering an empty pocket. 'I'm not in luck today.'

And on subsequent days more evil fortune befell him. For instance, it was a great blow to his self-respect that the messages he sent to Clifford Oakleigh, requesting an interview, were unanswered. In addition, a Duke whom he knew but slightly, and to whom, immediately upon the announcement of his engagement, he had sent round a wedding present, had not invited him to the ceremony. For three days in succession important newspapers appeared without containing any mention of his name. But the worst blow of all was the behaviour of Miriam.

One night he was dining at the Savoy with the Duchess of Quinton, one of the leading Duchesses of our day . . . and Mr William Gillett.

Suddenly Lashbridge reduced the table to silence by exclaiming:

'Isn't that your niece dining over there with George Harding, the K.C.?'

All eyes were turned in the direction of the table, at which the two were sitting alone. They were making no concealment of the fact that they were in love with each other, they were gazing *les yeux dans les yeux*, each, apparently, enjoying to the utmost the other's conversation. His eyes glittered with admiration, and hers with amusement. Then the women began to operate. Within five minutes her character was gone.

'What a pity!' said the Duchess.

'My dear Mr Parker,' exclaimed a pretty little American blonde, with an accent like a beatified banjo, 'so your niece has entered for the nuptial stakes.'

'I know nothing about it,' replied the great social despot. 'I . . . I hope they are engaged.'

Lashbridge's comment was that it seemed to him a mésalliance. 'A girl like that,' he said, 'could have married anybody. Nobody ever marries a K.C.'

'No,' exclaimed the Duke of Quinton, 'because K.C.s are always married. I believe they marry before they become K.C.s. I think they have to by the etiquette of their profession. In fact, I understand,' he added, 'that no man could ever become a K.C. unless he was married to a solicitor's daughter.'

'Oh, that's quite an exploded idea,' interposed the Hon. Otho Trigg, who was a pupil in Willie Campbell's chambers. 'Solicitors don't have elderly ugly daughters nowadays. They have elderly ugly sons, whom they teach the tricks of the trade in their offices, and then send them to the Bar to take the bread out of our mouths. Still, Harding is an awfully good sort, and he's got a very good practice.'

The Duchess put up her lorgnette and critically examined the couple.

'Do you know,' she said, 'they don't look as though they were engaged. They look as if they were on their honeymoon.'

And the Duchess, as usual, was right.

In the cosy, red-carpeted hall with marble pillars Miriam and George Harding sat drinking their coffee. The table was near the door.

As the Duchess, accompanied by 'Bee' Plymborough, neared Miriam, she rose, and although the Duchess made a noticeable effort to avoid her, yet her eyes were magnetically drawn towards the handsomest woman in the room.

'My dear Duchess,' she exclaimed, 'I want to introduce my fiancé to you.'

Instantly the Duchess's eyes glanced at the girl's left hand. The engagement finger performed its duty satisfactorily.

There was a touch of a regretful verdict of Not Guilty as she said:

'I'm so glad. Let me congratulate you both. I have heard so much of you, Mr Harding. In fact, I once actually heard you in the Divorce Court and I said, oh, I forget now what I said, but something that I thought was quite worthy of the *Sporting Times*, only the next time I saw Lieut.-Col. Newnham Davis it had quite gone out of my head. Can't you remember what it was, "Bee"?'

'Bee' could, for the simple reason that she herself had been responsible for the scenario of the 'witticism'. After a particularly brilliant piece of cross-examination by the K.C. she had said to the Duchess:

'Never you let the Duke retain that Mr Harding.' But she feigned forgetfulness.

The Duchess turned to Mr Parker:

'My dear Mr Parker, I do trust that you will forgive me for being before you in congratulating your dear niece?'

Mr Parker could forgive anything to any Duchess.

'But surely,' said Miriam, 'you saw the paragraph in the *Daily Mail*? The announcement will not be made in the *Morning Post* until tomorrow, but the *Daily Mail* always gets hold of things before they happen.'

'It often gets hold of things that are never going to happen,' chimed in the Duchess.

For the last two or three days the *Daily Mail* had been in evil odour with Mr Parker. He had sent to the office explicit details of his movements. But it had declined to print the fact that he had walked in the Park on the Tuesday, or perhaps the more interesting fact that he had not walked in the Park on Wednesday.

'And when is the wedding to be?' asked 'Bee' Plymborough.

Mr Parker produced his engagement-book from his pocket.

'I am disengaged on the 19th of next month,' he said.

Harding smiled.

'I'm afraid the wedding will not be ... for some time at least.'

'And, judging by the look in their eyes,' the Duchess whispered to 'Bee' Plymborough, 'I don't see why they should be in any hurry.'

CHAPTER XXVIII

DISAPPOINTMENT

THE next day, as he was returning from the Temple, he caught sight of the contents bill of the *Pall Mall Gazette*. On it appeared:

SIR CLIFFORD OAKLEIGH'S ULTIMATUM

So Clifford was issuing ultimata, was he? Eagerly he bought the paper. The news, startling news, was to the effect that the eminent surgeon would undertake the Emperor's case, but only on condition that he came to Harley Street.

How would the Emperor receive that? How would the public receive that? It seemed to him that this was a unique act of impertinence. What had come over Clifford lately? Was it not rumoured that he had been commanded to proceed to Badschwerin and that he had deliberately disobeyed? It could not be on the ground of money, for naturally the Emperor would offer him any fee. Besides, Clifford was not of a grasping nature. He felt an acute desire to see his old friend. Presumably he would find him at Harley Street. He got into a cab.

There was much business with his card. The butler maintained that Sir Clifford was too much occupied to see him. He pleaded for five minutes, and as he entered the library the great man's watch was in his hand.

'Five minutes,' he said, 'if you have come to see me about myself. Five years if it's anything to do with you. No, no,' he added quickly, 'you're not ill: not even love-sick.' Then he smiled.

'You know?' exclaimed Harding, in surprise.

'Oh, yes, I know,' was the answer, accompanied by a hand-shake, 'and I wish you every sort of happiness.' With a curious look in his eyes he continued, 'I shall be able to spare time to come to your wedding, George, and I shall not insist on the nuptials being celebrated in my house.'

Harding laughed.

'That is extraordinary modest, for you.' Clifford turned away impatiently.

'Of course, I know what you've come about.' And he rambled on. 'An Emperor's life is the same as anybody else's life. I've only got a certain amount of time to devote to the curing of patients. It takes some time to cure a patient, not so long as it takes to try a case, of course, but then a human life is not so important as litigation, is it? Anyhow, I am in a position to make my own terms, and I shall make them or I won't do a deal. I can't spare the time to go to Badschwerin. It's impossible for me to go to Badschwerin.'

'But it is possible for you to vanish.'

The other flashed at him:

'In Heaven's name, isn't it possible for you to attend to your own business? If the Emperor wants to be cured, let him come here and he will be cured. If he doesn't want to come here, let him remain in Badschwerin and die: that is if he has got cancer. I don't know that he has got cancer; but, at any rate, the German doctors have certified that he has got cancer. That being the case I am prepared to cure him. Whether the German doctors will be prepared to certify that he has been cured or not, I don't know. Possibly, for the sake of their reputations, they may find it necessary to let him die . . . of cancer.'

'You really think that they . . . ?'

'Look here,' said Clifford, earnestly. 'In these matters of high politics, complicated with disease, anybody may do anything. I know what I can do, and I'm going to do it in the way that is safest for my reputation. If you're defending a woman, say for murder, who has been unfaithful to her husband, would you make arrangements to have the case tried by a judge who is a puritanical crank? No. You look after your reputation. I look after mine.'

Calmly Harding gave him the lie. He did not speak as though he were jesting.

'Clifford,' he said, 'your reputation has nothing whatever to do with it. Your action is governed simply and solely by some new interest that has come into your life.'

'That closes the matter,' answered the other, his hands tight clenched. 'You are my oldest friend. But, my God, this is too much for friendship. You can leave the house, please.' There was a sinister glare in his eyes as he added, 'And I don't think it is necessary for you to consult further with Reggie Pardell as to my habits.'

The K.C. stammered:

'My dear Clifford, you don't mean to say that after all these years we're going to have a serious row?'

The other's face relaxed.

'I really don't know,' he replied. 'Can't you let me lead my own life? . . . I'm helping you to lead yours.'

As the barrister walked away from the house, he pondered on these words: 'I am helping you to lead your life.' What did he mean? How was Clifford helping him to lead his life? Clifford was so strange that he felt it would scarcely matter to him at all if he never saw him again. The only person who was helping him to lead his life was Miriam. He would go and see Miriam. Perhaps she would dine with him and go to the theatre. He knew no greater happiness than going out at night with her.

Disappointment met him at 69 Pembroke Street.

Miss Clive was not at home.

When would Miss Clive be at home?

The butler did not know.

Would she be at home for dinner?

No, she was out of town.

Where was she staying?

The butler did not know.

Impatiently he turned away. Miriam would certainly have to mend her ways. He would compel her to account for her movements.

Then he walked indignantly to his club, and by way of consolation played Bridge and lost money.

CHAPTER XXIX

REGGIE LOSES HIS JOB

HE returned to South Audley Street in a bad temper, and found Reggie Pardell waiting for him in the library.

Reggie was smoking a cigar in a noticeably despondent manner.

'My dear chap,' he said, 'I've been waiting for you two hours. However, your cigars are excellent.'

'So Clifford allows you out in the daytime now, does he? You don't have to do any work at all, apparently.'

'I've finished work. I've retired from work. I doubt whether I shall ever do another stroke of work in my life.'

Harding raised his eyebrows.

'Come into a fortune?'

'No. Got the chuck.'

'The chuck? When?'

'Just now. Clifford sent round for me to Harley Street, paid me a month's wages, and dismissed me from his service.'

'Phew! Did he give any reason?'

'No reason.'

'Did you ask for one?'

'What in the name of common sense is the good of asking a man like Clifford for anything?'

'Has he got another . . . servant?'

Mysteriously Reggie replied:

'I don't think he's going to have another servant.'

'Do you mean to say,' inquired the barrister, 'that he's going to sleep there alone?'

Reggie shrugged his shoulders. 'There's nothing too absurd for Clifford Oakleigh to do. He is the most mysterious man I've ever come across. And, upon my soul, he gets worse and worse. I can't make head or tail of this case, can you?'

Harding lit a cigar and threw himself on to a sofa.

'My dear Reggie, I'm completely baffled. At first when you told me the story of his lying dead in his house and I found that the body had disappeared, it struck me that you had gone mad. But now I think that he has gone mad.'

Reggie shook his head with determination.

'You're wrong there. Completely wrong. No one has ever been saner than Clifford. Do you fancy that you detect anything odd about him? His manners are exactly as they always are.'

'Yes, yes, I admit that there is nothing odd in his manners, but there is something extraordinarily strange in the things he does and the life he leads.'

'Don't make any mistake, George. We are face to face with a unique problem.'

For a moment the K.C. paused. 'You know it's a most astounding thing,' he said at length, 'that the twentieth century is the century of mysteries. Murders are committed and the murderers are never traced; people disappear and civilisation is powerless to discover them; a man behaves in a manner which is inexplicable by the ordinary rules that govern the behaviour of the sane, yet that man is not mad. Within the last few days in my small circle two phenomenal things have occurred. One is the behaviour of Clifford and the other is the disappearance of my clerk's daughter.'

'There's a third,' interposed Reggie.

'A third?'

'And it's perhaps even more extraordinary than the other two. You've fallen in love.'

Harding laughed.

The other continued:

'Has the possibility of these three extraordinary things being connected struck you?'

'Of course not, man.'

But Reggie persisted:

'Think. It is not impossible that they should be connected ... these three events entirely out of the common should take place in your environment within a few days.'

'Reggie, you're a fool,' said the other, impatiently.

'How can the disappearance of Mingey's daughter have anything to do with me? How can an extraordinary death that was not death in King Street be connected either with Miss Mingey or myself?'

Then Reggie recalled the episode of his meeting with the servant next door; of the interview with Nellie in the public-house.

The K.C. pooh-poohed the idea.

'The whole facts of the case make it extremely unlikely that there is anything in the girl's story. My dear man,' he added impatiently, 'what could be the motive? Why should Clifford, an habitually temperate man, suddenly take to drink and be fetched away from his house by the ugly daughter of a barrister's clerk? Of course, the girl made a mistake. You know how quick some people are at seeing likenesses that don't exist. For instance, the other day a man told me I was like that ass Robinson the whisker-crank. Or again, it is quite possible that the girl lied. Experience teaches us that directly the police offer a reward the liars come out of their shells. There are lots of people of a low type of intellect who would sell their souls to have their pictures in a Sunday paper. You know the sort of thing—"Picture of Nellie So-and-So, the last person who saw the vanished girl".'

Reggie yawned.

'Where are we going to dine?' he asked, as though tired of the subject.

'We?' inquired Harding in surprise.

'Oh, yes,' said the other, calmly. 'I forgot that I didn't tell you I'm staying with you.'

'The deuce you are!'

'Yes. My dear chap, I'm doing this simply and solely to please you. Now that you're engaged, you'll want someone to whom you can talk with complete self-abandonment about Miss Clive. Don't be afraid of boring me. I give you *carte blanche*.'

Harding frowned.

Reggie reproached him. 'My dear fellow, that isn't the way to receive a favour. But don't think that I'm putting myself out. I shall be quite comfortable in your spare bedroom. My things are up there, and there's everything I want.'

'You've got the devil's own cheek. You talk about not being put out. I'm not sure that you won't be.'

Suddenly he remembered that Miriam was away from town, so Reggie's presence would not seriously inconvenience him.

'Well,' he said, after a minute's thought. 'I can put you up for two or three days, but I may have to turn you out at a moment's notice.'

For two days Reggie remained in South Audley Street, and Harding seemed to exhibit a certain pleasure in talking about the girl he loved. This was his first love affair, and he showed infantile joy in describing the charms of Miss Clive. He did not, however, tell him of the anxiety which her peculiar absences caused. They were sitting in the library, discussing the usual topic just before dinner.

The telephone bell rang.

'Yes, I'm Mr Harding . . . And you?' A smile of delight came over his face. 'Oh, it's you, darling, is it?'

'Don't mind me,' said Reggie in a whisper. 'All this sort of thing is chestnuts to me.'

'Will I take you out to dinner tonight and a play afterwards? Certainly.'

'Three is company,' interposed Reggie, 'two is merely compromising. I can easily come.'

'Keep quiet,' growled Harding.

'. . . All right, darling . . . I'll fetch you at seven-thirty . . . All right, if you prefer it . . . Fetch me in the motor seven-thirty. Till then good-bye, dearest . . . Wait a minute. Where have you been? Curse! She's rung off.'

He looked at his watch.

'Well, Reggie, I'm awfully glad you've enjoyed yourself here.' He reflected for a moment. 'Do you know, if I were you I think I should go to 78 Half Moon Street. A butler who used to be with Lashbridge has got very good rooms. I don't think you could do better than 78 Half Moon Street.'

Reggie knew that his visit had come to an end. Disappointed though he was, he felt that he could not further foist himself upon his friend, who was telephoning to a library for a box.

'People have caught awful chills in boxes that were not properly filled. Two are practically lost in a box.'

'Confound you, shut up!' roared the K.C.

Then he relented.

'Oh, yes, if you like, come to the box. But I'm hanged if I ask you to dinner.'

'All right, old chap, I'll come. But I think you're deucedly inhospitable.'

CHAPTER XXX

AN UNFORTUNATE MEETING

RADIANTLY beautiful she looked, seated in the motor, nestling, a fluffy mass of pink chiffon and lace, against the fawn leather upholstery.

As the car sped silently towards the Savoy he put his arm round her and kissed her tenderly.

'My darling,' he murmured, 'how good of you to let me take you out.'

He felt that her heart was throbbing against his chest as she answered:

'My dearest, I couldn't wait. I was longing for you.'

There was a catch in his throat, as he began what he intended to be a hostile and aggressive cross-examination as to her absence from town. But the words he chose were: 'My dearest girl, where have you been? Why did you go away and leave me?'

Her lips tightened and her eyes looked almost coldly upon him.

'My dear George, that's nothing whatever to do with you.'

'It has everything to do with me,' he replied hotly. 'I'm in love with you.'

'Therefore you should trust me. . . . Don't you trust me?' She spoke with a metallic note in her voice.

'Oh, of course I trust you, but I want . . . to know.'

'I have been away.'

'That is no answer.'

'George, understand once and for all, that is the only answer I can give you.'

'But my position is intolerable. No man would stand it.'

She smiled. 'You must take the bad with the good. We are none of us perfect. I have a curious habit of absenting myself from town. If you can't stand a woman who has that curious habit, you must break it off with her. This is a matter for you to decide for yourself.'

Bitterly he answered: 'But there's nothing to break off. Apparently, you are never going to marry me. We are not really engaged at all.'

'Oh, yes, we are,' she laughed. 'We're engaged to be engaged. We're not engaged to be married, I admit, but our engagement should be, at any rate from the man's point of view, the best possible sort of engagement.'

'It's unheard of,' he replied.

'Are we so conservative,' she asked, 'that there are to be no innovations in the world? I have given you everything, as the saying is. When you are tired of me, you can cast me aside like a soiled glove or dove—whichever it is.'

He reproached her.

'You talk in a most extraordinary way.'

'I am an extraordinary woman. I say it without egotism, I am extraordinary.'

'Oh, yes, I admit that you're deuced extraordinary.'

She bridled: 'The fact that I'm in love with you doesn't entitle you to be rude to me.'

'I beg your pardon. My dear Miriam, I want to understand . . . if I can. Am I never to know where you go to when you disappear?'

'You are not,' she answered firmly. 'Those are my terms. Unless, of course, you employ . . .'

He supplied the word 'detectives'. 'Of course I shouldn't do that.'

'No,' she said, 'you're a gentleman. If you were to have me watched—well, of course, if I found out that you were not a gentleman . . . well, then, I shouldn't miss you so very much.'

'Miriam!' he cried.

As the car arrived at Piccadilly Circus he caught sight of a contents bill:

THE EMPEROR ARRIVES TOMORROW

'By Jove,' he exclaimed, 'that's a triumph for Clifford Oakleigh! A triumph for impertinence.'

She contradicted him volubly.

'My dear George, you're talking absolute nonsense. A man who has subdued disease is a greater man than the conqueror of a country. There are two things in the world worth having—money and health. The millionaire has discovered his power: the medical man will soon assert his. He will assert it even over the millionaire. When the Emperor and the plutocrat are standing by the jaws of death, the man of science can ask his own terms.'

'My darling,' he said, fascinated by her beauty, and scarcely listening to what she said, 'you'll come back to South Audley Street tonight . . . and have some sandwiches?'

A delighted nod was her reply as she nestled to his side.

Gratefully he pressed her wrist.

'What's that?' he asked, as his hand touched a large gold heart-shaped locket.

'Only an ordinary thing that I got at Percy Edwards'.'

Though she tried to withdraw her arm he seized the heart.

'That's an awfully out-of-date sort of thing. These things have been out of fashion for about six years.'

They had, indeed, been invented by an actress, and for a time were all the vogue, but he had not seen one on a well-dressed woman for years.

'That heart opens,' he continued.

'No, it doesn't,' she answered, putting her right hand on it.

'Of course it does,' he persisted. 'I can see the hinge. What have you got inside? You must have had this for six years at least.'

'My dear George, you're becoming a nuisance. Your suggestion is that I had a love-affair when I was a flapper . . . Well, even if I did . . . You know. What does it matter?'

Imperiously he told her to open it.

'George, you're intolerable. I'm not going to open it. It has nothing whatever to do with you.'

Querulously he answered: 'Nothing has anything whatever to do with me! I suppose there's a man's photograph in there?'

She looked at him curiously out of the corners of her eyes.

'There is.'

'Ah, I knew it.'

'You haven't asked whose photograph.'

'Naturally. You wouldn't tell me.'

'Oh, yes, I should.'

'Well, whose is it?'

'My Uncle Gussie's.'

'That brute's?'

'There you are!' she said, laughing, laughing with laughter that overcame her pretended annoyance. 'You abuse my relatives.'

'Let me see it.'

'Certainly not,' she pouted. 'I shouldn't dream of it. Why should a man wish to see a picture of an avuncular brute?'

'Will you swear that the photograph is Augustus Parker's?'

With a movement of weariness she turned her head away.

'For God's sake, George, do remember that I'm not in the witness-box.' Then, with a flattering smile, she said: 'I have come out to enjoy myself. I'm going to be happy all tonight. Will you swear not to worry me any more?'

His arm slid round her waist, and of course he promised. But his self-respect was wounded to find that she was in a position to dictate her own terms. Laughingly he said:

'You are as imperious as Clifford Oakleigh.'

'I am,' she admitted.

After a delightful dinner they went on very late to the Criterion, where they found Reggie Pardell awaiting them in the box. It gratified Harding to see the impression that his fiancée made upon his friend. Altogether he enjoyed himself very much. He felt prouder of himself perhaps than he had ever felt before. Had he not secured the love of one of the most beautiful women in England? Was he not supposed to have secured her hand? He delighted in the unmistakable look of envy that Reggie deliberately threw at him.

As they were coming out of the theatre, he walked ahead of the other two in order to catch sight of Miriam's footman. As he stood on the pavement while the man had gone in search of the motor he was conscious of something in the nature of a disturbance taking place in the entrance. Following a natural instinct, he rushed back and saw Miriam looking in complete perplexity at . . . Mingey.

Mingey's eyes were darting from his head. He was gesticulating wildly. He had the appearance of a man bereft of his wits, and in a loud tone was addressing her as 'Sarah' and appealing to her to come home and to 'leave this life of shame'.

Instantly Harding had him by the collar.

'Mingey, what the devil do you mean?'

In complete bewilderment the frail, startled man looked into his master's face.

'Oh, Mr Harding, it's her; it's my Sarah. I have watched at a different theatre every night and now I've seen her again.'

Miriam, with her eyes wide open, questioned Harding:

'Do you know this man?'

'This is my clerk,' he said, and then added quickly to Reggie, 'Put her into the motor. We can't have a scene here.'

But the people were crowding round. Eager faces were pressed towards the quivering clerk and the beautiful woman.

Mingey tried to shake himself free and raised his hands heavenwards.

'It's my daughter,' he cried, 'it's my daughter! Let me go, Mr Harding. I tell you, all of you, it's my daughter—the daughter who disappeared. My name is Mingey. You have all heard of her. Now I have tracked her down.'

'For Heaven's sake keep quiet,' said Harding, without releasing his grip. Then by way of an explanation, which was eagerly desired by the crowd, he said:

'This poor fellow is my clerk. His daughter vanished— the Bayswater mystery, and the poor fellow's mind is quite unhinged.'

Mingey wrung his hands.

'It's not true. It's not true. It's my daughter. It's my Sarah. But she doesn't know me, sir. The poor thing doesn't know me. And she has sunk to this. But I would take her back, even now.'

Two red spots burned on Harding's face.

'Keep quiet,' he said, through clenched teeth, 'this lady is my fiancée. You'll be in a madhouse in a week.'

Then he left him and entered the motor.

CHAPTER XXXI

THE DISMISSAL OF MINGEY

THE next morning a painful interview took place between Harding and his clerk in King's Bench Walk. The barrister felt there was but one possible course open to him. He therefore told Mingey as kindly as might be that, after his behaviour of the night before, he would have no further use for his services.

'I'm very sorry, Mingey, very sorry indeed. You have been with me for many years, and you have worked admirably, but . . .'

The clerk pleaded with him.

'Oh, sir, I'm not a young man. I shan't be able to get another job.'

In all honesty he admitted that he had saved a certain amount of money. But the Temple was the Temple, and a barrister's clerk is always influenced by the romance of his surroundings. It may be that he himself is unaware of the fascination the old buildings exercise. Be that as it may, it is almost always his ambition to die in harness. He finds it almost impossible to retire.

'Besides, sir,' he continued, 'it was my daughter: it was my Sarah. I ask you, sir, could a man make a mistake over anything of that sort?'

'No man,' replied Harding sternly, 'who possesses all his faculties, to such an extent as a barrister's clerk should possess all his faculties, could make such a mistake. Still, that's the mistake you have made. The lady you believe to be your daughter is, as a matter of fact, Miss Clive of 69 Pembroke Street, Mayfair, and she is also engaged to be my wife.'

That should be sufficient for the clerk.

Mingey was unshaken.

'She's my daughter, sir. As sure as there's a God above, she's my daughter.'

Harding became impatient. 'Don't talk nonsense. You showed me a photograph of your daughter. She was a plain girl in spectacles. Miss Clive is a beautiful woman, and she doesn't wear spectacles. Indeed, no beautiful woman wears spectacles,' he continued, struck with an idea.

'It's an extraordinary thing that only plain people suffer from defective eyesight.'

The clerk persisted. 'But her eyesight was not very bad, sir.'

Harding struck in. 'Then she must have been very ugly. No girl, unless she had given up all hope of presenting a pleasing appearance to the world, would wear spectacles.'

'Any girl, sir, would look pretty dressed up as she was.'

Sternly Harding answered:

'No girl could ever be as pretty as Miss Clive ... except Miss Clive. I have every sympathy with you, Mingey. You have been through a great deal, and I am afraid you haven't come out of it. Of course, I will give you a good character. But I should advise you to go to the seaside for a bit. Here is a cheque for £50 to pay your expenses.' Mingey took it between trembling fingers and toyed with it for a minute. 'You'll promise me, sir ...'

'Yes, yes.'

'You'll excuse my saying, sir, what I'm going to say.'

'For Heaven's sake, say it.'

'You will really marry her, won't you, sir?'

At the end of his patience, he exclaimed:

'Whom? Marry whom?'

'My daughter, sir.'

'No, damn it, I won't.'

'Then I can't take your cheque, sir.'

Mingey replaced it on the table.

'Oh! you ass! You complete ass! Take the cheque. Don't be a fool.'

'No, sir, I can't take it! It seems to me . . . like the price of shame.'

With an imperious gesture, Harding motioned him towards the door.

That terminated the interview.

Harding sat down at his table and began reading a brief.

In a few minutes, the door opened and Mingey glided in.

'Please, sir, how long have you known this Miss Clive?'

Harding sprang to his feet, pallid with indignation.

'What the devil do you want to know for?'

'I thought, sir, that if you only got to know her after my Sarah's disappearance, well, it might help to clear matters up, to make you understand.'

This was the last straw.

The barrister stood towering over the frightened clerk.

'Get out of my chambers, here and now. Take your hat, take anything that belongs to you, and go.'

'You will marry her, won't you, sir?'

Harding banged the door, strode to the fireplace and rang the bell.

His junior clerk entered.

'Thomas, I have been obliged to get rid of Mingey. The sudden disappearance of his daughter has destroyed his nerve. He is to leave here at once, poor man. He's got some strange ideas in his head. But remember this, that under no circumstances is he ever to be admitted to these chambers.'

'Yes, sir.'

'That will do.'

It is a strange thing how out of a conversation which seemed to us at the time to be but slightly important, we often remember a phrase or a word destined to have considerable influence on our lives. On the previous night Harding had been roughly indignant at Miriam's suggestion that he might employ detectives. At frequent intervals, the possibility of employing detectives had occurred to him, but he had thrust the idea aside as unworthy of a gentleman. And, now, Mingey had made the absurd suggestion that the disappearance of Sarah and the coming into his life of Miriam might be contemporaneous. 'Curse detectives! Confound Mingey! Let us get to work.'

But it was impossible to work. He couldn't: points of law—even the simplest—became cloudy and elusive. Only two points seemed worthy of consideration. Should he employ detectives? Was it possible that the disappearance of Miss Mingey and the appearance of Miss Clive had taken place at about the same time? He reflected for a minute: and then he remembered that this was actually the case. But two events. Well, supposing the two events had happened at the same time, it did not follow that one had anything to do with the other. A man commits a burglary on Tuesday the 18th March: at precisely the same moment on the same day a torpedo destroyer is lost in the North Sea. These two incidents have no bearing upon one another. And yet that imbecile Mingey suggested that his dull, drab daughter was Miss Clive. Harding roared aloud. 'Mingey thinks that I'm in love with his daughter. Good God!'

Still, he couldn't work. He would have a few words with Miriam.

He rang her up on the telephone.

The usual answer was given him.

'Miss Clive is out of town, and I don't know when she will be back, sir.'

Impatiently he put the receiver back on the machine.

Then he took a sudden decision. He looked up Smallwood in the book.

Of all the detectives who, having earned their pensions at Scotland Yard, had gone in for private business, Smallwood was the best. He was absolutely reliable, and against his reputation no word had ever been breathed. Smallwood promised instant attendance.

He came, a keen-faced, middle-aged man, with somewhat indefinite features and a porterhouse moustache.

Harding glanced at his boots. They were not of the square cut used habitually in the Force.

Briefly he gave his instructions.

'Now, look here,' he said, 'I know perfectly well that all you fellows in the D division when you are once in a house make a point of finding out everything that goes on in that house. You know who loves who, which is each inhabitant's favourite vice, and so forth and so on. All these facts you tabulate. I know that Mayfair has no secrets from the D division. I understand that you are in touch with Inspector Clegg, about the smartest man in the Force now. Anything he knows he will let you know. I want you to find out all you can about Miss Clive. She lives at 69 Pembroke Street. She is at present out of town. I want her house watched night and day. I want to know the moment she arrives. I need not talk to you, Smallwood, about expense. I'm not anxious to be ruined . . . but anything in reason. Let me know the moment she returns. Mind you, you must look after this job personally.'

Smallwood expressed his gratitude at being entrusted with the matter, and left.

Within two hours, Harding was rung up on the telephone. Smallwood informed him that Miss Clive had not left the house, and was, as a matter of fact, at 69 Pembroke Street. That she had come in at three o'clock in the morning and had not been out since.

CHAPTER XXXII

THE ASSISTANCE OF SMALLWOOD

EVERY day, Smallwood made his report. Every day, his report was the same. Miss Clive had not left 69 Pembroke Street.

On three occasions Harding called at the house and asked to see her. Invariably he was informed by a servant that she was out of town. After a week of terrible anxiety, he summoned the detective to King's Bench Walk.

On that shrewd man's face was written bewilderment.

'Frankly, sir,' he said, 'I can't understand this case. The lady has not moved out of her home since you instructed me. She was there at the time, and she is there now.'

'But how do you know?'

'Well, sir, I have had the house watched. I have watched the house myself. I am prepared to swear that she's never left it.'

'But,' interrupted Harding, 'she may have left it before you began your investigation.'

'I don't think so, sir. Morally speaking, I am prepared to swear that she is there now. Last night there was a light in her window.'

Impatiently Harding exclaimed: 'The fact that there was a light in her window doesn't prove that she was in the room. Haven't you managed to get into the house?'

Regretfully Smallwood admitted that he had not.

'I have tried, sir: and my men have tried. But these servants are extraordinary. I've got a young man, a very promising young fellow, who works for me: he has never failed with a housemaid yet. He is a well-set-up, good-looking young fellow, but he couldn't make any headway with the servants at No. 69. They are different to ordinary servants.'

'How do you mean? In what way?'

'Well, sir, they are on their guard. Directly you begin speaking to them, passing the time of day or what not, they seem to suspect. I can't get any information at all.'

Harding put his hands behind his head and thought with closed eyes.

'Assume that you are right. Assume that she is in the house. Does your experience suggest any explanation?' Suddenly he added, 'Wait a minute. As to the people who go into the house, of course, you have found out who they are?'

The detective shook his head.

'No one has gone into the house. Many motor-cars and broughams have drawn up: a great many cards have been left. Oh, Miss Clive knows a lot of fashionable people. But no one has absolutely entered the house.'

A burden was taken off Harding's shoulders.

'You're prepared to swear that no man has gone into the house?'

'No man, sir.'

'You are quite sure about that?'

'Absolutely.'

'Do you see any solution?'

'Well, sir, there's . . . one solution that suggested itself to me. But I don't like . . .'

'Oh, out with it.'

'Mind you, sir, I've never seen the lady.'

'Go on, go on,' commanded Harding.

'It would be a great help for me if I could see the lady.'

'Let's have your suspicion.'

The detective was not anxious to express it. However, at last he found words.

'It seems to me, sir, mind you, this is only the vaguest suspicion in the world, that perhaps the lady gives way to drink. She may have drinking bouts. She may be, if I may say so, a dram drinker. You know what women are, sir; when they take to that, they will drink anything, from Eau-de-Cologne upwards. If I'm right, what more natural than when she's under the influence of drink she should tell her servants she's out of town.'

'There's nothing in that,' answered Harding, dismissing the idea with a wave of his hand. 'If you'd seen the lady you would know that she's not a drunkard.'

'They are very crafty, sir,' said the detective, shaking his head, 'and if it's not drink it might be worse.'

'How do you mean?'

'Drugs, sir. It might be drugs—morphia or cocaine, or something of the sort. When a woman does anything that one can't make head nor tail of, it is nearly always drugs at the bottom of it. Half the women who get into trouble in the Divorce Court or in shop-lifting cases are morpho-maniacs.'

Against his will, it occurred to the K.C. that Smallwood had hit upon, at any rate, a possible solution. He drew a deep breath, and then shuddered. In his own walk of life he knew of many cases where women had ruined themselves by morphia. He had known pretty little Mrs Bernstein, the wife of the money-lender in Berkeley Square. He recalled her hideous tragedy; how she had prosecuted her best friend, Cecily Allardyce, for stealing jewels which she herself had given to the man she loved. He recollected her hideous collapse in the witness-box at the Old Bailey. He remembered the shock he had sustained on realising, perhaps, for the first time in his life, the terrible power for evil possessed by that drug. The case of Violet Tarrington, with the marvellous soprano voice, who had died in a mad-house, was of later date. So he, the eminent King's Counsel, an acute judge of human character and of human vices, might have been deceived in the ordinary way by a woman. But for the life of him he could not call to mind any symptoms in Miriam's conduct. She had not, as far as he knew, ever shown any symptoms of taking morphia. Anybody who has ever had the misfortune to come in contact with a morpho-maniac, anybody who has the slightest faculty of observation, knows the unmistakable signs in the eyes of a person addicted to the drug habit. However, the suggestion was so monstrous that he did not desire Smallwood to think that he accepted it, even for a moment.

'There's nothing in that,' he said drily. 'Miss Clive is not a "druggist". I'm afraid, or rather I'm glad, that you're on the wrong track.'

'I hope so, sir,' said the detective. 'But I don't know what else to think.'

'By the by, have the Yard got any information about the disappearance of Miss Mingey?'

The detective shook his head: 'Nothing, sir.'

'You know, Smallwood, it seems to me that the police never discover anything. Every now and then a man confesses that he has committed a murder that has baffled them for years, and then the police, instead of taking his word for it, prove that the man is wrong. They are much better at proving that men have not committed murders than they are at proving that they have.'

'The police is not what it used to be,' the detective admitted.

'No,' laughed Harding, 'not since you left the Force, eh?'

'I didn't mean to suggest that, sir.'

'Oh, yes, you did. But now tell me exactly, do you see any hope of solving the mystery of No. 69? Can't one of your men get in, as an electrical engineer, or as a waiter, or something?'

'We've tried everything, sir, but the servants are . . . Well, they're not like any servants I've ever met. You can't get round them any how.' Impatiently Harding rose from his chair.

'Look here, the butler uses some public-house in the neighbourhood. Do you mean to say you can't get into conversation with him, stand him a drink, stand him several drinks, and then pay a visit to him in the servants' hall?'

Despairingly the detective replied: 'I've tried everything, sir. With an ordinary butler it wouldn't be any trouble to get him to have as many drinks as I would pay for. I could put him on a winner perhaps, and then I could have the run of the basement. But with this man, sir, it is no good.'

'Have you been able to find out anything about these servants? Surely the men of the C division must know something about some one of them?'

Smallwood shook his head.

'I've been working hard for a whole week, sir, over this matter, and though I say it, as perhaps shouldn't, I've wasted my time. I've done nothing for your money.'

'Well, well,' replied Harding, 'at any rate, you're not wasting a great deal of money. Go on keeping watch. And, mind you, the moment you hear anything go to the nearest public telephone-office and telephone me either here or at my house.'

With that he dismissed the detective.

CHAPTER XXXIII

MORPHIA?

THAT afternoon, as he walked westwards, it struck him that it might be as well to go and see Clifford Oakleigh. He had a favour to ask of him.

He reached Harley Street at six-thirty and was instantly shown into the great man's consulting-room. Without going directly to the subject, he inquired about the Emperor; and, indeed, the condition of the Emperor was the great topic of the moment.

Here was a European potentate who had come to London, and, who had, without any personal attendants of his own, taken up his quarters in a doctor's house in Harley Street.

'How is he doing? Do you think you'll succeed?'

Clifford's eyes were glittering with enthusiasm. He shook Harding's hand.

'My dear fellow, he's safe! He's cured! The leading men of London, two of them that is to say, will examine him tomorrow, and they will pronounce him absolutely free of any suspicion of cancer.'

'By Jove!' exclaimed Harding, 'you're a miracle-worker!'

'Miracles of one century are commonplaces of the next.'

'What are you going to get for this?'

Clifford smiled his sad smile.

'Oh, a great deal of abuse,' he answered. 'I shall be universally attacked because I don't cure everybody. But do you know, I don't think that everybody ought to be cured. There are an enormous number of people who don't deserve to be cured. Of course, some people get more than they deserve. Don't you run away with the idea that curing a man of cancer is to me the simplest thing in the world, that it is done without a vast expenditure of . . . what shall I say? . . . vital energy. I shall issue no recipe for the cure of cancer; a patent pill will not cure cancer; the cancer cure will not be "within the reach of all". Do you know, Harding, that it's quite possible that my secret will die with me?'

There was something uncanny in his enthusiasm.

'There are moments,' he continued, 'when it seems to me that God has endowed me with super-human powers. I certainly can do things that no other man has ever been able to do. I have discovered secrets that I am the sadder for discovering. I often fancy that I have peered too deeply into hidden things, and it may well be that some day I shall pay the price.'

'How do you mean?' inquired Harding; 'everything you have done has been for the benefit of Humanity. If you have cured the Emperor you have practically done an immense service in the cause of peace. You have saved the lives of millions.'

The great surgeon became pensive.

'One does what one can, but what will be the verdict of posterity?'

'Oh, confound posterity!' cried Harding; 'let the judge who has seen the prisoner try the case.'

'You speak of me as a prisoner?' asked Clifford with raised eyebrows.

'I used a legal metaphor,' replied the other. Then he changed the subject back to the old subject.

'What will you get for this, Clifford?'

'Anything I want,' he answered; 'I don't know that I really want anything. This morning his Majesty suggested £50,000, a cart-load of orders and decorations, and a promise that the King would give me a peerage.'

'Anything else?' asked his friend, smiling.

But the other's eyes were far away.

'It would be a curious thing if I were to get, or rather if I were to take, no reward.'

'Deuced curious,' commented Harding, almost with a sneer. 'So curious as to be pretty well inhuman.' But he was struck with admiration at the triumph of his friend. 'Now, then,' he said suddenly, 'I want you to do something for me. You know what an enormous number of drug-takers there are about.'

'Good Heavens, yes.'

'Now, you, with your experience, could detect the drug habit in anybody at once, couldn't you?'

'I don't think I should have any doubt about a person who was in the habit of taking, say, morphia or cocaine?'

'How would you tell?'

'Oh, I should examine the body, wrists, ankles and knees for punctures.'

Harding interposed:

'No, but there is some other way besides that. I don't want you to make an examination.'

'The eyes,' said the surgeon, 'are practically convincing evidence.'

'Thank you,' said Harding. 'Now I want you to meet a friend of mine. I want you to talk to my friend and to give me your opinion.'

'Yes.'

'Will you do that?'

'By all means. When do you want me to do it? I can come round now, if you like, anywhere.'

'No, not now. The lady is out of town.'

'Oh, it's a lady?'

'Yes. As a matter of fact,' he added, 'it's Miss Clive.'

Clifford made an abrupt movement and turned away. He whistled. Then he said briefly: 'I can't do it.'

Harding was surprised at his refusal.

'Good God, man, this is a matter of the greatest importance to me!'

'And to *her*,' said the surgeon. 'If you think that she takes morphia, as you suggest, you will . . . break it off. That will break her heart. Why should I break the heart of a woman I've never seen?'

'Because,' answered the K.C., 'you are my friend. You've never seen her. What is she to you?'

Clifford smiled.

'The fiancée of my great friend is, theoretically, at least, a great deal to me.'

Harding became indignant.

'Look here, no one knows better than you the agony that results to a man who's in love with a morpho-maniac. I have my suspicions about Miss Clive. I want these suspicions cleared up.' Clifford whistled. Then he said, deliberately, with a forefinger raised:

'Don't you worry. Although I've never seen Miss Clive—but from what I hear—I should say that she *doesn't* take morphia. I'll bet you a thousand to one in sovereigns that she's never touched it.'

'You really mean that?' asked the K.C.

'I mean it absolutely.'

'But who is to decide whether the money is payable or not? I should like you to decide.'

'I tell you I can't. I won't have anything to do with it. There are reasons which make it impossible. But she doesn't do it.'

'You say reasons; what do you mean?'

'I mean that I'm not going to do it. I don't want to do it.'

'That's a woman's reason.'

Clifford put his hand on his friend's shoulder. 'Women are not always fools. Miss Clive, I presume, has her own reasons for loving you. You don't scoff at *them* because they are a woman's reasons.'

Harding reflected for a moment; then he said:

'You know, Clifford, you're a most extraordinary man. I never, for one moment, thought you would refuse this very trifling favour. I can't understand why you *have* refused it. Can't you give me a definite reason?'

Clifford answered him slowly:

'No, I can't. But this much I can tell you—I admit it isn't very much to tell you. Some day you will know. Or you will never know.'

Harding stared at him. 'In return for that valuable piece of information, Clifford, but for the fact of your being engaged in curing the Emperor of cancer I should be tempted to assault you with considerable violence.'

'Oh, nonsense,' replied the other, smiling. 'Harley Street is swarming with doctors. For this matter you don't need a specialist. Get any doctor to meet Miss Clive—any general practitioner—and in five minutes he will set your mind at rest. But don't bother about assaulting me, old chap. Some day, as I hinted, the whole thing will be made plain. Or, as I also hinted, it will not be made plain.'

In spite of the irritation he felt towards Sir Clifford, his old friendship for that fascinating man prevented him from losing his temper. In a few seconds he was sufficiently self-composed to say with a laugh:

'If I were to kill you, I suppose the Emperor would die?'

Clifford nodded.

As Harding left the room he said:

'I've no wish to be a regicide.'

CHAPTER XXXIV

A POSSIBLE CLUE

THE daily reports he received from Smallwood were always the same. The eminent detective had no news. All efforts to communicate with the servants at No. 69 Pembroke Street proved futile. On more than one occasion Harding lost patience.

'If you're a detective,' he said, 'why the deuce don't you detect?'

Smallwood could offer no defence except the fact that he had done his duty. He had sent one of his men, disguised as a gentleman, to call at the house, and to inquire if Miss Clive was at home. The man had been informed, in the usual way, that she was out of town.

'Were you watching at the time?' asked the K.C.

'Yes, sir.'

'Did you notice whether the servant who answered the door was slovenly, after the manner of servants when their employers are away?'

'I noticed particularly, sir, that he seemed very spruce and, well, sir, what you call servant-like.'

'Have you been able to find out the names of any of these servants?'

'Oh, yes,' answered the detective, briskly, producing a note-book from his pocket. 'I've got all their names.'

'How did you get them?'

'Oh, in the ordinary way, sir, through the postman.'

'Do you know anything about them?'

'No, sir; nothing at all. That is, I do know something, in a way, about the cook. She's been in trouble. A long time ago. That is, she wasn't exactly in trouble, but Mary Baker was tried and acquitted at the Old Bailey.' He continued the perusal of his notes. 'Mary Baker was tried and acquitted for theft.'

Suddenly the K.C. sprang up.

'Mary Baker! I seem to recollect something of that case . . . I was in it myself.'

He put his hand to his head, as though searching his memory.

'Yes, yes, I remember. It was one of the first cases I ever had. I defended Mary Baker, and I got her off. But my own recollection is that she was guilty. Yes, yes, all the facts come back to me. She was accused of stealing four five-pound notes from a house in Portman Square. It was a deuce of a job to get her off. I remember that my success in that case brought me a lot of work that was very welcome in those days.'

The detective's eyes glowed. He stretched his hand towards the barrister. Then he hesitated . . .

'No, sir, I don't suppose you would do a thing like that, sir.'

'Like what?' asked the other, sharply.

'Well, sir, I think I see daylight, or a possibility of daylight. If you got that woman off and she was guilty, well, she might be willing to tell you the truth about this Miss Clive.'

At the suggestion, Harding whistled.

'Oh, I couldn't do anything like that.'

'It is for you to decide, sir. But I think it's our only chance.'

Harding sat down.

'What do you suggest?'

The detective hesitated.

'Well, I don't like to make a suggestion of the sort to you, sir, but I think it would be a good thing if you were to see this woman.'

'Mary Baker?'

'Yes, indeed, I think it would be a good thing. I don't think she would conceal the truth from you.' Harding threw back his head and stared at the ceiling.

'I don't like doing it. It's playing it rather low down for me to interview a servant.' Smallwood stared curiously at him.

'I don't know, sir,' he said with a smile, 'that it's playing it lower down than employing a detective.'

Harding's eyes twinkled. '*Facilis est decensus Averno.*'

'Beg pardon, sir.'

'Nothing.'

It was ten days since he had seen Miriam. He had been parted from her for a longer period than ever. Previously, her absence had only been for three days. But ten days! The position was intolerable. Suddenly he rose from his seat.

'I'll do it. But how shall I get at her?' The detective thought for a moment. Then he said:

'Would you mind giving me a note, sir, and I could go to Pembroke Street and arrange everything?'

'Yes. But what shall I say in the note?'

'Simply recall the facts of the Old Bailey to her and ask her to arrange an appointment with bearer.'

'I don't like doing that,' said the barrister. 'It sounds very much like blackmail, digging up a woman's past. It's a beastly thing to do.'

The detective shrugged his shoulders. Again he said, 'It is for you to decide, sir.'

Harding, being very much in love, decided to write the note.

'Now, then, Smallwood, where am I to see her?'

'I think the best place would be your own house, sir. It's handy, and it wouldn't take her long to get there at any time she could pop out.'

'All right. Fix up any time you like and I'll be there.'

Within two hours, he received a telephonic message from the detective to the effect that the cook would call at South Audley Street at seven o'clock.

He reflected. At seven o'clock! That obviously meant that, in spite of Smallwood's opinion that Miriam was in town, it would be the hour when the cook would of a certainty be engaged, if her mistress were dining at home. And he could not for one minute imagine that Miriam would be so rash as to risk dining out when she had assured him that she was not in London.

'Do you want me to be present at the interview?' asked the detective.

'What do you think?'

'I don't think it matters, sir. I've every confidence in your doing the right thing.'

Harding smiled at the compliment.

'Thank you, Smallwood. But be at my house at eight o'clock.'

'All right, sir.'

Then he put back the receiver.

As he walked home, he tried to recall the appearance of Mary Baker. But search his memory as he might, he could not produce any more vivid picture than a slight suggestion of a thin, unattractive woman standing in the dock in the New Court. He was vague, also, as to who had tried the case. He rather thought it was the Recorder. Yes, undoubtedly, it was old Tommy Chambers. He remembered that Tommy had rather helped him in the defence. As to the prisoner's guilt he was certain, and he was sorry that he was certain. It seemed to him a disgraceful proceeding to address this woman practically as a criminal who had escaped from justice. He thought that his hold upon her would be sufficient, if he had merely secured the acquittal of an innocent woman. In his note, of course, he had merely said:

'You will no doubt remember me. I defended you on a charge of theft some twenty years ago.'

Supposing it was not the same Mary Baker?

Ah, but if it was not, of course she would not come. No other Mary Baker would come.

Then the thought flashed across his brain that if ever Miriam found out, she would be indignant, and rightly indignant. Still, her behaviour in the matter had been extraordinary, too extraordinary. Her behaviour was responsible for his conduct. She was not entitled to attack him. Still, no matter on which side the greater blame lay, he felt that she would in all probability break off all relations with him.

Because he was very much in love, however, he was prepared to risk it.

CHAPTER XXXV

HARDING MAKES HEADWAY

HE dropped in at his club for half an hour, and, on the stroke of seven, reached his house.

In a few minutes, an elderly woman, with the figure of a successful cook and the clothes and the bugles and the black silk of a successful cook, was shown into the room. In her rubicund, shiny face were frightened eyes. She came in, as she would have described it, 'all of a tremble'.

When they were alone, the K.C. stood staring at her.

'Be seated, Mrs Baker,' he said.

But she was too nervous to sit down. Her plump hands in her white cotton gloves fidgeted awkwardly: her umbrella dropped to the ground. She picked it up, and became redder in the face. Still, he did not speak.

At length she broke the silence:

'Oh, sir, I ought to thank you for what you did for me many years ago. You saved me, sir; indeed, you did.'

'Yes.'

'Oh, yes, sir. You've no idea what I went through then. I've never done anything wrong since, sir. I've been an honest woman ever since, sir.'

'I'm very glad to hear that.'

'Both the police and the warderesses told me that I shouldn't get off, sir. It was only you that did it. You worked for me, sir, just as if I was a real lady. I can't tell you how thankful I am, sir.'

'Yes.'

She appeared to find relief in speech, and continued:

'After my trial, sir, I had a deal of difficulty in getting a place. I couldn't get any character from my last situation, if you take my meaning. But I've never done anything dishonest since, and I've never touched a drop of drink. It was the drink that brought me to it. But I've never done nothing of the sort since.'

'I'm very glad to hear it.'

She was on tenterhooks to know why he had sent for her.

'Directly you sent for me, sir, I come.'

'But how do you manage to get away when you ought to be cooking the dinner?'

She gave a startled movement. She hesitated. His eyes were upon her. She was compelled to tell the truth.

'There wasn't any dinner to cook, sir.'

'But your mistress is at home?'

'I don't know, sir.'

'Good Heavens!' he cried, 'you don't know whether your mistress is at home or not.' Then he added, and there was a touch of feigned sadness in his voice, 'I'm surprised, Mrs Baker, that you lie to me.'

'Beg pardon, sir, I'm not lying . . . far from it.'

And strangely enough he believed her, though he didn't show it. He smiled:

'I don't know why you should treat me in this way. You're the cook to Miss Clive and you don't know whether she's at home or not.'

'No, sir, I don't.'

'I know you're a good cook, because I have often eaten your dinners. But it seems to me a strange thing that a cook doesn't know if her mistress is in London or not.'

'It's this way, sir,' she said, 'I shouldn't like you to think that I've told a lie to you, after what you've done for me. I shouldn't like you to suspect it. But I'll tell you the whole truth so that you'll know I'm an honest woman.'

He affected boredom. He expressed with his hands a desire to be spared Mrs Baker's defence. But she persisted:

'No, sir, it's my right to tell you the truth.'

'As you wish.'

'And, mind you, sir, the truth is strange enough. I oughtn't to tell you. I'm on oath not to tell you.'

He had a terrible fear that the power of the oath might seal her lips.

'Oh, if it's incredible!' he said, with a forensic sneer on his lips.

That determined her.

Rapidly she spoke:

'It was like this, sir. Sir Clifford Oakleigh cured me of a tumour when I was in the hospital. He was that kind to me, sir. He was as good to me as you. It's strange that the two people who did me the greatest kindness, yourself and Sir Clifford Oakleigh, should be such friends. Well, sir, he's always kept in touch with me. He used to send me a little present at Christmas time. And do you know, sir, I believed then that I was his favourite patient. Of a sudden, a little while ago, he sent for me to go to Harley Street, and he said that he wanted me to take the place of cook to a friend of his, a Miss Clive. He told me I was to leave my situation at once. Well, sir, naturally I couldn't refuse going to Sir Clifford. So then and there I packs up my things—Lancaster Gate my situation was, only a Jew stockbroker, sir, as I wasn't very keen on.'

From the weary movement of the K.C.'s head one would have imagined that, to his thinking, of all subjects the most tedious was the history of the Clive *ménage*.

'Well, sir, he told me that I wasn't on no account to tell nobody, them was his very words, of anything that went on in the house. He said that Miss Clive was a little erratical in her movements, that she needed to go in and out of the house without nobody knowing that she went out or came in. Very mysterious it seemed to me, and I wouldn't have done it for anybody except Sir Clifford. Oh, he's a good master, I tell you. So I packs up my things and I comes to Pembroke Street. And then I had a sort of a shock. I found that all the other servants thought they was his favourite patient. Each one of them said as how Sir Clifford had saved their lives. And it's my belief that he'd put them all on their oaths, the same as he'd put me. So Miss Clive comes and goes as she likes, and we don't know when she goes or how she comes. Orders was given that the front door is never to be locked or bolted, so she can always open it with her latchkey.'

'Tut, tut!' said the K.C. 'How extraordinary.'

'I know it's extraordinary, sir, but I give you my word it's true. She may be in the house now. She was there last night.'

'Did you see her?' he asked.

'No, sir, I didn't see her. She was in her bedroom. Her bedroom is always kept locked.'

Earnestly she looked at his face.

'You do believe me, sir, don't you?'

He pretended to be thinking.

She whispered:

'It's my belief as how the lady's a Russian spy, sir. I do hope that you won't marry a Russian spy. Not that I've got a word against the lady. She's the kindest mistress I've ever had. But it's very peculiar.'

'Yes, it's very peculiar.'

There was a pause. Then he said:

'Oh, yes, Mrs Baker, I believe you.'

'And might I ask, sir, what you sent for me for?'

'Oh, nothing, Mrs Baker, nothing. I was only curious to know how you were getting on. As a matter of fact, my defence of you was almost the beginning of what has been not altogether an unsatisfactory career.'

A great weight fell from her shoulders.

'I thought as how you were going to tell Miss Clive.'

'Oh, dear, no.'

'And you won't tell her, sir, what I've told you, nor yet Sir Clifford Oakleigh?'

'If a couple of sovereigns to buy a new dress are any good to you, Mrs Baker, take them. No, let it be guineas. I think that is what you paid me for your defence.'

'And the best two guineas' worth I ever had in my life, sir.'

'I'm glad you're doing so well, Mrs Baker. Good-night.'

'Good-night, sir.'

CHAPTER XXXVI

THE RETURN OF MIRIAM

WHEN Smallwood appeared that evening, he listened attentively to Harding's account of his interview with Mrs Baker. Both men looked at the matter from every point of view. But the only light which the cook had thrown on the case was that there must be some sort of connection between Sir Clifford Oakleigh and Miss Clive. What that connection might be baffled them.

Why had the doctor denied any knowledge of the lady? Why, if they were so intimate, were they never seen together?

'My own view,' said Harding, regretfully, at last, 'is that the lady is in the habit of taking drugs of some sort.'

'But,' interposed the detective, 'Sir Clifford Oakleigh denied the possibility, didn't he, sir?'

'Yes, of course, he denied it. But why should he admit it? It seems to me that, in all probability, Sir Clifford has taken every sort of precaution to prevent the poor lady's unfortunate habit from becoming known. You see he has obviously engaged servants in whom he has complete trust. For days at a time, Miss Clive indulges in orgies of morphia or cocaine, or whatever the cursed stuff is. When she's in this state, she remains in her room and the servants are instructed to say that she is out of town. How does that strike you, Smallwood?'

'It seems to me perfectly possible, sir. May I ask how long it is since you saw her?'

'I have not seen her for over a week. But I have telephoned every day and always had the same answer, to the effect that she was out of town.'

'Do you think, then, sir, that she's been under the influence of the drug for a whole week?'

Harding shivered with horror.

'I'm afraid so,' he replied. 'It's the longest time that she's ever been "out of town". As a rule, her absences only last for three days.'

Then, suddenly, he shot out, 'You've never seen Sir Clifford Oakleigh enter the house?'

'No, sir.'

'It's an extraordinary thing,' said the K.C., 'that if he is aware that she is a morpho-maniac he should not visit her.'

'Hasn't it struck you, sir, as curious that he hasn't been able to cure her? He can cure everything else, it seems. Isn't it extraordinary that he can't cure a simple thing like the practice of taking morphia?'

'It isn't a simple thing.'

'I think it is to him, sir. Anyhow, it is simple compared with cancer, and they say that the Emperor is completely cured. At any rate, that's the rumour.'

After three or four minutes of silence Harding exclaimed:

'I wonder if it would be any good for me to ask her uncle, Augustus Parker, about it?'

The detective shook his head.

'I don't think so, sir. The thought had occurred to me, but I don't think it's a matter on which an uncle would give away his niece. Mr Parker would probably pooh-pooh the whole idea. Anyhow, sir, I haven't got a very high opinion of Mr Parker.'

'You haven't, eh?'

The detective hesitated.

'Well, sir, as a matter of fact,' he said, 'we all know that he takes money for introducing ladies into Society. As a matter of fact, one of the Inspectors in the C division told me that Miss Clive had paid him £1000.'

'What infernal nonsense!' cried Harding, indignantly. 'Why should a girl pay her uncle such a sum of money for such a service? If you had heard any such story, why didn't you tell me?'

'Inspector Clegg only told me so today, sir.'

At that moment there was a sound of shouting in the street.

Harding moved to the window. A man was rushing along with the contents bill of the *Evening News*. As he went he shouted out some indistinct words. The only ones intelligible were 'Emperor . . . completely . . . cured.'

'Rush out and get me a copy, will you?' he said to the detective. Meantime he opened the window and stopped the man. On the return of the detective he read the paper. Here, indeed, was marvellous news. Three of the most eminent doctors said that there were no symptoms of cancer in the Emperor. Sir Clifford Oakleigh had cured him. The Emperor, in gratitude, proposed to confer on him the Order of the Treble-Headed Eagle. His Majesty had already left Harley Street to pass three days with the King at Windsor before returning to Badschwerin.

'What an extraordinary man!' commented Harding. 'Clifford is a genius.'

'Yes, sir,' said the detective, 'he is a genius and a gentleman. I did some work for him five or six years ago and he was most liberal in his payment. He will get a peerage for this, sir.'

'The only use of a peerage,' said Harding, 'is to make an eminent man commonplace. Clifford Oakleigh is now one of the biggest names in the world.'

At that moment the telephone bell rang. Harding went to the machine. No sooner had he taken up the receiver when his face flushed with enthusiastic delight.

'Is that you, Miriam? . . . Of course. Certainly . . . By all means . . . Come at once. I haven't had dinner myself. I've been too busy. We will get to the Carlton by nine . . . You will call for me in the motor? . . . Right.'

Quickly he turned to the detective.

'Miss Clive is coming here at once. Have you ever had any experience of morpho-maniacs?'

'Oh, yes, sir. I've seen lots of them.'

'I want you to be present when Miss Clive is shown in. You must enter into conversation with her, and see if you detect anything suspicious.'

'Yes, sir.'

He took down from a bookshelf a volume on forensic medicine, and eagerly read the pages dealing with the effects of morphia. Then he handed it to Smallwood. 'Just you read this carefully,' he said.

'I shall be dressed in ten minutes. Wait here.'

Then he went out of the room. He told his servant to ask Miss Clive when she arrived to come in.

The servant showed her into the library.

She was handsomer than ever. Her eyes flashed more brilliantly. When she caught sight of Smallwood she made a sudden movement of surprise.

'Oh, I beg your pardon,' she said. 'I didn't know there was anybody here.'

'Mr Harding has gone to dress. He will be ready in a minute.'

She appeared conscious that the man's eyes were staring at her attentively. But was there anything unusual in a man's eyes staring attentively at so beautiful a vision as Miss Clive? Obviously not.

'Wonderful triumph of Sir Clifford Oakleigh,' he said at last.

'Marvellous!' she answered.

'I suppose,' he continued, 'that there's practically nothing that man can't do?'

Miss Clive smiled.

'Well, if a man can cure cancer, I should think he would have no difficulty in curing a cold in the head.'

'It is proved,' said the detective, 'that he can deal with disease. I wonder whether he would be successful in cases of bad habits.'

'Such as?' she inquired.

'Drink or drugs,' he hazarded.

She looked curiously at him. A questioning glance came from her eyes.

'Do you know of anybody who suffers from either of these curses?'

'No, no,' he answered quickly. 'No one in particular. I only put the question generally.'

Harding entered.

With the words, 'Ten o'clock tomorrow at the Temple,' he dismissed Smallwood.

He was on the point of flinging his arms round Miriam when she drew back.

'What did you ask me in here for?' she inquired.

'I wanted to kiss my darling.'

'No doubt,' she responded, with something very like a sneer on her lips. 'But why did you require the presence of a detective?'

He was on the point of lying.

'That man is not . . .'

'Pardon me,' she interposed, 'Smallwood is one of the smartest detectives that ever retired from the Force.'

He was baffled.

How on earth did Miriam know that Smallwood was a detective? He put the question:

'Yes, he's a detective. But how did you know?'

She laughed:

'I flatter myself that I can always detect detectives.'

'Yes. But you can't detect their names. How did you know he was Smallwood?'

'I will tell you,' she answered, 'if you will tell me why you had him here.'

He lied awkwardly.

'A friend of mine wants to employ him.'

'What friend?' she asked quickly. 'Tell me immediately. Don't stop to think.'

At a venture he answered: 'Frederick Robinson.'

She patted him on the face with her fan.

'What the dickens does he want a detective for? I suppose he wants to find out why Sir William Clarke-Odgers wears whiskers. George, you have lied to me,' she continued. But she did not appear angry. 'You have not told me the truth in this matter. I shall not tell you the truth as to how I know that Smallwood is a detective.'

'Confound it!' he replied, 'these are nice relations between a man and a woman who are in love with each other! Miriam, I insist on an explanation. No man can stand this sort of thing.' He looked carefully at her. But to his delight he detected none of the symptoms mentioned in the book on forensic medicine.

She pursed her lips and sighed prettily.

'You're not going to throw me over, are you? And you're not going to make a row, are you? I love you very, very much.' She threw her arms around him, and kissed his face passionately. 'Darling, it's ten days since I saw you.'

'Why is it ten days? It's your own fault.'

'Sit down by me on the sofa,' she pleaded. 'Don't let us go to the Carlton yet. Order the dinner in half an hour. The motor can wait.'

He hesitated. She drew his head down, and pressed his lips against her neck.

He was conquered. He telephoned to the Carlton, ordering dinner in half an hour.

'But what will your servants think?' he asked uneasily.

'I don't care a damn,' she replied, 'what the men think. I have not seen you for ten days.'

CHAPTER XXXVII

THE ACCIDENT

THE thing happened in an instant.

When he came to, he found himself surrounded by useless people with wide-open eyes. He fainted again, and when his eyes opened he found himself in a four-wheel cab with a policeman and another man. His first words were:

'Where is she?'

The other man said:

'Oh, she's all right. How are you feeling yourself?'

Harding answered that he felt very much shaken.

The other man passed his hands over his arms and legs. 'Do you think that any bones are broken?'

'I don't think so.'

'Are you sure?'

Harding nodded.

'Where are you taking me?'

'To Charing Cross Hospital.'

'I would sooner be taken home.'

'I think the best plan would be to take you to the hospital. Do you live far from here?'

'Oh, no,' he said, 'South Audley Street. Excuse me, but who are you?'

'I'm a doctor,' and the man gave his name, Dr Oakley-Williams. 'I happened to be passing when the accident occurred.'

'Frankly,' Harding said, 'I don't think there is anything seriously the matter with me. You had better take me to my house.'

So he was driven home. The doctor and the policeman helped him up to his room. He gave the policeman a sovereign, and the two were left alone.

The doctor administered brandy, undressed him, and put him to bed. Then he examined him with great care, and the result was very satisfactory.

'You've had a marvellous escape. A few flesh wounds, and that's all. I'm afraid you'll be horribly stiff for a day or two. But, all things considered, you've had a wonderful escape.'

'What happened?'

'I was standing just by Swan & Edgar's when your motor-brougham came along Piccadilly. A motor-'bus coming up Regent Street skidded and crashed into your brougham and overturned it.'

'And the lady?' he asked, sitting up in bed eagerly. 'What has happened to her?'

The doctor looked thoughtfully at him before answering.

'She isn't hurt. But as she was insensible, it seemed best to take her to Charing Cross Hospital.'

'Are you quite sure,' he asked, 'that nothing has happened to her? She is my fiancée.'

'No, no, no. Make your mind easy on that point.'

'And the servants?'

'I can't tell you,' he replied. 'I was so busy looking after you. I'm afraid they've both been hurt. Now, don't you ask any more questions. What you need is sleep. Can I do anything more for you?'

'No, thanks. Yes, stop. There is something you can do for me. I shall be very much obliged if you will go down to Charing Cross Hospital and see how Miss Clive is.'

The doctor hesitated. Then he said at last:

'Certainly, if you wish it.'

'If I wish it! Good God, certainly I wish it! A man naturally wants to know how his fiancée is.'

'And do you want me to come back tonight?'

'The sooner the better, sir.'

'Would you like your man to sit up with you?'

'No.'

'Try and get some sleep.'

'I shan't get any sleep until you come back.'

The doctor was gone an hour. Directly he opened the bedroom door he felt the barrister's eyes upon him. Nervously he spoke:

'I have just ascertained from your man that you are Mr Harding, the—if I may say so—the eminent K.C.'

Harding frowned.

'I hoped you had ascertained the condition of Miss Clive.'

The other answered:

'She's going on as well as can be expected.'

Harding sat up in bed.

'Look here, there's nothing the matter with me. I'm in full possession of my faculties, and there's no earthly reason why you shouldn't tell me the truth. Mind you, if you don't tell me the truth—and I'm perfectly convinced that you don't want to tell me the truth out of mistaken kindness—I shall know at once. Out with it, man. What is the matter with her? Tell me; is she alive?'

There were beads of perspiration on his forehead, and his hands were gripping the bedclothes in agony.

'Oh, yes, she's alive.'

'Thank God! But is she in danger?'

'Her life is not in danger.'

'Out with it. Tell me, what's the matter.'

'Her leg is broken.'

'You are still keeping something back.'

'And her skull is . . . fractured.'

He moaned, and fell back, pale as death on the pillows.

'What a fool I was to tell him,' said the doctor to himself. 'But he's the sort of man one has to tell the truth to.'

But Harding had not fainted.

With a great effort he spoke again.

'Swear to me that you have told me the worst.'

On this point he was reassured.

'I will go and see her at once,' he said, sitting up laboriously in bed. But the effort was too much for him. 'No, I'm weaker than I thought. I must wait till tomorrow.'

The next morning Smallwood appeared at nine-thirty. But before that, Harding had read the papers. The accident was described at great length, and the description of Miriam's condition tallied with the report made by Dr Oakley-Williams. The papers, however, he was pleased to see, exaggerated the misfortune which had befallen him. According to one, both his legs were broken, according to another, his skull was fractured; according to a third, it seemed improbable that he would recover. If they exaggerated in his case, it might well be that they would exaggerate in Miriam's case.

Smallwood was all sympathy.

'I suppose, sir, you don't want me to watch the Charing Cross Hospital?'

'Oh, no.'

'You're looking a little pulled down, sir, but not much, after what you've gone through.'

'I'm not in the least pulled down. I'm getting up in a minute and going to the hospital to see Miss Clive.'

Then an idea struck him.

'I want you to take a note round to Sir Clifford Oakleigh. I want him to go immediately to the hospital and see Miss Clive.'

The detective shook his head.

'There is a curious rumour about Sir Clifford Oakleigh. It seems that the King sent for him last night and no one knows where he is.'

'That isn't curious in the case of Sir Clifford. Probably, after the tension of the last few days, he has gone somewhere to amuse himself.'

'I'm afraid he's very erratic, sir.'

'Not for a genius,' answered his friend. 'Get me that blotting-pad and my stylographic pen.'

Thereupon he wrote a note.

While he was writing it, Smallwood stated that from his observations made last night, he was perfectly convinced that Miss Clive did not take morphia.

'So am I,' said the K.C. 'Take that round to Sir Clifford and wait for an answer. Go in a cab. By the time you're back I shall be dressed.'

The detective went out.

On his return, it was evident from his face that he brought grave news. The butler at Harley Street had informed him that his master had gone out the previous evening at about seven o'clock, a few minutes after the departure of the Emperor, and that he had not returned.

'I know where we shall find him,' said Harding.

They drove to King Street. They rang once, twice, three times, but could get no answer. Five times, six times they rang. The house appeared entirely deserted.

'Well, it's no good,' said Harding at last. 'I'm only wasting time. I had better go down to the hospital. Can I drop you anywhere?'

'No thank you, sir.'

He got into a cab and went down to the hospital.

The house-surgeon received him very sympathetically.

'I'm afraid,' he said gravely, 'that you won't be able to see Miss Clive.'

'Has there been a relapse?' he asked.

'I'm afraid I have very bad news for you, Mr Harding. Mind you, there's no danger. But we have been compelled to amputate Miss Clive's leg.'

'Good God!' he cried, ghastly pale. 'How far up?'

'Above the knee.'

'How far above the knee?'

'Only just above the knee.'

'Poor woman,' he murmured. 'And the fracture?'

'Oh, the fracture's very slight. She has a wonderful

constitution. She has been considerably shaken, of course, but there is really nothing at all to be alarmed at.'

The K.C. stared at the surgeon.

'But she will be a cripple for life.'

'Oh, my dear sir,' said the other, 'in these days the loss of a leg is not much.'

Harding interposed. 'It is a terrible thing for a woman.'

'Not at all,' replied the other, cheerily; 'with an artificial leg she will be able to walk with a scarcely perceptible limp.'

'When can I see her?'

'I should think in two days. I will send you a report every two hours, if you like.'

Harding thanked him, and gave him his address in the Temple.

'Can I do nothing? I hope she is comfortable.'

'Oh, yes, far more comfortable than she would be at home. She has a private room, of course, and she has the best care in the world.'

'Without casting the slightest disparagement on you or the staff of Charing Cross Hospital I should very much like my friend Sir Clifford Oakleigh to see her.'

'That can easily be arranged.'

'I'm afraid it can't.' Harding explained the difficulty that stood in the way of securing the great man's presence. 'By the by, I want to ask you a question,' he added. 'This is, of course, entirely between ourselves, but I have heard it suggested that Miss Clive takes morphia, or has taken morphia.'

The other shook his head and laughed.

'My dear sir, dismiss that idea from your mind. There is not a mark of a syringe on her anywhere. Besides, her eyes prove that she has never been addicted to drugs. Oh, no, no. Don't worry about that.'

'Thank you, thank you, that's a great relief to me.'

Then he went back to the Temple.

CHAPTER XXXVIII

'SOMETHING IS ON HER MIND'

THE great topic of conversation during that day and the next was the disappearance of Sir Clifford Oakleigh. The fact that an eminent K.C. and his fiancée had narrowly escaped death sank into insignificance in the face of the astounding behaviour of the greatest surgeon in the world, who had vanished suddenly, when the King had sent for him with a view to bestowing on him some great honour. Telegrams from all parts of the world, offering huge sums, were despatched to Harley Street. A pork king in Chicago was alleged to have offered him a million pounds to cure his daughter of consumption.

But there was no Clifford Oakleigh.

The butler at Harley Street could only say that his master had gone out on the Tuesday evening, wearing a frock-coat and top-hat, and carrying a gold-headed cane.

On Friday morning Detective-Inspector Johnson, accompanied by P. Barlow, forced the door of his house in King Street. The house, such parts of it as were furnished, appeared in good order. P. Barlow pointed out to Johnson that in all probability a charwoman attended to the house. Johnson glared at Barlow.

On the hat-stand Barlow found a pair of gloves. He suggested that these might be Sir Clifford Oakleigh's gloves. Johnson assumed that they were, but denied that their discovery had any important bearing on the case.

P. Barlow felt discouraged. He hesitated to point out that among the sticks in the hat-stand were two gold-headed ones. Johnson maintained that eminent surgeons were often presented with gold-headed sticks by grateful patients.

'But,' said P. Barlow, 'don't you think that one of these might be the stick he brought with him from Harley Street?'

'On the contrary,' said Johnson, 'if he had a gold-headed stick here why should he bring another from Harley Street?' Then he added something which sounded very like 'pooh'. Nevertheless, he took the two sticks and the pair of gloves, told Barlow to remain on duty, and left the building.

He proceeded at once to Harley Street, where he saw the butler.

Instantly the servant identified one of the sticks and the gloves as those which his master had worn on the night of Tuesday. Thereupon Johnson informed the newspaper men of the wonderful clue which he had discovered. Sir Clifford Oakleigh had gone from Harley Street to King Street. That much was clear. From King Street he had gone, without gloves and without a stick, somewhere which was not clear.

The papers were loud in the praise of Johnson, not only for his wonderful skill in discovering clues, but for his admirable sense in communicating them to the police.

When he returned to King Street he blamed Barlow for not having had a lock put on the door.

Barlow said a new lock was not necessary, because there were bolts on the door. Johnson explained to Barlow that he was not a man of great intellectual calibre. Barlow became so downhearted that he scarcely liked to mention the fact that he had found a silk hat on one of the chairs.

'Now that is an important fact,' said Johnson. 'Why the dickens didn't you tell me of that before?'

P. Barlow said he did not know.

Then Johnson examined the hat.

'This,' said he at last, after opening the leather lining, 'is Sir Clifford Oakleigh's hat.'

'How on earth can you tell?' inquired Barlow.

Johnson explained.

'On the inside of the hat is written in ink, in ink, mind you, "Sir Clifford Oakleigh", and underneath it "17RI". Now, that alone,' he added, 'would be sufficient to make one suspect that the hat belongs to Sir Clifford Oakleigh.'

'But what does "17RI" mean?' inquired Barlow.

Johnson considered.

'That is probably put there to throw us off the track. I have no hesitation in saying that that is Sir Clifford Oakleigh's hat. I must, however, proceed by steps. Have you noticed anything further about the hat, Barlow?'

'It is to my thinking,' replied the other man, 'an ordinary gent's top-hat.'

Johnson looked scornfully at him.

'You have failed to observe that the hat was made, or, at any rate, sold, by Lincoln & Bennett. I will proceed at once to Lincoln & Bennett's and inquire if they are in the habit of supplying hats to the gentleman. You, Barlow, will remain here tonight. In the morning, if the charwoman comes, you must detain her. I will order some food to be sent in to you.'

Then Johnson went off to Lincoln & Bennett with the hat, and having ascertained that this eminent firm was in the habit of supplying Sir Clifford Oakleigh with hats, he went a step further, and showed it to Sir Clifford's butler, who unhesitatingly asserted it to be the one that his master wore when he left the house on Tuesday.

That morning the house-surgeon had telephoned to Harding asking him to come to the hospital at once. The surgeon said:

'Mr Harding, I don't know that I'm doing the right thing. Miss Clive is progressing favourably. She is, however, so anxious to see you. She repeats your name so often that I am perhaps justified in allowing you to see her. But only for a few minutes, mind.'

In accents of deep emotion the barrister thanked him.

He was shown into a small but airy and intensely clean room.

Miriam's white face, with its wealth of black hair streaming from under the bandages, lay upon the pillow. As he entered, the nurse rose. The sound of the opening door roused the patient. Her huge eyes turned towards him.

'Oh, my darling, my darling!' he cried.

Her colourless lips did not burst into a smile. She seemed very, very weak. He fancied that the heavy smell of chloroform was struggling with the perfume of the flowers that he had sent her.

She made a motion of her head to summon him to her side.

Very tenderly he bent over her and kissed her. Her lips opened, and she could just say—he thought—'Dearest.'

With marvellous self-control she managed to speak firmly: 'Take me home.'

So surprising was the request from one so frail that he could make no answer.

A wild look, a cross between horror and determination, shone in her eyes.

'Take me home,' she repeated.

The house-surgeon was standing by the door.

Harding went up to him and said:

'She asks to be taken home.'

'Impossible,' he said, 'absolutely impossible.'

Miriam's eyes caught the movement of negation.

'It would be impossible to move her,' continued the other. 'I'm sure she's comfortable here.'

Harding returned to the bedside.

'George,' she said in a low voice, 'I tell you I must be taken home.' Then, as though her strength were waning, she uttered in a faint voice, which he just succeeded in catching, these curious words, 'It's a matter of life and death.'

'My dearest,' he said, 'I'm sure it would be death for you to be moved.'

She said something, but he could not grasp it.

'What was that you said, dear? What was that about Clifford Oakleigh?'

But she had fainted.

The surgeon looked very grave.

'I'm afraid your visit hasn't done her any good,' he said. 'I think she has got something on her mind. She is always saying, "What day did the accident take place? What day is it now?" She seems to think I am deceiving her about it.'

CHAPTER XXXIX

AN ASTOUNDING DISCOVERY

THE papers on Saturday morning were enthusiastic over Johnson's marvellous discovery of the hat. He became the most popular detective in the kingdom.

'Ah,' said one paper practically, 'Mr Johnson would prefer that a hundred innocent men should be convicted rather than that one guilty man should escape.'

The papers said nothing about P. Barlow. Yet that morning, at six-thirty, Barlow, ever alert, had detected the sound of somebody attempting to open the door. With catlike tread he had gone to the door and suddenly drawn the bolts. A startled old woman, obviously of the charwoman class, stood on the steps, aghast at the sight of a policeman in uniform.

'Lor' bless me,' stammered Mrs Widgeley, 'what's 'appened to the door, and 'ow did you get in, constable?'

Barlow produced his notebook.

'Not so fast, old mother. First of all, name and address, please. No, first of all, you come in, mother.'

Barlow laboriously wrote down the fact that Mrs Widgeley, who proved to be very deaf, lived in George Street Mews, that she was employed as charwoman by Sir Clifford Oakleigh, that she daily arrived at six-thirty and worked till about ten, or until such tune as she had fulfilled her duties.

Suddenly she got tired of interrogation.

'Say,' she said, 'what's all this talk about Sir Clifford Oakleigh 'aving disappeared?'

Barlow regarded this as a question of a guilty person. Although he did not suppose, one may presume, that she had actually done away with the great surgeon, he rather fancied that she had 'had a hand in it', whatever *it* was.

Fortunately, before he had actually come to the conclusion that it would be a wise scheme to arrest her, the admirable Johnson arrived.

He strictly examined the old woman. All the information, however, that he extracted from her was that occasionally when she arrived in the morning she would find Sir Clifford's hat on the hat-rack. She would then take up a cup of tea to his room at eight o'clock. That would be the last she would see of him, unless he happened by any chance to pass her on the stairs when she was cleaning up. Sometimes he would sleep in the house for three nights at a time. But his movements were very erratic.

'Bless me,' she said, 'when I come 'ere in the morning, I don't know whether he's upstairs in bed no more than the man in the moon.'

'When did he sleep here last?'

'I couldn't say, not being no scholar. It might 'ave been last week or the week before. You see, it's only a matter of making a bed if 'e's 'ere, so it's not the sort of thing one would be expected to remember.'

Though pressed to the utmost of Johnson's ability, she could not be more definite.

'But were you not,' he inquired with knitted brows, 'somewhat surprised when you heard that he had disappeared?'

'No, I wasn't. You see it's this way. He's always disappearing as you might say. In fact, he disappeared twice for every once that he appeared; if you take my meaning.'

Johnson tried to take her meaning.

Barlow took her meaning—in writing—all wrong.

Johnson came to the conclusion that it was no use wasting further time with the old woman.

In the course of the next few days public opinion became less favourable with regard to the merits of Johnson. The greatest of all surgeons disappears. The matter is placed in the hands of Inspector Johnson. He fails to find the greatest of all surgeons. Johnson is not so bright as we thought him.

A certain interest was now aroused in Miss Clive. A beautiful woman, engaged to one of the most brilliant men at the Bar, owing to a motor accident is crippled for life. The public wanted to talk about that. This terrible disaster was due to a motor bus. People wanted to say unpleasant things about motor buses.

Twice daily Harding called at the Charing Cross Hospital. Whenever he was allowed to see Miriam, she repeated her request to be taken home. The house-surgeon informed him that the poor girl became hysterical in her demand to be taken home. This absurd desire must, in his opinion, retard her recovery. Harding urged her to be resigned. He implored her to explain why she wanted to be taken home. Had she any fault to find with the Charing Cross Hospital?

Petulantly she cried, 'No, no.'

She did not complain of pain. She did not seem affected at the terrible outrage that had been inflicted on her body. The prospect of being a cripple for life did not seem to worry her. Her sole desire was to be taken home, 'Before it is too late.' She was for ever asking what was the day on which the accident occurred, and calculating the number of days that had passed up till now. The white fingers were constantly tapping the bedclothes, Tuesday, Wednesday, Thursday, Friday, and so on. It was a terrible time for Harding. He hated to go to his club because he was tired of sympathy.

But one evening as he was in White's, nominally reading the *Saturday Review* but actually thinking of Miriam and her terrible position, a man came up to him with a face tense with excitement.

'I say, do you see that they've found the body of Clifford Oakleigh?'

Harding jumped from his chair.

'No. Where? The body? Dead? You say Clifford is dead?'

'He has been dead some days. They found the body in a house in Pembroke Street.'

'Good heavens! What has happened?'

The man explained. He was a bore who rarely found it impossible to obtain a listener and who enjoyed his explanation.

The gist of it was this:

The servants in a certain house had detected a curious smell for which drains could not be held responsible. The butler had gone to Vine Street police-station; detectives had examined the house and had located the smell. It came from a secret cupboard on the ground floor.

'Secret cupboard!' exclaimed the K.C., incredulously. 'People don't have secret cupboards nowadays. Whose house is it?'

'Bless me, I forget for the moment. But it's in the evening papers. Ah, I remember now. It is 69 Pembroke Street. The house of a Miss Clive, I think it was.'

Harding sank back in his chair, ashen white.

CHAPTER XL

MIRIAM'S DEFENCE

In a few minutes he pulled himself together and rushed out of the club. He jumped into a hansom and drove to Charing Cross Hospital. There he found the house-surgeon.

'I must see Miss Clive at once,' said he.

The other shook his head.

'I'm afraid it's impossible, Mr Harding.'

'She's not worse?' he inquired.

'No, she's not worse. In fact, she's doing very well.'

'Then why can't I see her? I insist on seeing her.'

'We have strict orders from the police that no one is to be allowed in her room, except, of course, the staff.'

'Good God, why?' he inquired.

'Surely, surely, Mr Harding, you, as a barrister . . .'

He gasped.

'You don't mean to say that the police suspect her?'

'My dear sir, I know nothing. I only know what I have read in the papers. Of course, at the inquest tomorrow some light may be thrown on the affair.'

They were standing in the hall. The whole horror flashed on Harding. Miriam might be tried for murder. Of course, she was innocent. But she would be tried . . . in all probability she would be tried. The moment had come for action. No effort must be spared. He himself would attend the inquest in her interest. But he must see her first. He would go to the Home Secretary and get a special order. The house-surgeon was too much a man of the world to make any attempt at consolation. He saw in front of him a stern, gaunt man prepared to face the situation.

At that moment Johnson, accompanied by Barlow, entered. The house-surgeon nodded to him.

'Johnson,' said the K.C., 'I presume you have this case in hand.'

'Yes, sir.'

'I understand that no one is allowed to see Miss Clive.'

'No one, sir.'

'I don't know whether you are aware that I'm engaged to this lady?'

'I know that, sir.'

'Under the circumstances, I don't see how you can object to my seeing her.'

Johnson reflected for a moment. He spoke to the house-surgeon.

'Does Miss Clive know that Sir Clifford Oakleigh is dead?'

'Yes. One of the nurses told her.'

'The devil!' exclaimed the detective.

Barlow was on the point of taking a note of the exclamation.

'No, you needn't put that down, you fool.'

It appeared to Johnson that it would not be an unwise thing for her fiancé to be present . . . when he did what he had to do.

'No, sir,' he said. 'I don't think that I should object to your seeing Miss Clive. But, of course, you must not go near her.'

'Why the dickens not? She's not under arrest. You policemen are taking too much upon yourselves.'

'She is not under arrest now,' replied Johnson, slowly.

The man's tone irritated the K.C. He felt too impatient to speak to him.

'Let us go up at once,' he said to the house-surgeon.

'Certainly.' And he led the way to the patient's room.

When they were outside it, Johnson stepped forward.

'Excuse me, I must go first.'

Harding noticed a woman of the respectable caretaker type standing by Barlow's side. He shot a look of interrogation at the detective.

'Is she also of our party?'

'Yes, sir.'

Then Johnson opened the door.

Miriam, as she lay in her bed, looked even paler than when Harding had seen her last. There was in her eyes an expression of terror. The nurse rose, Johnson walked forward to the bed and stood at its side. He turned round, and motioned to the others to remain by the door.

'Miss Clive,' he said, producing a document from his pocket, 'I hold a warrant for your arrest on the charge of murdering Sir Clifford Oakleigh at 69 Pembroke Street.'

Harding shot forward. It seemed as though he was about to strike the detective. Miriam, in a faint voice that betrayed no surprise, merely said:

'I understand.'

Barlow made a note which afterwards read 'I don't understand.'

The nurse burst into tears.

'Oh, dear, poor thing!' she said, and sank into a chair in a huddled heap.

Then Johnson, in the ordinary way, cautioned the prisoner.

Her answer was, 'I have nothing to say at present.'

Barlow took this down more or less correctly, with a view to altering it afterwards.

During this scene Harding's eyes had been fixed on Miriam. He had had a great experience of criminals. But he could not for the life of him adduce anything from the demeanour of this frail woman. He kept an open mind. He marvelled at her self-control, but he could not form any conclusion as to whether it indicated guilt or innocence.

'May I,' she said in a voice that just reached him, 'speak to Mr Harding?'

'Certainly,' was the detective's answer.

Harding approached nearer to the bed. By straining every nerve he could just hear her say:

'Dear George, I want you to keep that little gold heart in memory of me. It is among my things . . . I was wearing it when the accident happened.'

She wanted to say more but her strength failed.

'I suppose there's no objection to that?' asked Harding.

'Oh, no, sir. It can't have any bearing on the charge.'

'Now,' said Harding, 'I presume the ordinary procedure will be followed in this case.'

'Oh, yes, sir.' And he beckoned to the lady of the respectable caretaker type.

'I have brought Mrs Parish, one of our most discreet warderesses. She will, of course, always remain in the room until she is relieved. Mrs Parish, you understand that nothing is to be done to inconvenience the . . .' He was on the point of saying the 'prisoner', but substituted 'lady'.

Mrs Parish curtseyed.

Then Harding spoke to Miriam.

'My darling,' he said, 'I will myself appear for you at the inquest tomorrow. You may rely on me to refute this monstrous charge.'

'Thank you, George. I am absolutely innocent.'

Then he turned to the detective.

'As I shall defend Miss Clive—of course, it will be weeks before she can possibly appear at the police-court—I shall have, I suppose, every facility for seeing her?'

'Only, sir, in the presence of Mrs Parish.'

'Of course, of course,' he replied impatiently, 'but not in the hearing of Mrs Parish.'

Johnson whispered to him.

'Well, you see, sir, it is very awkward. In a hospital like this there is no grating between the prisoner and the visitor.'

Harding sneered at him.

'I, sir, am a King's Counsel. That lady is innocent. You don't suggest, I suppose, that I should attempt to convey poison to her?'

'No, no, no,' stammered the detective. 'But formalities have to be observed.'

'Quite so,' answered Harding. 'You may rely on me to observe them.'

Then he approached the bed.

'Is there anything you want to say to me now, dear?'

She made a great effort. She moved her hand in the direction of the detectives.

Harding turned to them.

'Would you mind standing back?'

They moved to the far end of the room.

Then she spoke.

He bent down his head to hear her. The words came slowly.

'You must fix the date of the murder. My defence will be that he died . . . three days after my accident.'

He wondered whether he had heard aright. She seemed too weak to repeat the statement, so he said:

'I am to get them to fix the actual date of the murder? Your defence is that he died three days after the date of our motor accident?'

There was a slight inclination of the head.

These, indeed, were extraordinary instructions, given in an astounding way. That was all he had to go on. But somehow the way in which she spoke carried conviction with it. Her manner had in it the suggestion of a person conversant with the methods of police-courts. Truly, Miriam Clive was an astounding woman.

'Is there anything else you want to say?' he asked.

There was no answer.

The house-surgeon rushed forward.

'She has fainted. She can't stand any more. You must go away now.'

Harding went out, accompanied by Johnson and Barlow.

Then indignation mastered him.

'I consider your behaviour, Johnson, monstrously cruel, entirely unnecessary. You could have waited till the poor lady was a little stronger. I suppose it is so unusual,' he added sarcastically, 'for the police to be able to arrest anybody that they don't like to miss a chance.'

Barlow inquired if he should make a note of the observation.

Johnson told him a home truth. Then he said:

'We must examine the effects brought into the hospital by the . . .'

'Confound it,' roared Harding, 'don't say prisoner.'

'By the lady.'

'Yes, and you can give me the gold heart.'

'Certainly, sir.'

With tears in his eyes, Harding looked at Miriam's blood-stained clothes. He picked up the gold heart, and he remembered as he did so how he had questioned her about it. His heart bled for her in her pain and in her anguish. He put the heart to his lips. But as he did so, Johnson's hand shot out.

'Excuse me, sir.' He took up the heart.

Barlow's head craned forward.

'I think this opens,' said Johnson.

Johnson was right. The heart contained a small steel key.

In his excitement Barlow dropped his notebook.

Johnson, before handing the heart to Harding, said:

'Excuse me, sir, but I cannot let you have this locket.'

'Why not?'

'I may tell you, sir, that this heart contains the key of the cupboard in which Sir Clifford Oakleigh's body was found.'

With a limp hand, despair graven on his face, Harding gave the locket back to Johnson.

Barlow picked up his notebook.

CHAPTER XLI

THE day after the coroner's jury had returned a verdict of wilful murder against Miriam Clive, Harding went to the hospital.

He found Miriam still deadly pale, but a little stronger. Before he had time to speak, she put this question:

'How long has he been dead?'

'The medical evidence,' he answered, 'is that he has been dead ten days.'

A smile of satisfaction played over her face.

'They are quite certain about that?'

'Both the doctors agreed that there could be no doubt on the point.'

'Then,' she said, 'he died three days after the accident.'

'By Jove,' exclaimed Harding, 'I never thought of that.'

Here was a complete defence. Mysterious though the case was, this much was clear. If Clifford Oakleigh had lived for three days after Miriam had been taken to the hospital, where every moment of her time could, of course, be accounted for, obviously she had no hand in his murder, if murder, indeed, it was.

'What did they think he died of, George?'

'Heart failure.'

Again she smiled.

'Miriam,' he cried, 'for heaven's sake tell me all you know about this.'

Firmly she replied: 'My dear George, it's no good, I am very weak. What you must do is to go to the Home Secretary, who is a personal friend of yours, and get the warrant withdrawn.'

He shook his head.

'I don't think he would do that.'

But she disagreed.

'It's perfectly clear that I can't be convicted. What's the good of going on?'

Her demeanour astonished him. Her calmness seemed superhuman.

'My dear girl,' he said, 'in the present state of public feeling such a course would lead to a riot. Clifford Oakleigh at the tune of his death was the most popular man in England. The mystery surrounding his death has taken hold of everybody's imagination. Somebody has got to suffer. The whole country is crying out for a victim.'

A third time she smiled.

'But not, of necessity, me. You see that must be so; whoever did the murder, if it was a murder, and you yourself say the medical evidence points to heart failure, they can't convict me. A woman who has lost a leg and is lying in a critical condition in the Charing Cross Hospital can't go about causing people to die of heart failure, can she?'

He admitted that she could not, but he added: 'My darling, I'm afraid you'll have to stand your trial.'

She gave a slight shrug of her shoulders against the pillow, and in a tone of contempt said:

'It seems rather ridiculous that all the resources of civilisation should be employed to keep me alive in order that I may eventually be hanged.'

'Why,' he laughed, 'there was a man once tried at the Old Bailey for murder who went under an extremely severe operation, and had a silver windpipe inserted in his throat in order that he should be hangable.'

This time she laughed. It was only the ghost of a laugh.

'You're rather gruesome, aren't you?'

He pleaded guilty. But he defended himself.

'You know, darling, you are so completely sensible that I talk to you as though you were a man.'

'That is a high compliment.'

At this minute the nurse entered. The patient, she maintained, was overtaxing her strength.

Harding went away.

He devoted himself strenuously to the preparation of Miriam's defence.

The point as to the dates of the death and of the motor accident escaped the notice of the Press. The public is only capable of taking an interest in one sensation at a time. The accident had been almost completely forgotten in the mystery. True, people knew that Miriam Clive had lost a leg as the result of a motor collision. Their comment was: 'It's a pity she wasn't killed.' The facts of the mystery were really very simple. An eminent doctor is found dead in a secret cupboard in a house that he has let to a beautiful woman. The servants have not seen him enter. When his will is proved it is found that he has left every penny to the beautiful woman. These were all the facts. But the public asked itself what the eminent doctor was doing in the house of the beautiful woman. This question Harding had also put to himself. But in her present condition he hesitated to put it to Miriam. Everybody was very, very sorry for Harding. Everybody regretted that his fiancé should have received a doctor, however eminent, in her house secretly. Everybody admired Harding for standing by her. It is a terrible thing to be engaged to a woman who is even suspected of murdering an eminent doctor, or indeed of murdering anybody.

Harding acquired a great deal of personal popularity through this. He moved heaven and earth to get the warrant withdrawn. But he moved heaven and earth in vain. There would have been a popular outcry if Miriam had not stood her trial.

So it was that three months later a haggard woman, a plain woman, was placed in the iron dock at Marlborough Street police-court.

The kindly, white-haired magistrate treated her, of course, with every consideration. Harding appeared for the defence. There was practically no new evidence adduced by the police. He, on his side, had received no assistance from his client. Miriam had absolutely refused to tell him anything more of the matter. She had simply insisted that her defence must be based on the medical evidence. Time after time she had reiterated this statement: 'No jury can convict me after that evidence. If the doctors go back on it, we will consider the matter.'

But the doctors did not go back on it.

Harding rose to cross-examine them. He pretended that he desired them to antedate the death. They would not budge an inch. They would not give him a day, scarcely an hour. They were firm that the body had been dead ten days, no more and no less. Could they be wrong about it? They denied any such possibility almost indignantly. 'Why,' said they, 'your own doctor entirely agrees with us.'

'Really, really,' said the magistrate, with that charming smile for which he was so famous, 'are you not labouring the matter a little unnecessarily, Mr Harding? If your own doctor agrees, what is the good of going on? Here we have Professor Salt and Dr Duckworth, two of the most eminent authorities in England. You also have your own doctor, an equally respected authority. How can you get behind that?'

At this moment a cry rang through the Court.

A weedy, gaunt man rushed to the railings of the dock.

'Sarah, Sarah!' he cried.

Sternly the magistrate said, 'Remove that man.'

But Mingey gesticulated.

'It's my daughter, your worship. My daughter, Sarah. I'm Mingey. You remember the disappearance of Miss Mingey.'

Two constables seized the miserable man, on whom the prisoner turned dull eyes in which there was no recognition. Struggling violently, and shouting, 'Sarah! Sarah!' he was dragged from the Court.

'Is there anything known about that man?' asked the magistrate.

'Yes,' said Harding, 'he used to be my clerk, but he suffers from delusions.'

The reporters were busily describing 'Scene in Court'.

When the hubbub had subsided Harding said:

'Your worship thinks that I am only wasting time of the Court in disputing the statement that the deceased had been dead for ten days at the time of the discovery of the body.'

'I do,' replied the magistrate.

'That,' said the Counsel for the Crown, 'is my case,' and sat down.

'Now, Mr Harding, do you propose to open your defence here, because I need hardly tell you that I propose to take a certain course?'

'Your worship has intimated the course which you intend to take.'

'Now,' said the magistrate, 'with regard to the prisoner. I have considered the matter of bail. Of course, in a murder charge bail is out of the question, as a rule, but in this case, and I may tell you that I have consulted the Home Secretary about it, I shall be prepared—'

'Oh,' said Harding, standing up. 'I'm not going to apply for bail.'

The magistrate looked surprised.

The barrister continued: 'I understood that the course you intended to take would be to discharge the prisoner.'

The magistrate appeared astounded and shook his head.

'I have no notion what could have put such an idea into your head, Mr Harding.'

'Why, sir, the fact that you yourself stated that there could be no doubt as to the body having been dead for precisely ten days before its discovery.'

'What bearing has that on the point?'

'I have here,' said Harding, calmly, 'the house-surgeon at Charing Cross Hospital. Will you kindly go into the box?'

The doctor was sworn.

'You are a member of the Royal College of Surgeons?'

'Yes.'

'You are house-surgeon at Charing Cross Hospital?'

'Yes.'

'On Monday, the fifteenth of June, the defendant was taken to Charing Cross Hospital suffering from the effects of a motor accident?'

'Yes. And I amputated her leg. Her left leg.'

'When did she leave the hospital?'

'Not until today.'

'Really, Mr Harding,' interposed the magistrate, 'we are aware of this unfortunate accident and we have every sympathy for the defendant, but it really has no bearing on the case.'

'Pardon me, your worship, it has the greatest bearing. It is, indeed, the whole case. You will notice that the doctor said the fifteenth of June was the date of the accident. It was not, according to these two eminent experts, whose opinion you yourself stated could not be contravened, not until three days after that Sir Clifford Oakleigh died.'

The Counsel for the Crown hastily called the experts to his side.

There was a sensation in Court.

Very firmly Harding spoke.

'Your worship, this being the state of the case, it is absolutely impossible that the defendant could have any hand in the death of Sir Clifford Oakleigh. He did not die until three days after she was admitted to the hospital.'

The magistrate seemed undecided. He glanced down at the Counsel for the Crown to see if he could afford him any assistance; he consulted with his clerk, but the clerk had no opinion to offer.

'I submit,' persisted Harding, 'that in face of these facts no jury can convict.'

'What do you say?' the magistrate asked, turning to the Counsel for the Crown.

'Your worship, I must leave the matter entirely in your hands. This has come as a complete surprise to us.'

In the result the magistrate discharged the prisoner.

CHAPTER XLII

THE SOLUTION

On the release of the prisoner, public opinion underwent a change. Not a great change, but a slight modification. Nothing had been elucidated with regard to the mystery. How could the body have got into the cupboard—the cupboard of which Miss Clive alone possessed the key? How did Sir Clifford Oakleigh leave her his huge fortune? After all, she could not be a nice woman. But then the world was full of women who could not by any possibility be nice women. Besides, she had suffered terribly. She was a cripple for life. Harding was an honourable man. Harding had stood by her side in her peril. But would he marry her? If he married her, the public thought that he, as her counsel, knowing, as they assumed, all her secrets, would be providing a verdict of not guilty. Would he marry her or would he not?

One day as she lay on the sofa in Pembroke Street he called to see her. Nothing was altered in the room. The same servants were in the house.

He sat down by her side. The colour was beginning to come back to her cheeks.

'What are you thinking of?' she asked, patting his hand affectionately.

'Do you really want to know?'

'Of course I do.'

'Well,' he said, 'I was thinking that you are not really a beautiful woman. That you were not, even before your illness, a beautiful woman.'

'You're perfectly right,' she laughed. 'I never was really beautiful. But the secret of being beautiful is to behave as though you are beautiful. In England if a man thinks he is an actor or an architect people will take him at his word. Perhaps we English are so stupid that they think the man must know best. As a matter of fact, I'm a very peculiar type. If I were badly dressed I should be ugly. When I am well-dressed—as I shall be at the wedding—I shall be beautiful.'

She felt an almost imperceptible movement of Harding's hand.

'When are we going to be married?' she asked.

'My dear Miriam,' he said, 'there can be no marriage until you have explained all the circumstances leading up to Clifford's death.'

'Yes,' she answered, 'you are entitled to ask that. I want to ask you, in your heart of hearts, do you really think I had anything to do with it?'

Somehow he felt that she was amusing herself at his expense; that she was not serious. 'Of course,' she added, 'I can quite understand that you might be afraid of being found in a cupboard. And yet that would be very foolish of you. That cupboard trick is the sort of thing one doesn't do often.'

The flippancy of her tone irritated him.

'You forget that Clifford was my greatest friend. With regard to this tragedy I will be quite candid with you, Miriam. I have no opinion. I know nothing. But I can't believe that you would commit a crime. I have always regarded you as the noblest of women.'

'Thank you,' she replied. 'Now you must be prepared for a shock. I am going to tell you something that perhaps you won't be able to believe, but I'm going to prove it to you. Clifford Oakleigh is not dead.'

Petulantly he snapped, 'Oh, if you are going to talk nonsense.'

'I'm not talking nonsense. I am Clifford Oakleigh.'

He got up from his chair in his irritation.

'Sit down,' she said.

There was something imperious in her voice. He sat down.

He gazed at her with half-shut eyes, wondering whether she was in complete possession of her faculties. He would marry a cripple, but he wouldn't marry a lunatic.

'George, you and I were at Oxford together.'

He made a movement of weariness.

She looked at him intently, and said in a low voice:

'Her shrine is petalled like the rose
And set about . . .'

'Good heavens!' he exclaimed, staring fixedly at her, as she repeated the other lines of the only poem he had ever been guilty of.

'Clifford told you that,' he persisted. 'Why did Clifford tell you that?'

'My dear George, you composed that wonderful piece of poetry, if, indeed, it is poetry, in a punt on the Cher with me. It was a hot afternoon. I was punting. We were just by Magdalen Bridge.'

Harding's jaw dropped. There was something uncanny in this.

'Clifford might have told you,' he said.

She laughed a negative and then put a question:

'Do you remember Muriel Holtwhistle?'

'Vaguely.'

'Well, I remember her pretty definitely. She was afterwards ordered out of Oxford by the Proctors.'

Memory came back to him.

'Yes, yes.'

'And,' she continued, 'you and I were both flirting with her. But she—being, as she said, literary and romantic—was awfully affected by the poem. Now, you remember that we collaborated in this work. You haven't forgotten that. I chaffed you for having won—if I may use the expression—Muriel by our joint masterpiece.'

She paused; then she inquired:

'Aren't you convinced?'

'God,' he said. He was trying to imagine by what miracle the intellect and the memory of Clifford Oakleigh had entered the body of Miriam Clive.

'I'm not strong yet, George. I'll tell you the rest as shortly as I can. You know that I have always been ambitious. My success as a doctor was due more to curiosity than to love of medicine. I have always desired to get out of life all that there is in life. I believe that only a small portion of the secrets of Nature have been penetrated by men. I have cured cancer. In fact, you admit, everybody admits, that I am an unusual man. I am more than an unusual man. I have powers which are granted to very few. Indeed, I doubt if any but myself have ever been aware that they possess them. Early in life I discovered that I exercised a curious fascination over men and women. I only had to want to be liked in order to be liked. My personality was magnetic. I seemed to be able to mesmerise people into liking me. You know that with regard to popularity there is always an element of unpopularity. Many people dislike a man simply because he is popular. In my profession I employed mesmerism a great deal. I found that I could keep a person in a comatose condition for a week. Suddenly an idea occurred to me. Would it not be possible for me to transfer my own identity into a comatose man? How curious it would be to lead another man's life. And if a man, why not a woman? We all know the sensation of loving as a man loves. I was struck by the charm of being a woman, to experience the delight of being a woman, if only for a day, a night. I would have given my soul to satisfy my curiosity. I have satisfied my curiosity. What I have done with my soul I don't know.'

Spellbound, Harding listened.

'Go on,' he said.

'The result of my experiments was that I felt convinced I should succeed. But the difficulties in the way were enormous. I wanted to lead the life of a beautiful woman. It was necessary for me to find an unknown girl. It was necessary that I should have practically two houses. My preparations occupied a long time. I purchased the house in King Street, I purchased this house. I rebuilt this house. After an enormous amount of trouble I managed, by the assistance of obscure builders, to construct a secret passage between this house and the ground floor of King Street.'

'Then these two houses are back to back,' Harding interposed.

'Yes,' she replied. 'No one, apparently, has ever noticed that. In each house there is a black oak cupboard, the lock of which is concealed in the woodwork. I had arranged everything. My servants in this house are all people on whom I have conferred benefits. I had, let us say, fascinated them. They are willing to do anything for me. In King Street I installed Reggie Pardell. Everything was ready, except the woman. But something told me that I should find her. One day Miss Mingey came. Instantly I knew that she would suit my purpose.

'The girl—well—the body you see before you is Miss Mingey. I ascertained that the body was perfectly healthy. Her practice of wearing spectacles was, I gathered, due to the fact that she wished to give herself an intellectual appearance. At any rate, her eyes, which you see, are fairly good eyes. But Miss Mingey made the worst of herself. I had no trouble in curing her of her ailment. There was little difficulty in inducing her to come and visit me at King Street. When she appeared on the eventful evening I mesmerised her. I triumphed.'

Miriam sat up, the light of enthusiasm kindling in her eyes. 'I became Sarah Mingey. On the sofa lay the limp, practically lifeless body of Clifford Oakleigh. There was only one identity in that room where previously there had been two. Then a terrible thing occurred. I had forgotten the key of the secret cupboard. What was I to do? For a moment I thought of reincarnating myself as Clifford. But my eagerness to enjoy my womanhood overcame me. I would risk anything. The street was deserted. There was no one in the house. I took off my spectacles, they seemed to fidget me; my skirts also were a nuisance. I ran clumsily out of the house to look for a four-wheeler. I could not find one. How long I was away I don't know, but it must have been during my absence that Reggie came in and found the body. When I returned I bundled Clifford into a cab, telling the driver that he was drunk, and drove here. I let myself in with my latchkey and half carried Clifford along the hall. You have noticed that I am a strong woman. I placed him in the secret cupboard and went upstairs. Previously, through Mudge, the servants had been informed that the new tenant would arrive that night. I had ordered some dresses and things which would more or less fit Miss Mingey. They were in my bedroom. Now remember this, that the servants were devoted to me, that the entirely reliable Mudge had informed them that the new tenant was a wealthy woman who could afford her whims, that she desired to take up her new abode as if she had always lived there, and that she would enter her house with her latchkey as though she had only left it in the morning.'

'Did Mudge know?' inquired Harding.

'No,' she answered. 'Mudge was mystified but he didn't suspect. After all, how can one suspect? Even now that you are having the facts put before you, you can hardly believe the truth.'

'With difficulty,' gasped Harding, 'go on.'

'There is not much more,' she answered. 'Most of the rest you can imagine for yourself. You can see the frightful obstacles I had to get over. I provided for every contingency. I made a will as Miriam Clive, leaving everything to Clifford Oakleigh. I made a will, as Clifford Oakleigh, leaving everything to Miriam Clive. It was only possible for me to be

Miriam Clive for three days or Clifford Oakleigh for three days. I was playing a sort of battledore and shuttlecock with souls. I always had a fear that some disaster might occur, and that corruption would take place in the body I was not using at the time. Hence, I would not go to Badschwerin. Also, I would not marry you. When I began, I thought that I would only keep up the experiment for a week or two. But I was fascinated with being a woman. I loved it. Often and often I wondered, should the worst come to the worst, should something occur like the accident, which I would prefer to be, a man or a woman. For the life of me, George, I couldn't decide. But Fate has decided. And, I think, wisely.'

He sat with his face between his hands, paralysed with horror.

Reflectively she said:

'I have come out of it very well. I have only lost a leg, and . . . Miss Mingey's soul—which was scarcely an asset. But I have got you, George, haven't I?'

'Yes . . . damn it,' he replied.

THE END